P.S. I HATE YOU

KIM JONES

THE BEST WAY TO GET OVER ONE MAN
IS TO GET UNDER ANOTHER.

From Sinner's Creed by Kim Jones, copyright © 2016 by Kim Jones. Used by permission of Berkley, an imprint of Penguin Publishing Group, a division of Penguin Random House LLC

This book is dedicated to Georgia, Mattie and Maria:
I look forward to many more smoke-outs with you.

1
MR. DELICIOUS

Despite the warm interior of my car, I can't suppress the shiver that runs through me as I gaze up at the neon sign hanging half-hazard from the front of the bar. Checking the address on my phone again, I frown when it matches the peeling numbers on the side of the building. According to the reviews, *Pop's* is known for its rough customers and rowdy fights—catering to bikers and every other outcast in the greater Lake Charles area. If it weren't a two hour drive from campus, I'm sure it would be mentioned in the awareness class my parents demand I attend once a month—labeled as "places to avoid."

I dial Emily's number—my other hand lingering on the gear shift. My best friend of ten years will definitely tell me to abort my mission. But after all the courage it took to get me here, I somehow feel like I need her approval before I can leave.

"Are you chickening out?" she asks, disappointment evident in that voice that's dying to sing "I told you so."

"Um, I don't think this is the right place."

"Yes it is. He checked in there three times last week on Facebook. If he's hanging out with his new biker friends, then that's exactly where he is." I drop my gaze when a burly man makes eye contact with me from a few parking spots over.

"I know Jud...he wouldn't be caught dead in a place like this."

"First, you obviously *don't* know Jud. Second, he's a biker now. Bikers hang out in rough places. And three, the most important of all, he screwed half of your sorority sisters. Right under your nose." It's been four months, and although the reminder doesn't rip my heart out of my chest like it used to, it still hurts.

"Are you sure he's really a biker?" I ask, already knowing the answer. He might have blocked me off Facebook, but was too stupid to block Emily. I guess he thought her being five hundred miles away somehow made him safe from her stalking. It didn't.

"You want me to resend the screenshots?"

As she says the words, I scroll through my images and find the evidence in black and white. Or blue and grey—the colors of the riding club he's now a member of. Eagles—Lake Charles, Louisiana. I thought it took years become a member of a club. Obviously, I was wrong.

I guess Jud used his charm on his biker brothers like he had on me. And the entire Velta Di sorority on LSU campus. Because in less than a year, he'd managed to make friends with the club and become a member—completely reinventing himself. The motorcycle he'd had since high school. But gone was the Sperry, khaki, polo wearing boy I'd fallen in love with. Now he wears a leather vest and rides with outlaws.

I look down at my own attire and roll my eyes. I've been planning this night for a month. Now that it's here, I'm starting to feel a little ridiculous. In my head, it had been perfect. The moment. The scene. The mood. Even the song. I was going to give him a taste of his own medicine. He'd screwed my sisters, now I was going to screw his brothers—aka fellow club members. Or so Emily had said after doing a little research.

"Stop thinking, Carmen," Emily snaps. "Get out. Go in. Order a drink. Order another one. Then make that bastard pay." I nod with each command—willing myself to follow through.

"I'll call you when it's done." Hanging up, I blow out a breath and grip the steering wheel. I'm way out of my comfort zone on this one. But I've been good for too long. It's time for me to live on the edge. Take chances. Chase a thrill. Understand the feeling of danger—not just the definition.

Without giving myself time to change my mind, I step out of my car and into the dark parking lot littered with bikes and a few old trucks. I feel even more out of place when I hit the lock button on my keypad, and the two loud chirps of my alarm system echo in the night as the LED headlights of my E Class Mercedes illuminates the front of the building.

My head jerks from side to side—searching the lot for anyone paying attention to me. I'm all alone and the realization has me shoving my hands into the front pockets of my coat and sprinting toward the entrance. Although I'm not sure if I'm running from danger, or into the hands of it.

A cloud of smoke billows over my head as I pull open the heavy glass door. Loud music blasts from speakers hanging on the dark-colored walls which are covered in posters of half-naked women and neon beer signs. The bar makes a huge U in the center of the room. Nearly every stool is occupied with men donned in black leather vests covered in patches—some the same, some different.

Several tables are scattered to my left—most empty. To my right are a row of pool tables where another crowd of men are gathered. I quickly make my way to one of the empty tables at the furthest corner of the room and take a seat—feeling a little safer in the shadows.

"What ya drinkin' doll?" I jump, startled as I meet the inquisitive eyes of the waitress. She's smacking on a piece of gum, her pen tapping impatiently on the tray in her hands.

"Chardonnay, please."

The corner of her mouth turns up as she drags her eyes down my body. I swallow and shift in my seat. "We don't serve *Chardonnay*."

"Right." I let out a nervous laugh. "Sorry, I've never been here before."

"No reason to apologize," she says, pulling out the chair next to mine. "I'll fix you up somethin' good. But first..." She leans in, her jaws working overtime as she chews her gum furiously. "Tell me why a girl like you is in a place like this."

Her gaze is so penetrating that I'm forced to look away. My eyes scan the room for something else to focus on. That's when I see him. Jud. My ex-boyfriend. The man I'd been planning to marry since my sophomore year in high school. The guy with the dark brown hair that curls at the nape of his neck and around his face. The one with the golden eyes and small dimple that appears in his right cheek when he smiles.

His arm—the strong arm that once held me is now draped over a girl's shoulders as he shakes hands with several of the bikers at the bar. Not just any girl. Clarissa. One of my sorority sisters. Regret starts to sink in as I take in her tall, perfect frame—dressed to ride. Her hair is a sexy mess from her helmet. Her cheeks flushed from the wind. Her eyes bright with excitement. Could that be me if I weren't always so scared to ride?

"You know them folks or somethin'?" the waitress asks, looking from me to Jud and Clarissa and back.

"He's my ex. She was my friend," I say, unable to look away from them.

There's a brief moment of silence before she gives my arm a squeeze and whispers, "I'll get you that drink." She disappears through a door, leaving me in the darkened corner with only my thoughts.

Seeing them together, in the flesh, is a lot different than hearing the rumors or seeing pictures. It hurts more—deeper. My throat constricts. Stomach tightens. Tears prick the back of my eyes as the ache intensifies. That place in my heart reserved only for Jud is now hollow. And I realize it's the emptiness that makes it so painful.

The waitress appears and I grab one of the glasses from her tray, not bothering to even ask what it is before I toss it back. The welcome burn in my throat and belly helps to dull the agony. In hopes I can numb it, I reach for another shot...and then another.

"Figured you'd need those."

"Thank you." I manage to stifle the hiccup that bubbles in my throat. At least it's not a sob.

"Here." She takes a seat, passing me a plastic cup. "It's Diet Coke. Goes good with the whiskey." I sip the drink while she takes a seat and lights a cigarette—both of us watching the two lovers too caught up in their throes of passion to even notice anyone else.

There must be something special about Clarissa. He's never held *my* hands above my head, rocked his fully clothed body against mine or made out with me in a public place. Then again, I haven't slept with half of the guys on LSU campus either. She's an experienced slut. *Her sluttiness got her your man...*

I grab another shot from the tray, quickly chasing it with a sip of Diet Coke. When I lean back in my seat, I finally start to notice the effects of the alcohol. It's definitely doing its job. My buzz is numbing. And with every kiss, hair pull, giggle and hip thrust I witness, the sadness dissipates—replaced with anger.

The past four months of my life have been hell. Being betrayed by my friends and my lover has resulted in me having to move out of the sorority house. Change my classes. My routine. Schedule. Even my gym membership. I've had to rearrange my entire life to move past this. And because I refuse to burden my family with my personal problems, I've settled for a job as a waitress just to make rent this summer. Why? Because I'm a good damn person. And it's gotten me nowhere but here—front row seats to a dry humping show.

It's time for another shot.

Unlike the burning liquor, this one is sweet with a butterscotch flavor. When I set the empty glass down, my attention is drawn to a group of men standing around a table next to Jud and Clarissa—

one man in particular. He's looking at me. His head turned slightly as he appraises me, and even though I can't make out all his features through the cloud of smoke, I'm pretty sure he's smiling.

The waitress gives me a smirk when she catches me ogling him. "He's hot, huh?"

"Can't really tell from here." Even still, I can't seem to drag my gaze back to the ones I need to watch in order to fuel my anger.

"You know what they say..." She stands, tucking the tray under her arm before shoving a piece of gum between her lips. "Best way to get over one man is to get under another one."

Little does she know, that's exactly why I'm here. But I won't do to someone else what's been done to me. So I ask, "Is he married? Have a girlfriend?" She shakes her head. "Are you sure? Just because a guy doesn't wear a ring doesn't mean he's single."

She rolls her eyes. "Girl, I know everybody in here. He ain't married."

"You think he's interested?" She studies my face. Taking in my hazel eyes and pouty lips framed in perfectly curled, long brown hair. She slides them suggestively toward my cleavage which is nearly non-existent without the help of a bra, before taking in my legs which always receive compliments. Although I think they're a little too thick.

Muttering something under her breath, she raises a brow at me. "You really think he wouldn't be in to a girl who looks like you? Besides, who you think bought your drinks?"

When her lingering eyes start to make me a little uncomfortable, I look back at the guy. I wish I could make out more of him from where I am, but even from a distance, I can tell he's confident. And the waitress said he was hot. Although at this point, it really doesn't matter.

This is my night. My chance. An opportunity to make Jud feel what I've been feeling for months. Even if it's just a taste. I may not know Jud like I thought I did, but there's one thing I'm sure of. He's the most prideful, possessive, jealous guy I've ever met. And seeing me with someone else may not crush him, but it'll definitely piss him off.

"Do you have a...juke box or something?" She pulls an iPod from her apron. "Dangerous Woman. Can you play it for me?" With a swipe of her finger, the track playing ends. Several people shout their complaints, but their voices are soon lost to the song that gives life to the daydream I've played over and over in my head.

I'm acutely aware of heads turning as I cross the floor. Despite my wobbly knees, I'm able to place one stiletto in front of the other without wavering. My palms are sweaty. I can feel sweat trickling down the back of my neck. I can't believe I'm actually doing this.

Stay focused.

You can do this.

Make him suffer...

I force my eyes to stay on the stranger, who's amused smile becomes evident the closer I get to him. And his smile isn't the only thing becoming clear.

The man is gorgeous. Standing over six feet tall with light colored hair that's a perfect mess on his head. Long, sculpted arms hang at his sides. Thick, muscular legs covered in faded jeans. Dusty boots on his feet. Leather vest. Black T-shirt. Head still tilted. Chin slightly raised. Full lips curved on one side. Piercing blue eyes that pull me to him.

When I've closed the distance, I start to fidget with the belt at my waist. He gives me an expectant look, but waits patiently for me to say or do something. I cast my eyes sideways at Jud and Clarissa who have their backs to me, before I focus on the man's throat and take a breath.

"Hi," I squeak, then press my lips in a hard line, lick them and try again. "Hi." This time, I meet his eyes. They're intrigued, but friendly.

His smile widens and he nods his head slightly. "Hello."

Shifting my weight, I fidget like crazy—feeling even more odd and out of place now that I'm the center of attention. I try not to think of all the people who may be staring at us. Or what they'll say about me if this man takes me up on my offer.

Then his voice jerks me from my thoughts. "Can I help you with something, gorgeous?" I flush at the endearment and drop my gaze. A giggle erupts from behind me. I stiffen at the familiar sound of Clarissa's annoying laugh. It's enough to motivate me to get back to the reason I'm here.

Tentatively, I reach out and run my shaky hands up his strong arms and around his neck. I stumble slightly and the result is my body flush against his. My cheeks darken when a wave of heat crashes over my entire body. I shouldn't be embarrassed by my reaction, I mean, it's not like he knows. Then again, something in those darkening blue eyes tells me he might.

"I want you to have sex with me," I blurt, wanting to kick myself for not sounding sexier.

He raises an eyebrow. "Have sex with you?"

"Yes, please."

His smile is so wide his lips pull back to show his teeth—white and straight and pretty. Who cares that he's beaming at my expense? "Why don't you tell me what you really want." Suddenly I'm aware of his hands on my hips. His grip tightens slightly, then releases. Like he's fighting the urge to hold me closer...or push me away.

"I-I told you." I'm thankful that our voices are low enough not to be heard by those around us. Especially those to the right of us who still have yet to notice me. *Assholes...*

"Tell me you want me to fuck you," he says, keeping his eyes on mine. His grip on me. *Oh to feel those lips on my lips...my other lips...*

Oh my god. I can't believe I just *thought* that.

"I can't."

"You can't what?" He's teasing me. I don't care. He looks delicious when he smiles like that. *Mr. Delicious...* That's what I'll call him. "You can't tell me...You can't do this... You can't believe you're here...Tell me, gorgeous. You can't...what?"

I can't think. Speak. Move. Nothing... "I don't know."

"Yes you do," he says. Then he winks. I might die. When I don't, I finally tell him the real reason I'm here.

"I want to make my ex-boyfriend jealous." He looks impressed. And pleased. Very, very pleased.

"Well, the pleasure is all mine, babe. But..."

"But?" *What the hell is wrong with me?* That "but" sounded downright pitiful. This is going to turn into sympathy sex... I just know it.

"But you still haven't said it." Challenge is written all over his face. He wants to hear me say *that*. I've never said the words in all of my life. *Damn if I don't want to, though.*

"I want you to fuck me."

"Louder."

I swallow hard. "I want you to *fuck* me." Emphasis on the "fuck" does more than gain me attention from Jud and Clarissa, it earns me a seat around Mr. Delicious' waist.

No sooner are my legs around his hips, his mouth is crashing against mine. The kiss is poisonous. Possessive. I'm putty in his arms as he carries me...somewhere. I'll go anywhere he wants, as long as that tongue of his continues to caress mine in that soft but fierce way. It's the kind of kiss I've yearned for. Craved. The kind that claims you, owns you, makes your toes curl and your spine tingle. The kind of kiss I've never had.

"Car--?..." Jud's voice is cut off when the bathroom door is kicked closed, then my back is against it. Adrenaline has my senses heightening and I take in the heady scent of my stranger. His male scent is mixed with leather and a hint of cologne. Fresh laundry and a little smoke. Whiskey and mint. It should be bottled and sold as an aphrodisiac.

He pulls away from my mouth, kissing a soft trail down my neck before meeting my gaze. His hair is messy from my fingers. My face still tingles from the dust of hair on his jaw. Blue eyes blaze with lust. And those perfect, full lips are a shade darker and still curved up in a smile.

"Do you have a condom?" I don't know why I couldn't think of anything else to say. Amused, he nods. "Okay, good. And I might scream a lot, but that's just to make sure he hears."

"Oh, you'll scream, but it won't be for him," he promises, winking at me...again.

"You have to stop that." I meant to only think that.

"Stop what?"

"Winking."

"Why?"

"Because it makes my liver quiver." Meant to think that too...

"Liver quiver. That's a new one."

I groan, letting my head fall back against the door. I close my eyes, but immediately open them when the room starts to spin. "This was a lot sexier in my head. You know, me and you?"

His eyes drink me up. "Still looks pretty sexy to me." *Damn...I just want to lick him.*

My head bounces off the door when someone bangs on it from the other side. "Carmen, what the fuck are you doing?"

"Carmen, huh?" Mr. Delicious asks, shooting me that irresistible smile. "I like it." He backs up a step, causing me to tighten my hold before pressing me against another wall. "Well, Carmen. I don't know your story, or why in the hell that piece of shit would choose anyone over you, but right now I'd love nothing more than to make you forget him."

Sadness starts to resurface. I can feel it swimming through my veins—infiltrating all my other emotions. For a minute, I'd forgotten why I'm here. I'd allowed myself to get lost in the moment. Now that I'm remembering, I'm starting to regret my actions.

Just when I think I can't do this, lips find mine. Once again, that heated, passionate kiss erases all my doubt and repairs the damage inside me. Tonight, I want to feel wanted. I *need* to feel wanted.

"Please," I moan, breaking the kiss so I can run my tongue and lips down his neck. His fingers trail up my thigh, beneath my coat, then still at my bare ass.

"Tell me you're naked under this," he whispers at my ear. I nod as he pulls back to untie the belt at my waist. Then, my naked body is on display for his greedy eyes. He takes his time dragging those stormy blues to my lips, down my neck, across my breasts—finally stopping on my freshly waxed sex. I may be imagining things, but I swear I hear him let out a low growl.

Keeping his head down, he peers up at me from beneath his dark lashes. "You sure you wanna do this?"

"Yes." My fingers twitch nervously, but I hold his gaze. "I want him to know what it feels like."

His face darkens a moment before breaking out into a mischievous grin. "You ever fucked a guy in a bar before, Carmen?"

The dirty talk is as embarrassing as it is a turn on. Shaking my head, I have to bite my lip to keep from thrusting my hips in search of some kind of contact to alleviate the pressure building inside me. His grin widens and I wonder if it's because he's aware of my struggle.

Another bang sounds at the door and my eyes shoot to the flimsy lock that could give any moment. But when the pad of his thumb touches my clit, I suddenly don't care if the door is kicked in.

"There she is," he whispers, his lips moving across my jaw. "For a second there I was worried you had a change of heart."

"No change of heart," I pant. "Still here."

"Good." His mouth moves to my ear. "I've been dying to taste your pussy since you walked in here." Then, I'm lifted—my back easily sliding up the wall as his big hands grasp my thighs. Burying his face between my legs, his mouth covers me. There's no teasing. No urgent flicks or cautious strokes of his tongue. Like a starved man, he devours me. Eating me as if I were his last meal.

His caresses are greedy. His tongue moving to thoroughly consume me in long, toe curling massages. He starts at my clit, which he sucks hungrily before dragging his heated, wet mouth through my lips—stopping to thrust inside me, then continuing lower until he's between the cheeks of my ass. He repeats the movements over and over as I grip his hair in my hands and digs my heels into his back.

He groans from deep in his throat—the vibrations eliciting a whimper from me. I want more. Less. I need his mouth on my clit. No, inside me. *There…* Everywhere. And he's not disappointing.

He's feasting on me. Touching, licking, even nibbling in all the right places at the right time with just the right amount of pressure.

My entire body is on fire. I'm shivering. Sweating. Begging. Moaning. Too caught up in the feeling of pleasure to care about how naughty and forbidden what he's doing to me should be. I'm near the edge—so blissfully close to achieving an orgasm that I know will be like no other I've ever experienced.

I open my eyes and meet our reflections in the mirror. His face between my thighs. My hands on his head. The heels of my shoes digging into the threads of the sole patch on his back. *PROSPECT*. I have no idea what it means, but he wears it well.

The sight of us together. The scent of my arousal. The sound of Jud banging on the door...it's erotic. Forbidden. Dangerous. *Empowering*. If I'd have known revenge would feel this good, I'd have done this shit months ago.

Dropping my head, I find him looking up at me. My breath catches in my throat at the sight of his hungry, blue eyes. "Your cunt is fuckin' delicious," he growls, and with those words, I do just as he promised I would—I scream.

Loudly.

It's obnoxious.

And not the least bit forced.

I'm not swimming in a sea of ecstasy—I'm drowning in a tsunami of euphoria. There are no tremors of pleasure—it's more like an earthquake of rapture. And when he pushes two thick fingers inside me and curls them slightly...

Nirvana.

With every beat of my pulse, I feel it again and again until it slowly fades to nothing but a perfect memory. I don't know how long it lasted. Maybe hours have passed. But when I finally shake the fog and come back to the real world, I find Mr. Delicious looking at me with a very pleased smile on his face.

I'm standing now. His hands are at my waist. The weight of his body keeping mine from sliding down the wall and making it impossible for me to ignore the raging hard on pressed against my belly. My growing excitement at what's to come quickly fades when I notice that my coat is tied tightly around me.

"The disappointment on your face is messing with my ego, gorgeous," he says, that ever-present smile on his face. "Considering you just came on my tongue, I figured you enjoyed yourself."

"What? No!" My eagerness to reassure him has me shaking my head and searching for the right words to say.

"No?"

"I mean, no I enjoyed it. I was just..." My voice trails off. *I was just what?* I sound pathetic.

"I'm teasing you, babe."

"Oh."

A bang sounds at the door, louder than the others, followed by a yell from Jud, demanding I come out. Mr. Delicious is not at all effected by Jud's outburst. For some reason, it makes me feel better. Like what just happened, happened because he wanted it too—to hell with the consequences or repercussions.

"You good to drive?" he asks, his face so achingly close to mine I can feel his breath whisper across my lips. It smells like me. My cheeks flush.

"Are we...um..." My gaze drops to his lips. "Through?"

Placing his finger under my chin, he lifts my head until our eyes meet. Thoughtfully, he studies me. Meanwhile, all I can think about is how that same finger was inside me only minutes ago.

"One bad decision ain't worth a lifetime of regret." His brow furrows a moment before he laughs it away—shaking his head in disbelief. "There's something good about you, Carmen. And it's fuckin' with my game." His playful smile doesn't match the bemusement in his eyes, which confuses the shit out of me. "Whenever you're over that piece of shit, you know where to find me." He straightens, forcing me to lock my knees to keep from falling. Unsure of how to respond to that, I give a tight smile and step around him.

I pause at the door. I don't know if I'm ready to face what's waiting on the other side. Or rather, who's waiting on the other side. I quickly search the room for a window and find Mr. Delicious leaning against the wall smirking at me.

"Only one way out, babe."

"I know that," I snap. His grin widens. "And for your information, I am over him."

"Sure you are."

"No, really. I am."

"If you say so."

I really wish he'd quit smiling. It makes him appear cocky. And sexy. And edible. "Maybe I can just wait him out." At my suggestion, he pushes off the wall and saunters toward me.

"Or…" He towers over me—twirling a lock of my hair with his finger. *That* finger. "You can remember the reason you're in here." Pushing my hair behind my ear, he dips his head. That wicked tongue lazily strokes my lobe before he pulls it between his teeth. "And who knows?" His hand slips beneath my coat—his fingers easily sliding between my folds before they're thrust inside me. A low moan builds from deep in my belly. "Maybe he'll have the balls to say something to me. And when he does…" Fingers leave me and I let out a grunt of disapproval.

He straightens and I watch as he shoves the two digits soaked in my juices between his lips, licking them clean before saying, "I'll make sure he's close enough to smell the sweet scent of your pussy on my breath." Dropping his voice, he adds, "I bet it smells better than his."

It takes a moment for me to recover from the sight of him sucking his fingers. Then, as I replay his words, I'm sobered at the reminder of what got me here in the first place. I'm breathe out a thanks for the much needed kick to my lady nuts.

With more confidence than I thought I had, I unlock the door and come face to face with Jud. Just as I predicted, he's seething with rage. "What the fuck, Carmen?"

"What?" I ask, my tone dripping with innocence. It pisses him off further. Good.

"Seriously? Everyone in here heard you getting banged like some cheap slut." He looks over my shoulder. I fight the urge to turn and look at Mr. Delicious myself. Knowing if I did look, I'd find him smiling.

Instead, I point to Clarissa who stands with her arms crossed beside Jud, clearly pissed that he's so pissed over me. "So it's okay for you to dry hump that bitch in front of everyone, but when I do it I'm a slut?" I let out a disbelieving laugh. *The audacity of this jerk...*

He motions with his finger between the two of them. "We're a couple, Carmen." It's then I notice the patch *she's* wearing. Something about being his property. *How friggin' ridiculous...*

"Well you sure as hell weren't a couple when you screwed her four months ago." I motion with my finger between me and him. "*We* were. But not anymore. So I'll be doing whatever, whoever, whenever I want." Feeling brave, I close the two feet between us until we're nearly nose to nose. "Get used to seeing my face, baby. Because I'm about to make your life a living hell."

Before he has a chance to respond, I lose myself in the throng of people crowded around for the show—ignoring his demands for me to stop. And the ones that tell me to stay the hell away from here.

Beneath all his rage and anger, I hope there's some pain. I hope he feels as empty as I did. I hope he's curled in the fetal position, crying over losing the greatest thing he's ever had. But more than that, I hope he's talking to Mr. Delicious...

Close enough to smell me on his lips.

2
A NUMBER AND A NAME

"You heard anything yet?"

I let out an exasperated breath at Emily's question—the same one she's been asking for three weeks.

"Not a peep." I slam the door on the dish washer, taking my frustration of Jud's silence out on the piece of crap machine that refuses to clean the dishes the first time. Damn Waffle House. Surely they could afford a decent dishwasher. I mean, it's not like paying me is breaking the bank. I make less than three bucks an hour.

"Well...you're just going to have to do it again." Her suggestion seems so simple. Maybe because I made that night sound so simple when I called her on my way home. But that empowering moment quickly faded. And when it did, regret started to sink in. I've told her this, but she still just doesn't get it.

"Boss is here. Got to go," I lie, stabbing the screen on my phone to end the call. I check the time before shoving it in my apron. 5:28p.m. Thirty-two more minutes before my grades are posted. The semester is finally over and I've never looked more forward to summer. Between work and finals, I'm exhausted.

I'm pretty sure I passed all of my classes with flying colors—maintaining that 4.0GPA I've had my entire life. But I refuse to, as my Daddy says, "count my chickens before they hatch." And the not knowing is stressing me out. Along with everything else that is my life.

Like the apartment I can't afford to properly furnish. The job where I work crappy hours for crappy pay. My ex-boyfriend who's yet to send a text or call telling me how much that night three weeks ago bothered him. And thoughts of that night, Jud, Clarissa, bathrooms...pretty much every thought, reminds me of *him.*

"Customer!" Jeannie, my co-worker, yells from the dining room—breaking through the memory just as I start to relive it.

I rinse my hands and peek out the window as I straighten my apron, making myself a little more presentable for the customer sitting alone in my section. Pushing open the swinging door that leads to the dining room, I plaster a smile on my face, but it falters when I notice it's him. I blink a few times and shake my head, making sure I'm not dreaming. How strange that I was just thinking of him, and now here he sits. *But you're always thinking of him...*

"Psst!!!" I hiss, catching the door and hiding behind it as I wave my hands to Jeannie. Confused, she quickly makes her way over.

"What?"

I pull her into the back, letting the door swing closed behind us. "It's *him.*" The crease in her brow deepens as she stares at him through the dirty window. Fingerprints, smudges and last millennium's grime obstructs her view. She starts to crack the door and I nearly throw myself in front of her.

She narrows her eyes. "Dude...chill out."

"You don't understand, Jeannie." I jerk my head toward the dining room. "That's *him.*"

20

"Oh my god... Is that Mr. Delicious?" I nod. "As in your cunt taste fuckin' delicious, Mr. Delicious?"

She pushes me aside before scrubbing at the window to get a better view. Meanwhile, I'm trying not to die at her words. I knew I'd regret telling her. But after a long shift and a cheap bottle of wine last week, it felt right.

"You swore to never repeat that."

She waves me off. "I don't know why it bothers you so much. You sure didn't mind when he said it."

"That was different. It sounded better coming out of his mouth."

Clutching her chest, she turns to me. "Carmen, you wound me."

"Will you please just wait on him for me?" I ask, having zero time for her dramatics. The cook had already called for us twice.

"Fine." She walks out, and I take her place at the window.

My appreciation of her morphs to horror as she tells him I'll be with him in a moment. Widening my eyes, I shake my head. She only smiles at me before mouthing, "you're welcome." When he turns to follow her gaze, I duck behind the door—cursing her under my breath.

I know I'm being petty. So we shared an intimate moment. It's not like there's anything to be ashamed of. Sure, I never thought I'd see him again...sober. But he's here. This is my job. And when I'm not in a bathroom, against a wall with a man's face buried in my vagina, I'm a professional.

Squaring my shoulders, I take a deep breath and force my feet to walk to his table. While he keeps his face buried in the menu, I take the time to appreciate his good looks with a clear head--his light brown hair. Square jaw with a few days of scruff. Them Val Kilmer lips. Shocking blue eyes framed in dark lashes. Muscular, cut arms that are well defined even beneath the long-sleeved thermal he wears. When he notices me, he smiles. My knees go a little weak. *He's beautiful...*

"Carmen? Right?" I just stare at him—my thoughts going stupid. *He remembered my name. Or maybe he read my name badge. How could he forget me? The bastard...*

"If you weren't breathing so hard, I'd think you didn't like me." His words make me aware of the scowl on my face and my labored breaths.

I shut my mouth and straighten, forcing myself to breathe through my nose. "What can I get you to drink?" I ask, trying to ignore the deep tone of his voice that makes me ache. *I wonder what it would sound like if he told me to take my panties off...* My cheeks flush at my thoughts.

"Sweet tea." I can hear the laughter in his voice as I turn on my heel—keeping my head down until I disappear from sight.

"Oh, he is too fine," Jeannie says. Thankfully, she's too busy looking at him to notice my shaky hands as I fix his tea.

"He's okay." I feign nonchalance.

"Yeah. That's why he's got you so overheated. Your skin is the color of my hair." My eyes flit to her fiery red hair. I blush darker.

"I'm just hot," I blurt before realizing I'd given her even more ammunition to tease me with.

"I bet you are." She dips her head to my ear and slaps my backside hard. "Go get em', tiger."

I hate her. I hate her. I hate her.

I say the mantra over and over in my head as I make my way back to his table. I manage to set his tea down without spilling it everywhere, and regretfully, give him an expectant look. He's smiling up at me. I'm melting.

"Ready to order?"

"You on the menu?" *Classic...*

"Do you want something to eat or not?" Thankfully, he has the grace not to comment on my poor choice of words. But his smile turns wicked and his eyes darken. My stomach flips. He knows I'm remembering that night. Just like I know he's thinking of it too.

"Steak and eggs. Medium rare on the steak. Over medium on the eggs. Raisin toast. No butter."

"Watching your figure?" I quip, temporarily forgetting the awkwardness.

His eyes roam my body. He's seen me on a good day—up close and personal. But even covered in sticky syrup and bacon grease, he looks at me like I'm sexy. And it makes me feel sexy.

"You have a good figure. What's your secret?"

I drag my mind back to the present, and answer his question as evasively as possible. "Ramen noodles and the occasional waffle with burnt edges." My truth has him pulling his eyes back to mine—that sexy half smile still in place.

"A girl like you deserves better than a ten cent pack of noodles and a free waffle." The intensity in his voice is surprising. It's as if he actually believes I do deserve more. And he's pissed I don't have it.

"You don't even know me," I mutter, scribbling his order.

"I know enough." My tongue slides over my lips. *Like his did on my other lips.* "Head outta the gutter, gorgeous." Jerking my head up, I meet his cocky smile.

"You order will be up soon. Let me know if I can get you anything." I don't notice his reaction to my generic, monotonous line. I just walk away embarrassed and kicking myself for allowing him to tease me. Once again, I take my anger out on the dishwasher—stacking cups and slamming the door with a little more force than necessary.

If I'm being completely honest with myself, the cause of my frustration stems from my sexual need. Just the memory of what we'd done stirs the embers of desire inside me until it becomes a blazing inferno. I've masturbated more in the past three weeks than I have in my entire life. But no matter how hard I try, I can't reach that level of oblivion I experienced with him. It's infuriating. And I'm sure seeing him again will only add to the fantasies I have when I'm in bed. Or in the shower. At work. Everywhere.

Jeannie's laughter breaks through my thoughts and has me craning my neck to find her flirting with Mr. Delicious. He's standing at the register—his food now boxed up next to the grill.

"Carmen! I need a ticket for table six!" He's leaving? Why? Better yet, why do I care?

Jeannie is called away to another table while I make my way over, leaving me alone with the star of my fantasies once I get there. I can feel his eyes on me as I ring up the order. He's on the phone, telling whoever is on the other end, "I'm on my way."

I show him the total on the ticket, and my hand trembles when his cool fingers brush mine as he hands me a hundred-dollar bill and a slip of paper. As if the friction causes some sort of magnetic pull, I lift my gaze to meet his piercing, blue eyes.

They're touching me.

Caressing me.

Making love to me. Right here. In Waffle House.

Chill, Carmen…

"I thought we were gonna be seeing a lot more of you at the bar." He grins, crossing his arms and bringing my attention to the cords of muscle there.

"Things didn't go as planned."

He quirks an eyebrow. "Is that so?"

"I thought it would really bother him." *Could I sound any more pathetic?*

"Oh, it bothered him. Still does." He seems to be fighting a laugh, and I have a feeling he knows something he's not telling me.

"Well, he never called or texted."

"That's because he wants you to think he doesn't give shit. Trust me, babe. He gives a shit." Stepping forward, he drops his head. He's so close, I can feel the heat of his mouth on my face. "A girl like you walks in a bar. The piece of shit who cheated on her is there. He watches as she sways those sexy fuckin' hips right around another man's waist. Then she's screaming…" His voice becomes a whisper. "While a man tongue fucks her pussy."

I squeeze my thighs together. I'm silently begging him to ask for a repeat of that night. We don't have to go to the bar. He can do what he said right here. On top of the counter—I don't care.

When he pulls back, his eyes are stormy. "Sounds like something that would bother me. Just sayin'."

24

"Sounds like a Lori Morgan song to me." I cut my eyes to Jeannie who's been eavesdropping on our conversation. Unashamed, she offers a shrug. "Just sayin'."

I look back to Mr. Delicious who winks. The gesture erases the anger from his face. "Dinner's on me, gorgeous."

I watch as he strolls out. The loose fitting, faded jeans he wears have to be the sexiest thing I've ever seen on a man. Well, second to that PROSPECT patch that looks a little more worn today than it did three weeks ago. I make a mental note to Google the meaning.

I'm still holding the hundred-dollar bill, eighteen-dollar ticket and slip of paper in my hand. I ring up the order, pay for the food, then tuck the large tip in my apron. While Jeannie busies herself with her customers, I quickly disappear into the bathroom—making myself to wait until I'm behind the locked stall before I open the paper and read the note.

A phone number.

A name.

Cook.

A couple hours later, I'm pacing the small hall leading to the bathrooms—phone in one hand, Cook's number in the other. I do a mental countdown about a hundred times before finally punching in his number and hitting send. I squeeze my eyes shut, silently praying he won't pick up.

"Yeah?" Shit. He picked up. And he sounds delicious. *Delicious? I've got to find another word.*

"Um, hi. Cook?"

"Who is this." He doesn't ask. He demands.

"Yeah, hey. So. Um, this is—" the swinging door to the lobby opens, and without thinking, I end the call. I greet the customer with a nervous laugh while holding open the door to the women's room.

Noise from the dining area draws my attention as a huge crowd piles in. Slipping my phone in my back pocket, I walk out with a smile—thankful for the distraction. But while I busy myself with drink and food orders, high chairs, extra napkins and ketchup,

I can feel my ass vibrating from the constant ringing in my pants. When I get a second to check it, I already have three missed calls. From him.

"Miss, I need some more water."

"Young lady, reckon you can get us some jelly?"

"If my food isn't out in five minutes, I'm leaving."

"My eggs are cold."

With so much to keep my attention, I still can't seem to focus on anything but Cook. The missed calls. His voice. Hands. Mouth. Lips. Eyes. That *tongue...* It's official. I'm addicted. The orgasm he gave me is like a drug. If I don't get another hit, I may die. I'm too young to die. So for the sake of my health, I have to see him tonight.

The anticipation has me so worked up, I can't do anything right. After the rush dies down and the restaurant is empty, I have less than twenty bucks to show for it. And a gallon of spilled maple syrup.

I fall to my knees and start the grueling process of cleaning up the sticky remnants. It seems to be everywhere. The more I clean, the more it multiplies. By the time I'm finished, I'm exhausted. And the promise of orgasm isn't nearly as enticing as my bed that waits for me.

My mind made up, I clock out and leave—driving in the direction of my apartment. Sitting at the light, I hear my phone chime with a notification and dig it from pocket. There's a total of four missed calls, all from Cook. And one message from Emily.

I hate him

Hovering my finger over the attachment, I contemplate opening it. I know I'll regret it if I look, but curiosity gets the better of me and I press the screen.

My mind spins when I see a picture of Jud and Clarissa smiling at the camera. The caption reads, "One day, I'm gonna marry this girl." And to make it even more sickening, Emily has been kind enough to make a collage which includes a picture from three years ago of me and Jud in the exact same pose as him and Clarissa—the caption being the same damn thing.

If Emily's intention was to piss me off, it worked. I'm livid. More at myself than him. Because my anger proves that I'm not completely over him. If I was, then things like this shouldn't bother me. But it's obvious that this is some kind of game to him—who can be the bigger jerk. He thinks I screwed one of his club brothers, so he posts a picture with one of my ex-sisters.

He knew it'd hurt me and it probably will. But right now, pain is the last thing I feel. Because in this moment...

I'm mad as hell.

3
TEQUILA WITH BIKERS

This time when I pull in front of Pop's bar, I'm not nervous. I waltz through the door and into the crowded building with confidence. Finding an empty stool between two men, I climb up and take a seat—searching the women behind the bar for the waitress with the great advice.

I hear her before I see her. Loud, smacking gum sounds in my ear and I turn to find her standing right beside me. "I knew you'd be back," she says with a wink. Giving me a onceover, she lets out a low whistle. "Only you can wear something like that and look good doing it."

Frowning, I look down at the cheap, black polo, black jeans and hideous nonslip shoes. I hadn't even taken my name badge off. I quickly unclip it from my shirt and shove it in my back pocket.

"I'm Kat. Short for...pussycat." At the mention of "pussy," the man next to her turns on his stool—his eyes dropping to her short skirt. "Ronnie, quit looking at my ass," she says without turning. "This here's Carmen. She wants a margarita."

Ronnie looks over at me. He's an older man with faded tattoos, glasses and a jean vest covered in worn patches. He shoots me an appreciative smile and nods. "Nice to meet you, Carmen. First drink's on me. The next one will cost ya."

I'm not sure what it'll cost me, but I don't think he's talking about money. I swallow nervously. Kat smirks at my reaction. "He's harmless. And he's loaded."

She moves behind the bar, and I watch in amazement as she interacts with all the customers as she makes my drink. She teases some, chastises others. Curses loudly and even threatens a man who reaches across the bar to playfully smack her—promising to cut off his "pecker" if he tries it again.

I envy her. I'd never have the nerve to speak so open and freely to a group of such harsh looking men. Sure, I approached Cook—*and let him eat me in the bathroom*—but he's a lot different than these guys. These men are rowdy and loud. Probably violent and mean. Likely on parole.

I should've went home. Got back at Jud by posting naked pictures of myself on social media. I just don't fit in here. I'm way out of my element. Too timid and reserved to act like I belong. And the one person I came to see, isn't here anyway. I'll finish this one drink so I don't appear rude, but them I'm out. Because all the tequila in Lake Charles couldn't loosen me up around this crowd.

"One, two...three!"
Lick.
Shoot.
Suck.
Hit the trash can target three feet away with the lime wedge.
It's the stupidest, most amazingly fun game I've ever played. And if it was an Olympic sport, I'd be a gold medalist.

"I win!" I announce, fisting my hands in the air as I sit cross-legged on the bar. The place is packed, and I'd given up my seat to Ronnie's buddy, Marshal, over an hour ago.

"I think you're cheatin'," Ronnie laughs. "How are you not shit-faced?" I stack my empty shot glass on the tower we've been building. I'd count them, but unbeknownst to him, I am pretty shit-faced.

"It's all about staying hydrated." To emphasize, I take a pull from my bottle of water. "More water. More liquor. More fun."

"More money," Kat says, holding her hand out. Ronnie peels off a bill from his money clip. "At this rate, I'll be able to buy new shoes after she pukes on these later." She juts her finger at me.

"I'm not puking. Guarantee it."

Kat raises a brow at me. "Mmm-hmm. We'll see." She looks over my shoulder—her eyes narrowing a moment before coming back to meet mine. "How drunk are you?"

"Shittttty..." *Really shitty.*

"Good." She walks away, not bothering to explain her question. I shrug it off--my focus on Ronnie as he signals for another round.

"I'm beating you this time."

"Yeah." I pat his cheek. "Keep telling yourself that."

It's amazing to me how easily I opened up. Sure the tequila helped, but six months ago I never imagined I would have the audacity to walk into a place like this, much less engage with the people who hung out here. And I'd done it twice. Once nearly naked.

But tonight, one margarita turned into two. Then Ronnie bought me a shot. Which led to another. And then a silly game. Next thing I knew; we were in competition with one another. Now, I feel like this kind of place is *my* kind of place. Like I'm a regular.

Lick.

Shoot.

Suck.

Score!

"Winner-winner, chicken-dinner, motherfucker!" *Motherfucker?* I've never said that word—out loud. But I like it. And it's socially acceptable here.

I wait for Ronnie to drill me. Accuse me of cheating. But his back is to me as he greets someone else. It's something he's done all night. It seems everyone who walks in, comes to shake his hand. He has lots of friends, obviously.

After the first twenty or so, I stopped paying attention to them. But as I stack my shot glass, I feel eyes burning into the side of my head. When I hear my name being spoken in that disbelieving, familiar voice, I roll my eyes.

"Ello Jud," I say, my voice accented. I have to blink a few times to focus my vision before I find his scowling face. "Where's your bitch?" I make a show of looking for her. "Ain't she like property of MVP Jud, or somethin'? You get her a collar and tag to go with that vest? I hear you can even put a chip in em' now."

Ronnie shakes his head—a smile on his lips. I grin back at him. *He thinks I'm funny.* Jud does *not* think I'm funny. He's fuming.

"She bothering you, Ronnie?" Jud asks, his tone full of authority. I hiccup a laugh.

"Nope. She bothering you?" There's a hint of something in Ronnie's voice. I may just be imagining it, but it sounds like a warning.

"No, but she's drunk. I'll get her out of your hair before she does something stupid." Jud starts around the bar, and he's nearly to me before I've fully processed his words. I need to drink more water. My brain is slowing down.

He reaches for my arm and I pull back. "Don't touch me!" I yell, my anger surfacing.

"Don't embarrass me, Carmen," he warns, glancing around nervously before leveling me with a look. I realize there are people watching us, and the noise has quieted down.

"I'm not even with you," I spit. "I didn't come here with you and I'm not leaving here with you."

"Let her be, Jud. She's alright." Ronnie's words have Jud retreating, but only after he shoots me a nasty look, which I respond with by sticking my tongue out like a five-year-old.

Once he's out of sight, I lean in to Ronnie. "You know...I was a good girlfriend. I loved him. A lot." My vision blurs slightly. *Damn tequila.* "I'd have done anything for him. Walked through hell wearing nothing but gasoline-soaked panties for him." He smiles at that. I wonder where in the hell the saying came from.

"I believe you, sugar. I really do." He hands me a napkin, and I realize I'm crying. I dab at my eyes, hoping Jud can't see me from wherever he is. I'm handed a shot by someone, and down it without bothering with salt or lime. Then I hiccup, wipe another fresh flow of tears and laugh.

"I'm drunk, Ron-Yay. Drunker than a piss-ant, as my daddy would say."

"Yes, you are. You about ready to call it a night?" I shake my head.

"Not until I do what Kat told me to do. I'm getting under him by getting over on someone else." This causes a round of laughter from the group of men around me—all who've been sitting in silence witnessing my drunken, emotional break.

"Well, I ain't gonna let that happen." I frown at him in confusion. "See, I'm the one who got you drunk, so you're my responsibility. And I don't tolerate men taking advantage of drunk women. But I'm sure we can figure something else out." He grins at me, which I return just because there's something about this kind man that reminds me of my father.

"Prospect!" If my limbs weren't like jelly, I'd have jumped at his outburst. Seconds later, a man appears behind him. I swear he has a halo of light surrounding his tall, muscular body. I don't know if I want to faint, cry or come at the sight of him. *Mr. Delicious...*

Ronnie keeps his eyes on me as he speaks to Cook over his shoulder. "Sugar here, wants to dance."

Yes. I. Do.

Eyes wide, mouth parted, I watch as Cook saunters behind the bar. He's all man—hard body. Strong jaw. Blue eyes. Amused smirk.

Then he's grabbing me under my arms, lifting me and steadying me on my feet. My hands go to his shoulders, gripping the firm muscles there as his hands slide to my waist.

"Hey, you," he says, darkly. Is it possible to orgasm from a voice?

"H-hey you..."

Grabbing my hand, he leads me through the crowd. I'm floating behind him. Eyes centered on his back. The smell of his leather thick in the air. I lift my gaze to the bright orange PROSPECT patch. *Damn...I forgot to Google that.*

I've heard a few Merle Haggard songs, and instantly recognize the one playing as *Misery and Gin*—a classic. Cook stops and turns, his hands sliding up my arms to place them around his neck. His touch feels so...*good.* I wonder if I've been drugged with Ecstasy.

"I called you back," he says, grabbing my hips and pulling me flush against him. His body is like stone, but warm and inviting. "Several times. You never answered."

"That was me. I called you." I sound like an idiot. My words make no sense. Cook just smiles.

"I knew it was you the moment I heard your voice. You have a sweet, southern tone. Even when you stutter, you sound polite and refined."

"Refined?" I laugh. "I'm drunk in a biker bar. In my Waffle House clothes. My hair is piled on my head because part of it is caked in syrup. And I can't remember the last time I peed." *Geeze, Carmen...* Why did I say that? Why don't I care that I said it? Why does the look he's giving me make me feel special? Or maybe it's the tequila making me feel special...

"Do you have to pee?"

"Well, I didn't until you said something." I squeeze my thighs together. The movement causes me to press further into him.

"We can stop dancing for you go to the bathroom," he says, baring all his pretty, white teeth in a wide grin.

"I'll pee on myself first. Unless..." I wiggle my eyebrows suggestively.

"Such a dirty girl. I've ruined you."

I nod in agreement. "Yes. You have. I've never had an *organism* like that." His body shakes with a laugh, tickling my nipples. *Nipples...* "I'm serious. I've been trying for days and can't make it feel that good. And him..." I motion over my shoulder with my hand toward where Jud might be. "Well, he's a selfish bastard. But you..." I poke him in the chest. "You are *not* a selfish bastard. You're a very kind and giving bastard."

"Why thank you, ma'am. I appreciate that."

"I mean it. Even if I didn't pretty much just use your face to piss him off. I still would say that. And I. Would do it. Again," I promise. "And next time, you're gonna do me. Which reminds me...why didn't you do me?"

"You mean why didn't I *fuck* you?"

"Yeah, that."

His lids become heavy and his voice drops. "Because when I fuck, I leave my mark." He leans closer. "You'll feel me for days. And your tight, little cunt can't handle it."

My breath is heavy when he pulls away. Visions of him in my bed flash in my eyes—him fucking me until I scream...*leaving his mark.* The thought liquefies me. I'm a pool of need...want...desire. And when I meet his eyes, my thoughts are reflected in them.

"I want you to fuck me," I say, the words flowing smoothly from my mouth without a trace of apprehension or doubt.

His response is robotic. "You're drunk."

"I don't care."

Cupping my cheek, he smirks as his thumb brushes over my bottom lip. "I do." There's a finality in his tone that might make me respect him for not taken advantage of me. But because I'm drunk, and super horny, his response makes me pout.

"I don't think it would matter if I wasn't drunk," I mutter. "What's a girl gotta do to get laid around here?"

His gaze darkens. "Ask me when you're sober and you'll find out."

"Such a gentleman to wait until I can think straight," I quip, but my tone is breathy.

"Trust me gorgeous, there's nothing gentlemanly about what I plan to do to you."

Ohmylordhavemercy.

I bet it's big. Maybe it will take my breath. Oh, I hope he talks dirty. And pulls my hair. I wonder if he's a spanker...

"Tell me what you're thinking," he demands. He might act chivalrous, but his thoughts are as perverted as mine.

"I'm thinking about what I want you to do to me."

The corner of his mouth lifts. This smile is deliciously evil. "You gonna tell me, or you want me to guess?"

"Guess," I blurt. There's no damn way I would tell him...I don't care how drunk I am.

"You been with anyone but him?" The question confuses me, but I shake my head in answer. Jud had been my first. *My last...* "I figured as much." He's silent after that, even though I'm staring at him expectantly.

"Well?"

"Well what?"

"Are you gonna guess?"

He shakes his head. "Don't need to. I already know what you want."

My eyes narrow. "How?"

"Intuition." He smirks.

"You don't know shit," I mumble. But his confident look tells me he probably does know.

"We'll see."

"Maybe." I shrug. "Who says I'm gonna ask you again?"

"Oh, you'll ask."

Damn right I will. Just as soon as I get this liquor out of my system. *Maybe I can fake being sober...*

"He's watching you." His voice breaks through my thoughts, and I realize I've been staring at his neck. Jerking my eyes to his, I find a storm brewing inside them.

"Who?"

He glances over the top of my head. "Jud." Cook spits the name as if it's venom. "He's pissed."

I don't bother turning to look. The view in front of me is much better. "Well he ain't got no right to be pissed at me." *Ain't got no?*

Cook shakes his head. "He's not pissed at you. He's pissed at himself."

"Why is he pissed at hissself?" I'm slurring. Spinning a little too.

"Because he let go of something every man in this room wants." Is he talking about me? Or what me and Jud had? Somehow I feel like it's a little bit of both. I also feel like the floor is crooked. And now *I'm* pissed because fighting to keep my balance is preventing me from enjoying the moment.

"Can we stop moving?" I ask, wishing the room was about fifty degrees colder. Although I'm sure that's impossible with Cook near. His presence is like an inferno.

"We haven't moved since we've been out here, gorgeous." His smile falters a fraction. Awe, he's concerned about me! *He should be...* I'm feeling a little queasy.

"I think I need some air."

"The moment you step outside, you're gonna feel a lot worse. So unless you're ready to feel the aftereffects of Jose, I'd suggest drinking some water and staying inside a little longer."

"I can't. I'm so hot." He grabs my arms from around his neck and tucks one of my hands in his.

"That's the fucking truth," he mutters, keeping me close to him as he pulls me back through the crowd.

I really want to look at Jud, give him the finger and then drag my tongue across Cook's face. Instead, I keep my eyes on Cook's back—seeming to feel a little more grounded as long as I keep my focus there.

While Ronnie and Cook exchange words, I thank Kat for the cup she hands me. The cold Sprite feels amazing running down my throat. And when I put the cup to my head, that feels fabulous too.

I'm faintly aware of Ronnie telling me bye. Kat telling me I killed it. Several of the men from the bar saying goodnight. I mumble something to them and force a smile.

Then, I'm ushered toward the door, and finally into the cool, night air. I moan at how good it feels. That lasts for about two seconds, then I'm spinning so fast, I have to cling to Cook's arm to keep from falling.

"I got you," he says, guiding me to the passenger side of my car. *He's got me.* How long have I yearned to hear those words? The thought is fleeting as I take a seat and lean against the door—thankful when the window rolls down and I can hang my head out of it.

Cold air blows from the vents in the car, as the wind from outside whips across my face. The car is moving, and I pray we catch all the green lights. As long as I'm being blasted with the frigid air, I might live.

I concentrate on surviving the entire drive. Surviving entails not only staying alive, but sobering up so I can get laid. And not puking. That would definitely ruin the sex he's going to give me tonight. I might be drunk, but a girl knows what a girl wants—Cook. Naked. Under me. So I can get on him.

Something like that...

4
PRINCE CHARMING

"I'm gonna die."

I hear a chuckle from behind me as something cold is pressed against my neck. Then I'm hurling again—promising the good Lord that if he'll just make it stop, I'll never drink again. Tequila is evil. Wicked. And doesn't taste nearly as good coming up as it does going down.

"I didn't even eat my steak," I whine, sniffling and crying and feeling sorry for myself.

"I'll get you another one."

"It's not the same." Sliding to the floor, I press my cheek against the cold tiles and keep my eyes on Cook's boots—knowing if I close them, I'll be spinning like I'm on the tea cup ride at Disney.

"It'll be better. I promise." I can hear the laughter in his voice.

"Are you smiling?"

"Always."

"Why?"

"Because I'm always happy."

I grunt. "Nobody is *always* happy."

He kneels next to me—pushing loose strands of hair out of my face while I study his knees. They're so...handsome.

"Well not everyone is fortunate enough to have such amusing company." I'm amusing to him? I guess that's better than disgusting considering I'm lying face down on a bathroom floor with puke breath. At this point, I have no humility left. I can feel the shame tomorrow.

Using my inebriation as an opportunity to say what's on my mind, I lift my hand and hold up two fingers. "Twice. I've asked you twice to have sex with me and both times you said no."

"I never said no, gorgeous."

"Then why am I not laying here screwed?" I snap, dropping one finger so only my middle is left in the air.

"Because you're drunk."

"Whatever." Huffing, I drop my hand over my eyes. "Take my socks off. Turn the air down. Why is it so hot in here? Just squirt me with the water hose."

"Demanding little shit, aren't you," he laughs, pulling my socks off my feet.

"Pretend I said please," I mutter, letting my eyelids flutter closed for just a moment. *If the world would just. Stop. Spinning.*

I hear his footsteps in the hall, and pray he's going to get the water hose. If he doesn't, maybe I can crawl to the tub and shove my head under the tap. Surely that will sober me up some. But I'm afraid to move. Scared to death that the nausea will resurface and I'll be puking my guts up once again. Even the thought makes me queasy.

"By the way, babe," he calls, coming back and setting the small fan from my kitchen in front of me. "You don't have a water hose." *Oh yeah...*

"The fact that you looked makes me love you more."

"So you love me?" He feigns shock—even taking his dramatics a step further by letting out a gasp, as he busies himself around my small bathroom.

"I love you so hard."

"You have no idea how long I've waited to hear that."

I smile, wishing I could see his face, but not wanting it bad enough to turn and look. But my happiness is short lived. Tonight is not going how I'd hoped it would. I'd envisioned hot sex. Sweaty, naked bodies. Moans of pleasure. Not me sprawled on the floor. Sweating tequila. Grunting and dry heaving and praying for death.

He leans over me and I'm blasted with cool air from the fan. "I had big plans for us tonight," I admit, my voice sounding robotic when it carries through the fan.

"Oh, I'm just waiting for you to pass out so I can sneak attack it," he says, placing another cold towel on my head.

"Sneak attack it?"

"That's right." He takes a seat on the side of the tub. "I'm gonna hit it and quit it. Get in and get out."

I laugh. "I thought you loved me."

"No babe. You're the one that's in love. I'm just in it for the sex."

"Hey...that's my role. You're supposed to play the romance novel guy who falls in love with me after we have sex. The modern day Prince Charming. The one who carries me to bed when I *accidentally* fall asleep. The one who takes care of me when I'm sick. And takes off my socks. And holds my hair back when I puke. And calls me perfect when I'm not."

"Babe..." he drawls. "I did all that. Except carry you to bed. Like I said, I'm just waiting for you to fall asleep."

My eyes flutter closed again. This time, it's tolerable. "You better not carry me to bed when I fall asleep. This floor is amazing," I mumble groggily.

"Okay, gorgeous." His voice is lower—soothing. Like he knows I'm drifting. But there's something else he didn't do. And I refuse to sleep until I call him out on it.

"You never called me perfect, either. Prince Charming would be offended. I'm offended. And I'm definitely not perfect."

He lets out a breath of laughter. I envision him shaking his head. "No...you're not perfect." Damn. Wasn't expecting that answer. "But you're pretty fuckin' close."

Wasn't expecting that either...

I'm freezing. I'm literally shivering to death on the bathroom floor. But at least the spinning has stopped and the nausea is gone. The only proof I have that last night actually happened is the sour taste in my mouth and the splitting headache. Oh, and those knees I referred to as handsome. They're still here too—staring back at me.

Cook is sitting on the bathroom floor. Knees pulled up. Back against the tub. Head lowered. Breath slow and steady. *Bless him.* He's asleep. Poor thing. Did he stay here all night? Or maybe it still is night.

I reach a shaky hand toward the fan, trying and failing to switch it off. But I do manage to knock it over and wake Cook. He blinks a few times then smiles. "How you feelin'?"

"Cold." With a flick of his fingers, the fan is off. "Thank you."

He stands, and my eyes follow him as he stretches. His shirt rising just enough to give me a peek at the V that's dusted in hair and skin and promise. *I bet it leads to something big....*

"Want me to carry you to bed, my damsel in distress?" I nod like an idiot. Knowing good and damn well I can walk. He just shakes his head and grins, then leans down and easily scoops me up in his arms. He's so warm. And smells so good. "How long you gonna milk this shit, princess?"

I pull my nose out of his shirt to answer him. "My book boyfriend wouldn't ask that. He'd simply take care of me." He laughs, his Adams apple bulging from his neck. I never thought they were sexy. His is. So is his neck—thick and masculine. Smooth and lickable.

"So you do remember last night."

The tequila—ugh. Dancing. Vomiting. Singing. His *not-so-gentlemanly* promise.... Yep. I remember. Flushing, I avert my gaze. He laughs but it's cut short when his phone buzzes in his pocket.

"Is that your wife?" I tease. "Girlfriend?" That smile falls just a fraction, and I know I struck a nerve.

"No. I don't have a wife or a girlfriend. And I don't want one. Women are too much trouble." He quirks a brow, dropping me onto the bed. My back doesn't hit the mattress before he's digging for his phone. I'd imagined him laying me down gently, tucking me in and saying something sweet, but whatever.

He's serious when he looks at me—pointing his finger in my direction. "Sleep. And no tequila." Then he's gone. Just like that. He didn't even say bye.

So I'd milked it a little. But I really was cold. And I do have a headache. I frown when I realize not only how petty I am, but how much it bothers me that he's no longer here. And that whoever texted him must've been more important than me. He didn't even ask if I needed anything before he left.

Pouting, I roll to my side and my eyes land on a folded piece of paper sitting on my nightstand. Next to it is a bottle of water, Gatorade and some headache medicine. I snatch the note—immediately forgiving him and grinning like crazy as I read it.

Love, Prince Charming

5
BREAKING AND ENTERING

"Details," Emily says the moment I pick up the phone. The incessant ringing had woken me from my deep, post-drunk slumber only minutes ago. I wanted a shower, some caffeine and brushed teeth before I spoke to her. But Emily can be relentless.

"Can I call you back, Em?"

"Why? Is someone there?" Her excitement is palpable.

"No. But I just woke up. I want a shower."

"You have ten minutes." Knowing she'll be counting down the seconds, I hang up and hurriedly undress, then step under the scalding spray. I moan at how good it feels on my tired muscles. Sleeping on the bathroom floor wasn't a very good idea.

The events of last night flash through my mind in a series of flashbacks. All of which are too embarrassing to pause on. Besides, I'll have plenty of time to relive my humiliation when I share the details with Emily.

I'm brushing my teeth when my ten minutes are up and Emily calls back. I make her wait until I'm dressed and have started my coffee before I finally return her call. Once again, she bypasses introductions—desperate for the juicy stuff.

"I got drunk. Hung out with bikers that looked like they belonged on Gangland, and puked everywhere." She's silent for a moment.

"Please tell me you didn't make an ass out of yourself in front of Jud."

"No, I waited until I got home."

"You drove?"

Rolling my eyes, I take a sip of my coffee—hot and very strong, just like I like it. I smile when I realize it's similar to my taste in men. One man in particular.

"Actually Mr. Delicious drove me home."

"Shut the fuck up!" Emily squeals, causing me to wince and pull the phone away from my ear. But I still feel a surge of heat at the memory. The way he looked at me. Took care of me. Promised me some not-so-gentlemanly action.

"I didn't mean that literally, Carmen. Give me more. All of it. Everything. Don't leave out a single detail."

She hangs on to my every word as I give her a step by step replay of last night and early this morning. When I tell her about our bathroom conversations, I have to pause for her laughter. By the time I make it to the part about the note, she declares that she's completely fallen for him. And so have I.

"There's one more thing he said to me." I'm pacing now, trying to burn off some of the adrenaline pumping through my body. Even when he's not here, Cook has the ability to work me up. I'm considering opening a bottle of wine.

"He asked me if Jud was the only guy I'd ever been with. When I said yes, he claimed that was all he needed to know to know how I want it. Like he's aware of my sexual fantasies or something. You think it's true?" I bite my lip—holding my breath for her answer.

I want my best friend to tell me that it is possible. That somehow, Cook has found my imaginary, little black book of

44

fantasies my mind crafted after reading Beatrice Small's *Pleasure Series*. But where I'm a dreamer, Emily is a realist. And she'll give it to me straight.

"I think there's only one way to find out."

She's right...

I have six unread text messages from Jud that I refuse to open. I won't let his nasty words hurt me or put a damper on my current mood. Which is a mixture of excitement, apprehension and horniness. There are still a few words in the first message visible to me, and they start with, "Having fun, whore?" But those don't hurt. Actually, they make me feel better about what I'm about to do. I mean, if I'm going to be accused of it, I might as well do it.

Without a second thought, I dial Cook's number. This time, I want him to answer. After about the fourth ring, I'm worried he won't. After the sixth ring, I'm preparing my voicemail speech. Then his voice comes over the line, fucking my name.

"Carmen." My clit literally throbs.

"Hello." It comes out almost a whisper, but it's packed with emotion. I might as well have screamed, "Give me your cock!"

"You feelin' okay, gorgeous?" he asks, his voice is gravelly and low—screaming beneath the surface, "Whose pussy is that?"

His.

Cook's.

This is Cook's pussy.

"I feel like I want some company," I breathe. Too worked up by the possibility of him coming over to care about how desperate I sound. The only noise I hear over the line is the sound of his heavy footsteps.

"You know what's gonna happen if I come over, Carmen." My limbs turn to jelly at the hint of promise in his tone.

"Yes. I know." I swallow back my nerves, but my next words flow like honey past my lips. "I want you to fuck me."

He speaks without hesitation. "Then open the door." I stiffen. *What the hell?*

"You're here?" His answer is a knock. I spin on my heel to face the front door. "But I'm not ready yet!" I squeak, panic filling me as I look down at my ratty T-shirt.

"Too late. Open the door." He's so calm. Meanwhile, I'm running around like crazy. Going from one room to another with no goal in mind.

"Fifteen minutes." I sprint toward the bathroom. "Ten," I counter when he doesn't respond.

"Now."

"But I have to shave!" I slap my forehead. *Stupid! He didn't need to know that.* Taking a breath, I calm down a fraction and try to reason with him again. This is my house. The door is locked. He can wait fifteen minutes.

"I wasn't expecting you so soon," I start, surprised at how relaxed I sound. "I need to do a few things first, but I'll call you as soon as I'm finished and you—" My words catch in my throat when his reflection appears in my bathroom mirror. As if I'm not fully convinced it's real, I turn and find him standing only feet from me.

This is the first time I've ever seen him look serious. There's no smile. No smirk. No winking or teasing or laughing. That may even be anger in his fiery, hooded eyes. But I give zero shits. This is bad-boy-biker Cook, in all his six foot plus, muscular glory. And he's here to fuck me—hairy legs be damned.

"Strip." The order has an edge to it—dominant and controlling, leaving no room for negotiation.

My heart is hammering. I feel light headed. Butterflies in my belly is an understatement. Panties soaked. Nipples hard. I'm two seconds from coming. And he wants me to strip. But I can't move. My eyes are glued to his ringed fingers. I want them inside me too.

"Strip. Carmen. Now." He doesn't yell, but I wish he would. Somehow, this voice is scarier. My nerves start to surface, diffusing some of that lust that's clouding my better judgement.

"You're not smiling," I whisper, as if to explain my apprehension. I guess it's better than, "You're starting to scare the hell out of me." But he doesn't soften. He simply lifts his lips in an evil grin. If it were possible for him to get any hotter, he just did.

46

"I'm going to give you to the count of three," he says, crossing his arms over his chest. The stance makes him that much more intimidating.

My mind is at war with my body. This is one of my fantasies. I want control. A little danger. I want him to grab me, strip me, spank me then fuck me. In that order. Or whatever order he wants. But my mind is screaming that this isn't normal. That I should call 9-1-1. Grab my scissors from the drawer next to me, stab him and run.

"One."

Shit. He's counting. I'm still deciding if I want to play this game. "Wait!"

"Two."

Shitty-Shitty-Shit-Shit... "If I ask you to leave, will you?" He quirks a brow. Shakes his head. And I know what's coming next.

"Three."

Quick! Gun to your head...do you trust him? Yes or no.

Yes.

The decision is made. This is happening. Not that it matters now, he's on his way over. I'm not breathing. And I'm not sure if I want to launch myself at him or duck and run. I'm not doing either. I'm just standing here like a deer in the headlights. Twisting my shirt in my hands. Trying to look at every part of him at once. It's impossible. For some reason, he looks bigger today. Like he ate one of Mario's magic mushrooms.

I'm expecting him to rip my shirt off. Grab the collar with both hands and tear it down the middle like they do in the movies. Instead, he slides his hands up my arms—slow and sensual. I concentrate on the rise and fall of his chest. His breaths are controlled, measured. Mine are erratic, loud pants.

His fingers trail up my neck. Fist in my hair. He pulls until I'm forced to look up at him. The pressure on my scalp. The hold he has on me. The parting of his lips and the dare in his eyes. All these things send a sinfully erotic charge through the room—erasing any and all doubt I might have had about him being here.

"You still want to ask me to leave?" My body flush against his, I can feel every word he speaks.

I try to shake my head, but his grip is too tight—forcing me to answer him. "No."

Then his mouth is on mine. Just like the first time he kissed me, he doesn't wait for permission. He takes what he wants. Exploring my mouth with his greedy, punishing tongue. He kisses like he's angry. Hungry. Like he can't get enough. *I* can't get enough.

My hands move under his shirt finding hot, hard planes of muscles that singe the tips of my fingers. His body is on fire. Heat radiates from his skin that is velvety smooth under my touch. I explore more of his chest, my thumbs dragging over chiseled, defined abs before lightly caressing his nipples.

One hand still fisted in my hair, he cups my ass with the other and squeezes hard. Gripping his shoulders, I lift my legs around his waist. His hard erection presses against me, eliciting a moan that's muffled by his mouth.

I feel like I'm floating as he carries us out of the bathroom. I've only read about sub space, but that has to be where I'm at right now. And he's only kissed me. My toes curl painfully at the thought of where I'll be when he pushes inside me.

With my hands trapped beneath his shirt, the only thing I can do is hold on when I feel us falling. Then my back is on the bed. He's between my legs. Cool, rough fingers are under my shirt. They tickle my skin—prompting me to bring my elbows down in defense. The moment my hands are free of him, he's pulling my shirt over my head.

Sitting back, he places his hands on my knees—parting them slowly. I fight the urge to close my legs and cover my breasts, but by the look in his eyes, I'm guessing he wouldn't like that very much. Although, I might not be so uncomfortable if he didn't have all his clothes on. *And if I could remember what underwear I'm wearing...*

"I'm gonna take my time with you, Carmen," he says, his gaze traveling over every inch of my exposed skin. He's so calm. I'm panting like I've just swam the Mississippi. But when he meets my eyes, I can't breathe at all. His look is feral. Predatory. So...dominant.

Have mercy.
He's a dominant.
He's going to spank me.
And I want him to.
But only if it doesn't hurt.

"What's goin' on in that head of yours, gorgeous?" His voice has me fisting the sheets. I'm nearly naked. Wearing who knows what kind of panties. And he just called me gorgeous.

"I don't think I've ever been so horny," I whisper, the endorphin rush has me so high I can't even hate myself for saying it out loud.

His eyes drop to my sex. "I can see how wet your pussy is." Heat spreads across my chest and up my neck before inflaming my cheeks. "I can smell it too." I cover my eyes and silently pray for death, while his finger trails the prickly path from my knee to my groin.

Despite how embarrassed I am by his dirty talk, my unshaved legs, strong scent, river of arousal and underwear, I find myself grinding my hips in anticipation. I need him to touch me. I'm afraid if he doesn't, I'm going to combust.

"You think too much," he says, his voice so low I wonder if he meant to speak those words out loud. *Been there...* He teases my skin along the hem of my panties. His touch just enough for me to know it's there. "Just relax, Carmen."

"I am relaxed," I mutter, twisting my body in an effort to urge him to get on with it. He simply moves his finger back to my knee and starts the agonizingly slow, torture of trailing it back down my leg.

Something between a grunt and a growl escapes my lips. Frustrated, I close my knees—capturing his hand between my legs. And like a bitch in heat, I tighten my thighs and grind my hips. I'm rewarded with some friction from either his rings or knuckles, right against my clit. The two seconds of bliss is nearly enough to push me over the edge. But before I can get there, his other hand grips my hip and jerks me to my side.

A loud smack sounds around the room, followed by a stinging sensation on my ass. I gasp in shock, still processing what happened as I'm pushed to my back, legs parted and his finger is again on my knee.

"I said I was gonna take my time." His tone has the same deep, sultry tenor. His eyes are still focused on my sex. He's acting like nothing just happened. I need a session with my shrink and a cigarette.

"You," I start, pausing to lick my dry lips and take a couple breaths. "You spanked me."

Head still bowed, he looks up at me from beneath his lashes. The corner of his mouth curves and he winks. "You liked it."

"I did not." *Liar, liar, crotch on fire. But don't worry, the flood happening down there will put it out.*

He doesn't respond to my obvious lie. But he does slip his finger beneath my panties and drag it between my lips before spreading the wetness on my thigh. I ignore his smirk and let my head fall back. Closing my eyes, I will my body to relax and focus on the lingering sting of his hand on me, the constant torture of his finger and the reminder that very soon, he's going to let me come.

"Maybe I should spank you more often," he says, pushing his finger inside me.

His suggestion is forgotten as I arch my back. "Please," I whimper, tossing the small amount of dignity I have left. "Please don't stop."

"You like me finger fucking you?" I let out a soft mewl and nod. He adds another finger, stretching me—slowly pumping them in and out of me. "Knees open, gorgeous." I hadn't even realized I'd closed them, and at his command, I let them fall back open again. "Good girl."

"*Son-of-a...*" *Damn.* How is it possible to feel this good? It's so good, I don't want to come. I don't want it to be over. The rhythm and pressure he's delivering is just enough to make sure that doesn't happen. And the dirty talk is like frosting on a cake—it's still edible without it, but not nearly as good.

"Fuck." The harshness in his tone has my eyes flying open just in time to see him reach inside his cut. I was so lost in the feeling of what he was doing to me that I hadn't even heard it ring, but now his ringtone, the sound of motorcycle pipes, fills my ears.

When the bed shifts, I know he's about to pull away. Before I think better of it, I'm begging. "Please." His movements never slow as he looks at me. "Answer it. Don't answer it. I don't care. Just don't stop." Without taking his eyes off mine, he presses the screen and puts the phone to his ear. I let out a breath when he continues fingering me despite the interruption.

"Yeah." It's the only word I hear. He's speaking, but the words are lost as I sink back into my happy place. I'm only there a few moments when his fingers still—prompting me to look up. I find him with a finger over his smiling lips. *Had I been moaning?* Flushing, I cover my mouth with my hand and squeeze my eyes shut. He rewards my obedience by moving inside me once again.

My obedience?

More aware of what's happening around me, I catch bits and pieces of his conversation. The words, "I'm thirty minutes out" have me wanting to yell to whoever is on the line that he's busy right now. *Selfish bastards.*

"Bad news, gorgeous."

"No," I snap. He shoots me an amused look. "You're not leaving."

"Greedy, impatient girl," he tsks, removing his fingers--leaving me feeling hollow and empty. When he puts them in his mouth, I nearly faint. *Why does that just get me?*

Embarrassment morphs to curiosity as he stands, but makes no move to leave. Instead, he takes off his cut, folds it and lays it on my nightstand. He places a condom between his lips, giving me a chin tip as he unbuckles his belt.

"Take your panties off." His command has my stomach flipping. I wondered what it would sound like for him to say that. Now I know. And it was better than I could've imagined.

"You're not leaving?"

51

"Fuck no." Reaching behind him, he fists his shirt in his hand and pulls it over his head. "But I don't have long, so either pull em' down or I'm tearin' em' off."

Puddle.

There's a puddle beneath me.

My nerves start to get the best of me and I do what I do best when I'm nervous. I ramble. "I-I thought you were going to take your time. Go slow." *Spank me more often....*

His jeans hang open revealing white boxers. When his hand disappears inside, I jerk my eyes to his. He winks. "Next time."

Next time? There might not be a next time.... My thoughts trail off as my eyes move to his naked torso. *OMG...*the man is not just built, but ripped. Corded deltoids. Sculpted pecs. Bulging biceps. Abs that could be the mold for an oversized ice tray.

His chest and stomach are smooth, but there's a fine line of dark hair that centers the notorious man V. But even in all its glory, the perfection of his upper body can't compare to what he holds in his hand.

It's big. *Really big.* I've never found a penis to be sexy, but then again, I've never called another man's knees handsome or an Adam's Apple lickable. And there's something about the way his ring covered fingers wrap around it that gives it an edge of danger. Maybe it's the skull that glares back at me—promising me death by orgasm.

"Not a fan of the panties?" I can sense his smile, but when I chance a look, there is none. He's back to looking predatory and determined. As nice as his cock is, because penis is now a word reserved for ordinary male sex organs, I can't look away from his eyes. They're darker—like a blue flame. And just as damn hot as one.

He holds my gaze as he sheaths the condom expertly. He's probably done this hundreds of times. I'll just be another notch on the ol' belt. Perfect. Maybe after he's finished with me, I'll never see him again. That way I'll never have to relive the humiliation of today. *Unless we elope and spend our days and nights having sex for the rest of our lives....*

"You're thinking again." His tenacious look hardens. Kneeling between my legs, he reaches for my underwear. My hips jerk, I hear a tearing sound, and then the head of him is against my entrance. "Let me remedy your wandering mind." He pushes through my tight opening until the head is seated inside me. "I like it better when you moan."

I'm expecting some quick, deep thrust that will likely render me unconscious. But I get a slow, consistent filling—inch by inch until his hands are on either side of my head, his nose is touching my nose and he's buried to the hilt inside me.

It's so overwhelming, it takes my breath. There's no pain, but the fullness of him is so intense, my body won't allow me to enjoy the pleasure. His mouth covers mine with a deep, yet quick kiss. When he breaks away, he pulls my lip between his teeth, giving it a light nibble. Then, as if he's in my head, he promises, "It gets better, gorgeous."

And somehow, I know it will.

Allowing me time to adjust to his thickness and length, his hips move slow at first delivering short, measured strokes that gradually awaken my pleasure points. Relaxing, I breathe deep and inhale the scent of my arousal lingering on his breath.

Sliding my hands up his arms, I curl them around his shoulders. He's in me. On me. Engulfing me with his heat. Burning me with his stare. Pulling me deeper into this moment, away from my erratic thoughts until my focus is only on him.

Sooner than I thought possible, I feel my knees fall further apart. My fingers curl into his hair, and I'm asking for more. His strokes grow longer. Deeper. Working me until he's nearly all the way out before filling me again.

"You have the sexiest fuckin' moans," he growls, and I respond with another whimper that begs for something. Anything. Dragging one hand down my side, over my hip and to my knee, he pushes it toward my chest. And with the swivel of his hips, something happens.

Sweat dampens my skin. Heat explodes from deep inside me. I don't know where the sudden blast of pleasure came from. There was no build up. No time to anticipate or prepare. Apparently, there really is a secret sweet spot. And he just found it.

"Harder. More. Deeper." I realize I sound like a phone sex operator, or the narrator of a cheap porn movie, but the thought is fleeting. Because when I asked, he gave.

He's relentless as he pounds into me. His drive is unmerciful. I can feel my arousal as it pours from me—prompting me to clench around him to stop it.

"Let it go, gorgeous," Cook says, moving his lips across my jaw. Unable to fight it any longer, I let go. My entire body goes slack as I come hard around him. Wave after exhilarating wave hits me over and over. My pussy tightens around him and his cock pulses in response with every jolt of pleasure that rockets through us.

I'm floating. Dropping. Spiraling out of control. The free fall is breathtaking. Consuming. I can feel it in my toes. Tingling in my spine. My mind is clear. Body liquefied. I'm sated. Happy. Complete. And if I can't walk tomorrow, it will still have been worth it.

Just like the last time Cook took me to orgasm land, it takes a moment for me to come back down to Earth. By the time I do, he has stilled inside me and is covering my face with sweet kisses. His lips brushing across my eyes. Nose. Cheeks. Across my jaw and the corners of my mouth. My stomach flutters from the show of affection. I expected the sex to be mind-blowing. The intimacy came as a surprise.

But the moment is lost when he pulls back and gives me a smirk. "You're a great fuckin' lay." I can't help but laugh. He looks carefree and boyish as he grins down at me. But the look is a façade. There's nothing boyish about this man.

"And you didn't even have to buy me dinner," I quip, attempting to shove him off me. Regretfully, it works. He pulls out of me slowly, and I cross one knee over the other the moment he does. *There's no telling what that thing looks like. He's probably ruined it.*

Nevertheless, his eyes drop and a sinful smile spreads over his lips. "Didn't peg you to be a squirter."

My eyes widen as I feel the blood drain from my face. *Is that what I am? Is that what happened? Is something wrong with me?* Horrified, I grab the edge of the comforter and cover myself. If I never see him again, it will be too soon.

Sitting up, I pull the cover tighter around me. "That's never happened before," I say in my defense.

"Hey." His cockiness is gone, replaced with a rueful expression as he stares down at me. "That's a good thing. A really, really good thing."

"I'm not so sure about that... I thought only porn stars had the ability to be...*squirters,* as you so eloquently put it."

He beams. "Never fucked a porn star before. Glad you were my first."

I throw a pillow that he easily dodges. "Shut up." I try to look angry, but my smile matches his.

There's something about his presence that makes me feel comfortable. Like I've known him all my life. Sure I embarrass myself every time he's around, but it's different with him. The moment happens, then it fades. There's no lingering sense of shame surrounding me. If I'd have repeatedly made an idiot out of myself around anyone else, I'd be drowning myself in the bathtub to escape humiliation.

"You got plans tonight?" he asks, disappearing into the bathroom. I crane my neck to watch him, but he keeps his back to me.

"I don't think so. Why?"

"I still owe you a steak."

"Don't you have somewhere to be?" I ask, just as he walks back in the bedroom. He's dressed now, and when he pulls his vest over his shoulders, he looks exactly like he did when he arrived. I look like I've been rode hard and put up wet—pun intended.

"Yes, I do. And I have seventeen minutes to get there."

"Will you make it?"

He shrugs, but he's confident. "I'll have to do about one forty the entire way. Shouldn't be a problem."

"A hundred and forty miles per hour?"

"Yep, so if I don't die, I'll see you at six." Before I can respond, he walks out of the room—his focus on his phone. Wrapping myself in the blanket, I follow him.

"Well, do I need to do anything?"

"Yeah," he calls over his shoulder. "Shave your legs."

Maybe I'll be drowning in the bathtub after all....

6
THE PLAN

Still wrapped in my blanket, I grab my phone and take a seat on the chaise lounge—the only piece of furniture in my living room. After all the excitement of yesterday, I'd completely forgotten to check my grades. Feeling a mixture of excitement and nerves, I start to log in to my student account, but the six unread text messages on my phone taunt me. Putting off my grades once again, I exit out of the screen and look at my texts.

Is that the best you can do, Carmen?

If you're trying to make me jealous, it's not working.

A prospect? Do you even know what that is?

Trust me, if you did, you wouldn't be fucking one.

You're going to have to do better than him to get my attention.

Never mind… You can't do better than him. Because a real brother wouldn't give you the time of day. If you weren't good enough for me, you sure as hell won't be good enough for them. Have fun with your toy, Carmen. I'm going to enjoy watching you make a fool of yourself.

Furious, I Google the meaning of Prospect. There are hundreds of articles that answer my question, but most of them say the same thing—a Prospect is someone who's trying to prove themselves to the club. They're not even a "brother."

Great. I went into this with one goal in mind. Problem is, both times I've tried, I've only managed to do just as he said—make a fool out of myself. I simply want to make Jud pay by hooking up with his brothers, like he hooked up with my sisters. If it weren't for the mind blowing, best I've ever had orgasms, the time I'd spent with Cook would've been a waste.

Frustrated, angry and a little hurt by Jud's words, I power off my phone. My day was perfect, but leave it to Jud to go and screw that up. He still manages to ruin my life even months after he's no longer a part of it. I hate that the wound is still fresh. I hate that I still think of him. I wish I could move on like he did. I thought I knew how.

But my scars run too deep. As much as I hate to admit it, a part of me still loves him. I want to be angry. I want revenge. But my plan has backfired. And Jud's betrayal was like venomous fangs piercing right through my heart. Not even "getting under" Cook could cure me from his poison.

"Don't you look..." Cook raises a brow, "cute."

I follow his gaze to my onesie pajamas that have the exact replica of Wonder Woman's costume printed on it. It even looks like I'm wearing the boots. They may not be the prettiest, but they're comfy. And reserved for only the shittiest or best of times.

"Shut up," I mutter, grabbing the bottle of wine out of his hand before leaving him at the door.

"Heroic?" he teases, joining me in the kitchen as I work to uncork the wine.

"I'm having a bad day."

He moves from behind me, placing his hands on the counter and boxing me in. Pressing his lips to my ear, he whispers, "You offend me, Carmen." My eyes flutter closed when his tongue licks the shell of my ear. Goosebumps cover my skin as I recall the words he said last night. He'd promised to leave his mark. He didn't lie. All day, every time I'd move, I was reminded of what we did. How it felt. How it still feels.

"I didn't mean..." I trail off when he presses his lips to my neck. The buzzer on my dryer goes off at that precise moment. He laughs as he pulls away from me—leaving me flustered and breathless.

"Is that the sheets?"

My desire vanishes just as quickly as it appeared. Scowling, I shoot him a dirty look. He wiggles his eyebrows. "I'm starving," I say, eager to change the subject. "Tell me you brought food."

He points to the two grocery bags on my counter. "No, I carry an armload of shit around with me everywhere I go."

"Smartass."

He laughs, taking the bottle of wine I'm still struggling to uncork. "Okay. I'll stop being a jerk and ask the big question. What's wrong?"

"Everything!" I fall dramatically on the chaise and cross my arm over my eyes. But I can feel Cook smiling at me from the kitchen. "Jud texted. And he's obviously jealous, but seeing us together didn't do the damage I was hoping for."

"You know I bought this wine to cook with, but if you need it that bad..." His voice drops to a mumble. "I don't know how you could want it after last night."

I shoot him a look. "It's wine. That's how." I refrain from telling him I may or may not be a wino. Or how I was raised in a house with a wine cellar that was bigger than our family room.

"Here." He hands me a glass of red. "Not sure if you'll like it or not."

"I'll like it," I assure him, taking a big gulp. And, of course, like it.

"So what makes you think he's not that damaged?"

As Cook starts to...cook, I power up my phone again and read him the messages. I'm expecting him to tense. Get angry. At least express some emotion that isn't happpniess as I tell him the nasty things Jud said about him. The only time he seems the least bit agitated is when I read the message where Jud claimed I wasn't good enough for him. But even then, he just shook his head and never said a word.

During the discussion, I'd made my way to the kitchen and am sitting on the counter next to the stove while Cook prepares dinner. Watching him work is distracting. He seems as comfortable with me as I am with him.

"Are we friends?" I ask, curious to know what he thinks of me.

He thinks for a moment. "You don't know enough about me to consider me a friend." The reality is a little unnerving. I knew absolutely nothing about this man, yet here he is. In my house. For the third time. *Which reminds me...*

"You broke into my house."

Grinning, he shakes his head. "Hardly. I used a key."

I blanch. "A key?"

"Yeah." He grows serious a moment, abandoning the food long enough to point a set of tongs at me. "Stop leaving the motherfucker under the mat. Do you want to get kidnapped and raped?"

Flushing, I drop my head—attempting to hide my red face. But of course, he saw it. "You're just full of surprises," he teases, pinching my nipple with the tongs. I swat his hand away and grab my wine—draining the glass.

I don't want just *anyone* to come in, kidnap and rape me. But role play is definitely something I'm curious about. And the thought of Cook wearing a black mask, kicking down my door, tying me up, ripping off my clothes...raping the willing. *Damn you, Beatrice Small!*

In an effort to distract my dirty mind, I decide to try and find out a little more about my fantasy rapist. "Tell me something about you."

"Like what?" I watch as he moves fluidly from the sink to the stove. Every step is graceful and precise, even though he's not familiar with my kitchen.

"Is cooking how you got your name?"

He smirks at my question. "Yeah, but probably not in the way you think." Tossing a dishcloth over his shoulder, he leans back on the island across from me—crossing his arms and ankles.

"Riding names are usually given to you during your prospect period. I got mine because for the first three months I did this. I was constantly fuckin' up and as punishment, I had to do all the event cooking. Since it was summer when I started, there was something every weekend. I counted every hamburger, hotdog and piece of chicken I grilled. I never thought the number would come in handy. Then one day Ronnie asked me how many of each I'd cooked."

"And you knew?" I cut in. He nods. For some reason, I'm captivated. I want to hear about everything he's done while prospecting. *Or maybe I just want to hear him talk.*

"So the name stuck. It was that or hamburger."

I laugh, unable to imagine him with a name like hamburger. Although I'm sure like everything else, he'd wear it well. *How in the hell is he single?* "Why hasn't some girl scooped you up yet?"

"Scooped me up?"

"Yeah. I mean, you're funny. Smart. You cook. You're semi attractive." I grin at him. He grins back.

"Semi, huh?"

I hold my fingers up and squint at the small space between them. "Just a little." For a few moments we just stare at each other. Smiling—waiting for something. Maybe he'll kiss me.

"Enough about me," he says, pulling the towel from his shoulder and straightening. He smacks my leg with it as he tends to the steaks on the stove. "What you gonna do about Jud?"

"I'm going to follow through on my plan."

"The plan...I gotta hear this, but first." He hands me a plate and I hold it dutifully as he forks a steak onto it along with some asparagus. Refilling my glass with wine, he looks at me out of the corner of his eye. "I've never ate a steak standing up."

I open my mouth. Close it. Look around the room. "Wait here." I sit my plate on the bar and sprint to my bedroom. It takes me a minute, but I manage to clean off my night stand and drag it into the living room. Then I grab two pillows—tossing them to the floor on either side.

Cook's watches me from the kitchen, impressed by my ability to improvise. "Now you don't have to eat standing up." I grab my wine and plate. Taking a sip, I wink at him over the top of my glass.

"Nope." He winks back at me. "Now I get to eat it while I sit...on the floor." I ignore his remark as I all but throw myself down and dig in. The food smells delicious and, no surprise, tastes delicious too. *Probably because it was prepared by Mr. Delicious himself....*

"I used to live in a house on campus," I start, feeling the need to defend my lack of luxury. "But when Jud started screwing the girls who lived there with me, it became a little awkward."

He looks surprised. "There was more than one?"

"Yep. Four that I know of. But I didn't find out until after we broke up. Clarissa, the skank he's with now, is the reason we split."

"So you moved out after Clarissa?" I nod. "Why would you move here?"

I shrug. "It's close to my job. And the neighborhood is quiet."

He smirks, shifting his eyes around the room. "I think your priorities are a little fucked up, babe."

My fork stills less than an inch from my lips. "What does that mean?"

"It means you're living in a shitty apartment and driving an eighty-thousand-dollar car." As always, he's amused by this. I'm not. If anything, my feelings are a little hurt and I become defensive.

"My parents bought me that car two years ago before I came to Louisiana. They also pay over a hundred thousand dollars a year for out of state tuition, because like a fool, I chose LSU instead of a university in Georgia, just so I could be with the man I loved." Angry tears burn my eyes, but I refuse to let them fall.

"Carmen..." He tries to intervene but I cut him off. My anger mixes with confusion at his cocky grin and laughing eyes. He doesn't look the least bit apologetic.

"So when I left my house on campus, I spent every penny I had getting this *shitty apartment*, and got a *shitty job* so I could pay for it. Want to know why? Because I'm a twenty-two-year-old, grown woman who refuses to ask her parents for help. They demand to pay for my education, and I can live with that. But I can't let them pay for my mistakes." I throw my napkin down on my plate and stand.

"Sure," I start again, waving my hands around the room. "It's cheap and simple and doesn't have any furniture. But it's the first thing I've done on my own. And I'm not ashamed of it." I stomp to the kitchen, plate in hand and toss it in the sink. My steak is only half finished, but I've lost my appetite. Besides, wine is better anyway.

"You through throwin' your bitch fit?" I spin around so fast I nearly lose my balance—finding him standing right behind me.

"Are you serious right now?"

He holds his hands up and tries to fight his smile. Lifting his hip, he sits on the corner of the counter. "I'm just messin' with you, gorgeous. I knew all that shit before you told me."

My eyes narrow. "How?"

"I'm not stupid, and I sure as fuck ain't blind."

"What does that even mean?" I shriek, starting to lose my temper. He wants to laugh, but doesn't.

"It means I pay attention to you." The exasperation I'm feeling on the inside must reflect in my eyes, because he elaborates. "Okay, for instance, the first time I met you, you wouldn't even say fuck."

"Fuck, fuck, fuck," I spit.

"Impressive, but I wasn't finished."

"Well fuck. Fuckin' hurry up." He covers his mouth with his hand. I know it's because the *fucker* thinks he can hide his laugh. But I'm not deaf. I can hear him. Fucking...laughing. *Damn. It still doesn't feel right.*

"When I got in your car last night, it was clean. Your gas tank was nearly full. I get to your place and it's neat. Everything in your cabinets is organized. Babe, those ugly fuckin' pajamas even have creases." He looks at me like I should understand what in the hell he's talking about. I'm glaring at him for insulting my clothes.

"Don't talk about my pajamas. They're awesome."

"Really, they're not."

"Whatever. I still don't understand how you can know about my situation based off of my organizational skills."

His smile is easy as he studies me a moment before he explains. "You don't say fuck because you were raised proper. Probably grew up in a nice neighborhood with two loving parents who instilled morals and values in you at a young age. Dad makes good money, but he worked for it. Taught you to appreciate things—like the eighty-thousand-dollar car you're driving." I roll my eyes. *I hate that he's right.*

"You're considerate and kind. You're proud of what you have and you take care of it. People like that are pretty easy to figure out. Mostly because they're conservative, which makes them almost always predictable."

I empty the rest of the wine in my glass, thankful that I have a few more bottles under the counter. "Well, Mr. Know-it-all, then I guess you already know my plans for Jud."

"The plan." He cocks his head to the side and narrows his eyes on me. "Nope. I don't think I do. But I'm *dying* to find out." *Smartass.*

I look at him over the top of my glass. "I'm going to fuck all his brothers." He pretends to be shocked and impressed. But I know he thinks I'm full of shit.

"*All* of them?"

"At least five."

"Wow. Five. That's a lot. But you can do it." He winks at me.

"Will you help me?" He laughs, it's deep and throaty and if he weren't laughing at me, I'd probably be turned on. *Okay...so I'm still a little turned on.*

"I can't help you fuck them, gorgeous. But I'll be more than happy to fuck you myself anytime you want. We can even fuck in the shower." He leans in and whispers, "Less cleanup."

Embarrassed, I turn on my heel in search of wine. As much as I'd love to let him take me in the shower, anytime I want, I'm determined to get back at Jud first. If it takes five brothers or fifty, then so be it. But I'm not stopping until I'm satisfied he's as hurt or as angry as I am. Then, if Cook's offer is still on the table, I'll take him up on it.

"Me and you...that won't work," I mutter regretfully.

"Because my position isn't important enough, right?" Peaking around the cabinet door, I expect to find him wounded. I breathe a sigh of relief when I see that signature smile.

"Exactly. But you can still help me." He shoots me an expectant look as I struggle to uncork the bottle of wine. "I mean...I know you're just a Prospect but don't you know everyone? And do you know their rankings? I want to make sure they're all ranked higher than him. That will really piss him off." He laughs again. Am I really that funny?

"Tell you what, gorgeous," he says, standing like he's preparing to leave. "Thursday night is bike night at Pops. They'll all be there. I'll make sure you're introduced to them."

"Really?"

"Really." My eyes zero in on his ass as he walks away. *I hate I didn't get to see it.* Maybe one day. But first...

"Do you think they'll be interested?" I ask, wringing my hands nervously. "You know, in me?"

He pauses at the door, turning to look at me over his shoulder. "Oh, gettin' them to fuck you won't be the problem."

I frown. "Well then what's the problem?"

"You'll figure it out. Besides, what do I know?" Lowering his sunglasses over his eyes, he shoots me a smirk. "I'm just a Prospect."

7
PATCHWHORE

"Shit!"

My voice echoes off the walls of my apartment as I sprint to the bathroom—shedding my Waffle House uniform as I go. After getting up at five and working eight hours, I was drained. It probably had more to do with the bottle of wine I consumed last night when I finally had the chance to look up my grades without interruption. But by noon, I was feeling the effects of my 4.0 GPA, solo, celebration party. Thinking I had time for a quick nap, I'd crashed. Now, as I furiously scrub under the scalding water, I mentally kick myself for not setting an alarm.

In record time I'm showered, dressed and in my car heading toward the bar. Worry starts to creep in on the drive. Just as it had last night. What if Cook lied? What if bike night was last night and he lied so I wouldn't go? His only reason would be he's jealous. The thought makes me smile. *He likes me.*

I'd called Emily and told her how my weekend turned out. She shared my suspicions of Cook being into me, and although thrilled that he'd been so amazing in bed, she didn't think any sex—no matter how great—was worth ruining "the plan." Sadly, neither Cook nor his magnificent cock was of any use in my quest for vengeance. He was merely a Prospect. He'd said so himself.

The idea that he might've lied fades as I near the parking lot. The place is packed. Bikes line up next to one another in row after row. I'm forced to park in the lot across the street and walk the rest of the way.

Beads of sweat tickle the back of my neck. Butterflies swim in my belly. My heart hammers against my chest as I plaster a smile on my face. Pulling open the door, I prepare to make my grand entrance. But there's not a biker in sight.

"Well, you're just becomin' a regular around here, huh?" Kat greets, leaning over the bar and exposing the tops of her large breasts. And I'm sure in her position, the cheeks of her ass can be seen from beneath her skirt. I thought my low-cut top, tight jeans and heels made me sexy. But after seeing Kat, my attire feels...conservative.

Damn Cook for putting that word in my head.

"I heard tonight was bike night," I say, climbing up on a barstool and looking around as if I might find a hoard of bikers gathered in a corner.

"You heard right. But they're in a meeting. Should be wrappin' it up soon."

"Oh." *So much for my grand entrance.*

She narrows her eyes on me—smacking that gum of hers. I'm starting to notice everyone here has some kind of nervous tick. Cook and his smiles... Kat and her gum... Ronnie and his tequila. Although, that might be alcoholism.

"What you really doin' here? You still tryin' to piss off Jud?" Even though a part of me wants to tell her everything, I don't want her to be aware of my ignorance when it comes to motorcycle clubs. So I decide to refrain from telling her how I wasn't aware that Cook's position in the club made my *interactions* with him, less painful for Jud.

"Clarissa, Jud's new girlfriend, was more than just my friend. We were sorority sisters."

Kat laughs, giving me a sideways glance as she tosses ice in a cup. "Did you just say *sorority* sisters?" I nod. "Like in the movies? Like pillow fights and a shitload of chicks in one house?" she asks, sliding me the drink. I take a sip—silently thanking her for not making it very strong.

"It's more than that, but yes. We lived in a house together. Although, I don't remember us ever having a pillow fight."

"So she was your friend and your...roommate."

What Kat's seen on T.V. is likely the only knowledge she has when it comes to sororities. Much like me when it comes to MC's. Keeping that in mind, I try to explain it to her without becoming frustrated by her stereotypical attitude.

"I know sororities don't have the best reputation. But there are a lot of us who really believe in the organization. We take our pledge seriously. We uphold our bi-laws. We are true sisters."

"Kinda like the MC, huh?" She's nodding in understanding. Suddenly realizing how similar the two are, I agree with her.

"Exactly. Of course, I don't know as much about an MC, but from what I do know the unity is the same."

Still nodding her head, her smile widens. "I get it. He fucked your sister. Now you're gonna fuck his brother."

"Yes." I take another sip of my drink to hide my disappointment. She'd just ruined my big reveal.

Rubbing her hands together, Kat bounces on her toes. "Oh this shit is gonna be epic. Girl, which one you want. I know em' all. And ain't none of em' married or got a girlfriend."

I'm glad I can get information from Kat instead of Cook. He's too damn distracting. And I have to stay focused if I'm going to do this. And probably drunk.

"Do you know Jud's rank?"

"He's not an officer. Just a patch holder." *Perfect.*

"Then I'll start with the lowest ranking officer in the club."

"Start?" Crossing her arms, she narrows her eyes on me. "What you mean start? How many you plan on gettin' with?"

I smile. Her mouth forms an O of surprise even before I say the words, "Every fucking one of them."

In the twenty minutes it takes the club to wrap up their meeting, I've consumed enough alcohol to calm my nerves. I've also doubled the amount of water I normally drink to ensure I don't end up face first on my bathroom floor. Again.

I watch as they pile into the main bar—entering through a door in the back I hadn't noticed before. And with the men, come the women. Of course Clarissa is here, looking so damn pretty it makes my stomach turn.

"I hate her," I mumble to myself.

"Me too." My eyes swing to the girl who takes a seat next to me. Her long, black hair covers more of her than her clothes. The T-shirt she wears is cut so short, the bottom of her breasts are visible. And the pockets of her cutoff shorts are longer than the shorts themselves.

She checks me out too then gives me a sweet smile when she finally makes it back to my face. "I'm Delilah. Can I buy you a drink?" *Is she hitting on me? Just being nice? Is she an ol' lady?* Confused, I just nod my head.

"She's straight, D," Kat says. "And if she changes her mind, you gotta get in line behind me." I turn my head as I toss back the shot Kat gives me in hopes of hiding the flush I feel in my cheeks.

"So what's your name and why do you hate her?"

Not giving me a chance to answer, Kat jumps in the conversation. "Her name is Carmen. And Jud is her ex. He cheated on her with Clarissa." Kat leans over and whisper shouts in Delilah's face. "She was her *sorority* sister."

"No shit?" Delilah shoots me a surprised look. "Like on T.V.?" I fight the urge to roll my eyes. "You sure she's straight? I heard crazy ménage shit happens in sororities."

"I can hear you," I snap. Kat laughs as she walks off, leaving me alone with the horny, beautiful woman. "And I've never had a ménage." She mistakes my admission as an invitation.

"There's a first time for everything." Delilah drags a long, red fingernail down my arm—leaving a path of goosebumps in its wake. *Damn you, body.*

"Are you playing nice, Delilah?"

My breath catches at the sound of Cook's voice. I try to appear unaffected, but when I see his arm slip around her shoulders out of the corner of my eye, I can't stop the urge to turn and look at him. Once again, he's just...*delicious.*

"I'm trying to get sorority sister over here to let me pop her bisexual cherry."

He laughs. "Well stop trying, babe. This one has other plans." I stare at both of them—his arm still around those shoulders and smiles on both their faces as they stare back at me. "I promised you an introduction, and who better than Delilah to help?"

He turns to look at her before going on to tell me about her. "She's from out of town. Here only for the weekend. She's familiar with the...*Eagles.*" His eyes drag back to me—sparkling with a hint of challenge. *Is he trying to make me jealous? Angry? Uncomfortable? Because it's working...*

"Good. Thank you." My tone is clipped. This makes them both smile wider.

"You know the MC gives names to people like you and me," Delilah says. "They call us whores." She picks up two shots from the bar. "Even if you change your ways, the title always stays with you. So to most of the MC, I'm a clubwhore. Can you believe they actually paid me to have sex with bikers?" She gasps dramatically. Inside, I'm doing the same. If she got paid to fuck Cook, well, *lucky her...*

"Now you, my little wet dream, are in a whole other category." Passing me the shot, she crosses her legs and leans forward. "You're considered a *patch*whore. Your form of payment comes in rank instead of money. And from what I'm hearing, your plan is to make it all the way to the top of the MC hierarchy. Right?"

I meet Cook's daring blue eyes before giving Delilah a nod. "Right."

She clinks her glass with mine and winks. "Well, then drink up sugar. You have some *boys* to fuck."

8
IT BEGINS

I follow behind Delilah as she weaves through the crowd toward the back of the bar. Standing on her toes, she waves to someone. I'm trying to keep up—still reeling from her very brazen description of her and Cook's relationship. *"When he was in town, I'd suck his dick."* It took a lot of willpower not to brag about what we'd done. For some reason, it made me feel like I had one up on her.

"Drake, this is Carmen. Carmen, this is Drake." The moment she's finished with the introductions she disappears back into the crowd. I start to follow her when he speaks.

"Hello, beautiful."

I look up at the tall, lanky, unattractive guy with a gap between his two front teeth—so wide you could drive a school bus through it. I'm unimpressed, despite his feeble attempt at trying to woo me. But, I smile anyway and offer him a simple, "Hi."

"Can I get you a drink?"

"Please," I blurt, looking nervously over my shoulder hoping Delilah will reappear, laugh and say she's just playing. That the real Drake is attractive and doesn't have a funky odor.

"Prospect!" I jump at the sound and he smirks. I'm expecting Cook to show up, but an older man appears. He's a lot easier on the eyes than Drake, and smells better too. "Carmen needs a drink, and I'll take another beer."

"Sure thing, patch holder." The man turns to me, a solemn look on his face. "Eagles Prospect Brett, Lake Charles." Holding his hand out, I take it, and offer him a kind smile. "What would you like, ma'am?"

"A margarita, please. But I can get it." It feels wrong asking this man to "fetch" my drink. When clearly it should be Drake.

He seems to relax a little. "I don't mind, Ma'am. It's an honor." *Honor? Ma'am?*

"Does he do everything you tell him to?" I ask Drake when Brett is out of hearing range.

"If he wants a patch, he does what he's told. We all have to do it. When the club decides he's ready, he'll be a full patch holder." Turning, Drake motions to the big patch that's centered on his back. Not surprisingly, it's an eagle.

"You're a patch holder?"

"I'm an officer. Road Captain." *Captain. I like it.*

He leans against the pool table—crossing his arms over his chest. Unashamed, he drags his eyes down my body and licks his lips. It's disgusting. A lot different than delicious. I look over his shoulder, hoping to get a glimpse of Cook. Instead, I find Jud glaring at Drake's back.

Smiling, I focus my attention back on the *captain*. "So what does a Road Captain do?"

"When we ride, I lead the pack. If someone's bike ain't runnin' right, I don't let them ride. I'll even cut a bad tire if I see one. It's for the safety of the club. Not just the rider, but the ones around him. I don't wanna ride next to a man whose rubber is about to blow."

I frown. "That doesn't make them angry? You cutting their tires?"

He shakes his head and gives me a cocky grin. "They can't do shit about it. I'm in charge." His grin fades when Brett appears, handing us our drinks. "That's all," Drake says, dismissing Brett with the wave of his hand.

"If you need anything, let me know."

Drake grabs his elbow, stopping him in his tracks. There's a hardness in the captain's eyes that makes me uncomfortable. "Anything?" Brett nods, and his reaction has an evil smile spreading across Drake's lips. "I want fifty thousand dollars, a brand new car and..." His gaze moves to me. He studies me a moment with lust filled eyes. "Since I already have a brunette, I want a redhead and a blonde to take home."

I have to bite my tongue to keep from telling him that I, am most definitely not his. And to avoid his molesting stare, I glance at Brett. He's white as a ghost. His forehead is dotted in perspiration, and I'm pretty sure he's not breathing. I chance a look back at Drake, and he's still watching me.

"You have an hour, Prospect. If you don't deliver, some other motherfucker will be wearing your patch." Out of the corner of my eye, I see Brett leave quickly. I sip my drink, somewhat impressed by Drake.

"You do realize he won't be back, right?" I ask, shaking my head at his confident smile.

"He'll be back. He wants this too bad."

"Why?"

He shrugs. "Why not? This life is great. Power...authority...women... we have it all."

"I doubt he has fifty grand, a new car and two women just laying around."

Smirking, he reaches out and twirls a lock of my hair. I try not to cringe. "You seem very sure of yourself."

I let out a laugh and give him a disbelieving look. "I have every reason to be confident." Glancing past him, I see Jud still watching us. Despite my disgust, I give Drake my best flirty-smile. "You're the one who shouldn't be so sure," I say, pushing my finger into his chest playfully.

"I'm willing to put my money where my mouth is." He leans closer, and I breathe through my mouth so I don't have to smell him. "If he delivers, you go with me to the poker run Saturday. If he doesn't, then I'll do something for you." Do something for me? *Eww...*

"Considering I'm going to win, I need to know what that something is," I say, and he grins at my words—dropping those boring, brown eyes to my breasts.

"You'll like it." *Doubtful.*

"How about if you win, I'll go to the poker run. But if I win, you take me to dinner." Surely I could stomach one night with this guy for the sake of my plan. Maybe if he thinks we're going out, he'll clean up a little. Take a bath. Wash his greasy ass hair.

"Dinner, huh?" I nod. "You really are a classy bitch." *And you're a tool.* He bites his lip, his head nodding as he surveys my body...again. "Jud's not gonna like this."

"You his Prospect?" My boldness earns me an angry glare. At least this time he's looking at my face.

"Hell no."

"Then we have a deal?"

His lips press into a thin line. "Yeah. We got a deal. And for the record, I don't give a fuck what Jud thinks. He's got property. And it sure as fuck ain't you."

On second thought, Drake isn't so bad after all.

He's bad.

Really bad.

I'm pretty sure I could look past his faults and find something good in him if he didn't smell so awful. And it took me a while, but I finally put a name to the odor—bologna.

For the last hour, he's kept his arm around the back of my chair, with me tucked close to him as we watch the karaoke singers on stage. He often dips his head to whisper in my ear, and I have to hold my breath to keep from gagging. In an effort to dull my sense of smell, I've been drinking heavily. Problem is, the more I drink, the more I want to tell him how repulsed I am.

I could leave. Get some fresh air. Take a shower. Burn his scent out of my nostrils. But there's an upside to standing my ground and refusing to bolt. For one, Jud's palpable anger. And because he's so focused on me, Clarissa is pissed, too. It's a win, win.

Then, there's Cook—a knowing smile on his face. I'm beginning to understand the problem he refused to share with me. He'd said I wouldn't have a problem finding one of Jud's brothers to have sex with me. But if they're all like Drake, the issue lies in finding one I could stomach having sex with.

I want to prove him wrong. I want to wipe that smirk off his face. See defeat in his eyes instead of challenge. If I thought I could do it without vomiting, I'd kiss Drake just to see Cook's reaction. But it's not worth the risk.

We're waiting on Brett, the Prospect, to return. As the minutes tick by, I'm afraid I'm going to have to go on a real date with Drake. Originally, I thought it was a good idea. But that was when I'd weighed it against having sex with him—something I'm now hating myself for even considering.

At least with the poker run, which he evasively explained as a club function, I'd be around other people. Have other scents to distract me. Like the lingering smell of Cook when he passes by. Or the scent of dog shit on the bottom of someone's shoe. Anything other than bologna.

Like an angel, and with only seconds to spare, Brett appears. I'm so happy to see him, I lean forward in my seat—giving my nostrils a temporary reprieve. I stare in awe as Brett sets exactly what Drake requested on the table in front of us. Fifty thousand dollars in *Monopoly* bills, a brand new *toy* car still in the package and two *Barbie's*; a blonde and a redhead.

Brett is proud. Drake looks cocky. And I'm being pulled to my feet. "Carmen here had little faith," Drake says, tucking me possessively into his side. Pretending to stifle a yawn, I cover my mouth and nose. "But I knew you'd pull through. You understand the lesson here?"

Brett nods. "Never offer anything I can't deliver."

76

Thankfully, Drake releases me to hug Brett. I take a breath—my gaze meeting Cook's from a few tables over. He's giving me that all-white-teeth-baring grin. I flip him the finger.

"You want me to pick you up Saturday?" I shake my head at Drake who you'd think just won a prize much greater than me. Little does he know, this is one bet I was more than willing to lose.

"No I'll meet you here," I offer, jerking my head toward the door. "I better get going."

Pressing his hand at the small of my back, he gives me a light push. "I'll walk you out." *Great.* If I have to kiss him...

"Drake." My head jerks up at Cook's voice. "Ronnie wants a word." Drake narrows his eyes, giving him a hard look. Cook only smiles. "Now." I'm surprised Drake doesn't put Cook in his place. Although I doubt he'd be as yielding as Brett had been. But still...he's a Prospect. *Maybe he's a high ranked Prospect.*

Looking down at me, Drake pinches my chin in his fingers. "Saturday. Here. Ten A.M. Don't be late." With that, he walks away and I all but bolt toward the door—my curiosity forgotten.

Once outside, I place my hands on my knees and drag in deep breaths. It's a little dramatic, but one taste of the fresh air has me hungry for more.

"What is that..." My head still bowed, I turn my eyes to Cook to find him fanning his face as he sniffs the air. "Turkey? Ham?"

"It's bologna," I snap. He smiles as I straighten, running my hands down my arms. "Here." I take a step toward him. "Help me get the smell off."

He sidesteps me. "Hell no."

"It's so bad," I whine, fearing I might have to torch my clothes.

"Wait 'till you fuck him."

I scoff. "I'm *not* going to do...that."

"Giving up so soon, are we?"

"I'm not...giving up. I'll just have to go with Plan B."

He quirks a brow. "Plan B?"

"Yeah," I say with more confidence then I feel.

"Can't wait to hear it."

Thoughts of him and Delilah invade my mind. I don't know where they came from, but they're more disturbing than I want to admit. She said she'd changed her ways. After seeing how she was dressed today, I'm not so sure. But just knowing she'd been with him sent a streak of jealously down my spine.

It's silly. I have no claim on him. We're not even friends. But the idea of him with her and me alone doesn't set well with me. If anyone is going to suck his dick while he's in town, it's going to be me.

"If you want, you can come over later and I'll fill you in once I work out the details."

He smirks. "That the only reason you want me to come over?"

Shrugging, I study my keys. "Maybe."

When the silence becomes uncomfortable, I peek up at him from beneath my lashes. But he's not looking at me. His eyes are narrowed on something behind me. Turning, I find a group of men across the parking lot.

"You should go, babe," he says, taking my elbow he guides me across the street to my car. "It's getting' late and you've been drinking. Don't want you to hit a road block."

"I'm not drunk."

He gives me a solemn look, and when he speaks, his voice is off. "You think I'd let you drive if I thought you were?"

"Is something wrong?" I ask, looking back over my shoulder at the men.

"Nah. It's all good." He's smiling. He even winks at me. But I can tell something is not right. His muscles are too tight. His eyes too aware. He's not as relaxed as he usually is—despite his efforts to appear so.

When we reach my car, he opens the door, ushers me in and even leans over to fasten my seatbelt. Wrapping his big hand around the side of my neck, he holds me in place as he gives me a hard stare. "Go home, Carmen."

"Cook, you're scaring me," I admit. "What's going on?" I try to move my head to look around the dark lot, but he holds me in place.

"Nothing is going on. I just need you to go home. I've got a lot goin' on tonight and I don't need to be worried about you."

Letting my nerves get the best of me, I have a mini freak out moment. "Why would you be worried about me? Did I do something? You shouldn't be worried about me. We're not even friends—"

"Damn, woman you're exasperating."

"Tell me why you're worried about me or I'm not leaving." I try to sound harsh, but there's a tremor in my voice. Cook must hear it too, because he softens a little and lets out a breath.

"I'm just doing my job, Carmen." I raise my brows expectantly when he doesn't continue. He seems to be struggling with what to tell me. It's so unlike him. He's always so confident. And his reaction is so unsettling, I'm on the verge of a panic attack.

"Just spit it out," I demand, impatiently.

"Ronnie told me to make sure you got to your car. He doesn't like the idea of you drinking and driving. I assured him you were fine. So if you leave here, go somewhere else, get drunk and get into a wreck, I'm gonna have to answer for it." *That's* what was so hard for him to say?

"Why didn't you just say that?" *Got me all worked up for nothing.* Those men were probably part of his ploy to get me to leave. *He damn sure didn't seem too concerned about them now....*

"I don't have the best track record when it comes to lookin' out for women." His jaw tightens. "I have a certain weakness, I guess you can say."

"Well don't go getting a weakness for me. I'm a big girl. I can take care of myself. And for the record, I'm leaving because I want to. Not because you told me to." *Told him.*

Rolling his eyes, he mutters something under his breath before saying, "I'll call you." When he straightens, I reach out and grab his cut before he can walk away—already forgiving him for scaring me into leaving.

"So you're coming over?" The hope in my voice erases the hard lines in his face and he grins. He drops his gaze and shakes his head before meeting my eyes again.

"Yeah, gorgeous. I'll come over."

I feel victorious as I leave. I may have lost the battle with Drake, but I just won my first ever whore-war. Retired or not, she'll be the one who's alone tonight. It's not that I'm jealous of him and Delilah. But I can't deny that I'm selfish. And If Cook's plan tonight involves sharing a bed with a whore, I want it to be this whore.

Me.

Carmen...

The Patchwhore.

9
THE DEAL

"...I'm gonna let him put his penis inside of me..." I sing, filling my hand up with shampoo for the third time. After thirty minutes in the shower, Drake's bologna scent is finally gone.

A few more spins, a couple dance moves and one verse later, I shut off the water and grab a towel—continuing my concert around the bathroom.

I don't remember ever feeling this hungry for sex. But now that I've had a taste of Cook and the tricks he can pull with his magic stick, I'm famished for it. The anticipation alone is thrilling. So much so, I have the urge to dry hump the vanity.

Squirting a generous amount of lotion in my hand, I start to massage it into my skin. He'll be happy to find I took his advice and shaved. Maybe this time he won't feel like he's having sex with a cactus.

No.

Not having sex.

Fucking.

"Fuck..." I say to the mirror, trying the word out on my tongue. I'm getting better at it.

Now that I'm smooth and smell like apples, I move on to step two of my pre-sex preparation routine—brushing my teeth. Then I need to dry my hair. Apply just the right amount of makeup to give me that natural look. And find something other than Wonder Woman pajamas to wear.

Then when Cook calls, I'll sound sleepy but insist he still come over. Run my hands through my hair to create bed head. Answer the door on a yawn, and lean against it wearing a sleepy smile. Just like they do in the movies.

The repeated track, *I Just Had Sex* by The Lonely Island, is interrupted by my ringtone. I'm sure it's Emily returning my call from earlier, but I nearly choke when I see Cook's name. Spitting the excess toothpaste out of my mouth, I try to dull my excitement and slip into sleepy voice when I answer.

"...Hello?" *Damn. I sound like I have strep throat.*

"Bad time?" My thighs tingle and I cross my ankles, grinding my hips into the vanity dramatically.

"No. I must have fallen asleep."

"You still up for company?" Grinning like an idiot, I nod, even though he can't see it. After a moment, his voice drops to nearly a whisper. "Was that a yes?"

"Yes. You leaving the bar now?"

"No." Good. That'll give me plenty of time to finish preparing. "I'm outside your door." I stiffen.

"Huh?"

"Your bathroom door." This time, his voice doesn't come through the phone. Instead, he's looking at me from only a few feet away, leaning against the door frame. And the sight of him has me forgetting that he caught me in a lie. In a towel. In my house. That he just entered without permission. *Again.* In his defense, I never moved the key. *Was it because I was hoping he'd use it again?*

"Glad you showered." He smirks, drawing my attention to his lips and the scruff on his masculine, square jaw. I imagine licking my way up his neck to his ear, biting his lobe and then whispering something dirty to him.

"I shaved, too." *Good grief, Carmen.*

"How considerate of you."

He's also freshly showered. The ends of his sandy blonde hair still damp. His jeans and shirt clean and crisp—a stark contrast to his weathered vest and dusty boots. I want to eat him. I've never wanted a cock in my mouth as much as I want his. I bet he tastes...*do* not *say it.*

Fuck it...*Nailed it!*

Delicious.

His eyes burn a hole through me as he pushes off the wall and slowly stalks over. My heart hammers harder with every step. The anticipation is almost too much. And to make it worse, he's taking his precious time and I'm nearly hyperventilating by the time he gets to me.

"So did you work out the details?" he asks. He's close, but not touching me.

I have to wet my lips before I can answer. "Details?" *Why won't he just touch me?*

"The reason you wanted me to come over?"

"Oh. Yeah. My new strategy." *One deep breath is all it would take for my breasts to make contact.*

Lifting his finger, he drags it across the seam of my towel. Which just so happens to run down the center of my chest. "Tell me about it." My mind scrambles to think as I follow the trail of his finger. But all I can think about is ripping the towel off so he can touch my skin.

"Carmen?"

"Um..." *Think, dammit!* "Well, I figured it doesn't really matter if I sleep with those guys or not." His finger stops at my belly button and trails back up.

"And why is that?" *His voice...It's like a friggin' drug.*

"I don't know," I whimper. I can't concentrate. How can I be so cool around him sometimes, and some wet, horny mess others? He's drugged me. Possessed me.

Focus. Focus. Focus!

"Jud is going to assume I'm sleeping with them whether I do or not. I think hanging around his brothers is enough." As if he's rewarding me, the tip of his finger makes contact with my skin, tracing the outline of my collar bone and the bare flesh just above the towel.

"So that's the infamous plan B...let the boys wine and dine you and then let a real man fuck you?" *It is now.*

"Yes." I nod. "That's the plan." I hadn't considered the second part. Or maybe I had just to ensure sleeping with Cook played a role in my newly devised scheme.

Tilting my chin up, he forces me to look at him. He's not smiling, which immediately makes it harder for me to look in his eyes. But I do and find them blazing. Hooded. Filled with lust and raw desire. For me.

"I don't share, Carmen."

Oh.

Wait.

What?

His admission snaps me out of my lust-induced fog. "I don't understand. I thought you and Deliliah..."

He tilts his head slightly when I don't continue. "You thought me and Delilah what?"

My hands fidget with the edge of my towel as I try to hold his gaze. Embarrassed, I search for words a little more appropriate than what Delilah had used to describe their relationship. "You share her."

"She's not mine to share. Never has been. Even when she was a whore. And she damn sure wouldn't have been a very good one if she was only exclusive to me."

"Well...I want to be a good whore too." His lips twitch at my admission.

"You're not a whore, babe."

"I'm not yours either."

This time, he doesn't fight his smile. But it doesn't quite reach his eyes. "No, gorgeous. You're not."

84

There's something about the way he looks at me. It's hypnotic. I feel like he's casting some kind of creepy love spell on me that makes my body and mind crave him. He has me so worked up...so turned on...so captivated. I may not be his, but I can see how easy it would be to fall for him. I guess it's a good thing I invested in that steel cage surrounding my heart. *Thanks, Jud.*

"But..." Cook takes a step back and crosses his arms over his chest.

I mirror his stance. "But?"

He gives me an evil grin. "Mine or not, I still won't share. You wanna flirt with these guys to make Jud jealous, fine. You wanna spend your weekends with a bunch of immature pricks, fine. But if you're fucking me, you're fucking only me."

At the mention of fucking him, my mind dips right back in the gutter. It would be so easy to let him take me right here in the bathroom. My skin heats as I think of all the ways we could do it. On the counter. In the shower. Me bent over, him behind me. It's what I'd expected tonight. What I hope to still get. But first, we need to clarify a few things about his demand for monogamy.

"You know," I start, leaning my hip against the counter. "My daddy always said what's good for the goose is good for the gander."

"Given what little I know, your daddy sounds like a smart man. I'd probably agree to whatever the fuck it is you're saying if I understood hillbilly."

I press my lips together to try and contain my smile. It doesn't work. "It means, that what's good for a woman is good for a man. So if I'm only screwing you, then you're only screwing me."

"You're *fucking* me," he promises. "Only me." Then he closes the distance, gripping my hips and pulling me flush against him. "And I only want to fuck...*you.*"

He stares down at me. I look up at him. "Well what are you waiting for?" I ask, my voice velvet. Body molten. Heart beating so hard...I can't even think of an idiom to compare it to.

"I'm waiting for you to agree." His patience is slipping. Still, he waits. Keeping me close. Daring me to say no. I won't. But I can't speak either. So I just nod. His eyes narrow. "Say it," he demands. The promise of what's to come when I do, burns in his eyes. And it's enough encouragement for me to find my voice.

"You," I breathe. "I'm fucking only you."

His hungry lips find mine—kissing, claiming, owning. My fingers seek out his skin, searching for the heat beneath his clothes. The moment they move beneath his shirt and brush across his hard stomach, a bolt of electricity courses through me. Fiery jolts of razor sharp passion shoot through every nerve. Through every fiber. I've never wanted something so much. My body has never felt so alive. And just knowing that it's going to get better—feel even better—has me climbing his body.

"Sexy, gorgeous girl," he growls, his mouth hot against my neck. "So eager." My back hits the bed. I didn't even realize we'd left the bathroom. "So hungry." His hands jerk the towel from around me. "So fuckin' delicious." I shake my head, wanting to tell him that's my word. But he's looking down at me. Famished. Then his face is between my thighs. He's eating me. Like I'm delicious.

Miss Delicious...

"Don't stop," I beg, my fingers knotting in his hair as his tongue swirls around my clit. Lips cover me. He sucks hard. My back bows. Hips jerk. And within seconds I'm coming. Moaning. Collapsing. Lost as bliss engulfs me. Rapture surges through me. It lasts for moments...minutes...hours...who knows? Time stands still.

Then the haze starts to dispel. Through the break, I see him naked. He's kissing his way up my stomach, to my breasts. Taking the tiny brown peaks in his mouth. Sucking. Teasing. Nipping. Eliciting another moan from me. Another wave of heat. Another electric current that wakes me. Makes me aware. Recharges my entire system.

"I'm gonna fuck you so hard," he promises, pressing his gloriously huge cock against my opening that still weeps from the onslaught of his mouth. "When you walk, you'll think of me."

In a single, harsh thrust, he impales me. It's so much. So filling. So *motherfucking* wonderful. Then he's still. Waiting. My body adjusts quickly, eager for more of him. I tighten. Clenching his massive length. Fervently begging for a reminder of him long after he's gone.

"Be careful what you wish for, baby." *Had I pleaded with him out loud?* He leaves no time for my thoughts to wander further. Instead he distracts me with long, powerful drives that immediately cause a tightening in my core.

The intensity has me squeezing my eyes shut. My mouth hangs open. Hands tighten around his arms—my nails digging into the hard muscles. The pressure borders on discomfort. Pain a hairsbreadth away from pleasure. I want to scream at him to slow down. I want to whimper my plea for him to never stop. But he seems to know just what I can't say. And his body responds to mine, giving me everything I never asked for.

My eyes flutter; I'm surprised by how much strength it takes to keep them open. Despite the overwhelming need to close them, or the desire that prompts them to roll back in my head, I can't pull them away from this man. The corner of his bottom lip is tucked between his teeth. A strange look of determination on his face. Those darkening blues are lava—fucking me with the same heated intensity of his cock.

"You remember me," he gravels. "When you're with them..." Sharp tingles of pain and pleasure burst inside me with a merciless jerk of his hips. "You remember who fucks you." I nod, lost in the abyss of his stare. "Remember who makes you scream." Gripping my hip in his hand, he lifts my body slightly before thrusting roughly. I scream—pleasure exploding inside me as he connects with my sweet spot.

"Right there," I pant, losing the battle with my eyelids as they flutter closed. But even in the darkness, I see his face. That look. Those eyes.

"That's right, gorgeous. You remember who knows how to give you what you need." His voice is smooth, confident. He knows I'll remember. Because he's making damn sure I won't forget. "You know who can make that sweet pussy come, don't you?"

"Yes," I whimper, so close to release. My hands tighten around him. Needing something to hold onto. Knowing I'm nearing the inevitable fall.

"Open your eyes." The urgency in his tone is clear. And with an energy I didn't know I had, I do as he says. There's a thick vein bulging from the side of his neck—pulsing with every beat of his heart. His jaw is tight. Nostrils flaring. Eyes narrowed. Voice strained and snarling when he speaks. "Say it, Carmen."

He pumps harder into me. I don't know what he wants me to say. I couldn't even if I did. I'm speechless. Unable to breathe. He's rendered me completely immobile.

I'm losing focus. Beginning my descent that will have me spiraling out of control. But he holds my gaze. Demanding I keep my attention on him. That I see who he is. Feel what he's doing to me. How he consumes me. Erases my every thought. Infiltrates my every fiber.

"Tell me whose pussy this is." The demand is rhetorical. There's only one response. Because in this moment, the only thing I can think of is him. I see only him. Feel and hear—him. And so I answer his demand on a strangled cry, using the only word I can formulate in my mind.

"Cook!"

I slowly blink my way back into consciousness. The first thing I notice is that I'm alone. The second thing is how cold the room feels without Cook. I look down at my exposed body, lying in a hot, wet mess on my tangled sheets. *The bastard didn't even cover me up.* But the thought is fleeting as I feel warmth seep into my pores at the sight of him walking through my bedroom door.

"Hey there, gorgeous." His sweet tone and boyish smile makes me feel shy. And he's looking at me with those clear, blue eyes full of appreciation. "You fell asleep on me." I'm expecting him to pull his cut over his shoulders and tell me bye, considering once again, he's dressed to leave. But he surprises me by coming to lay at my side—propping his head on his elbow as he leans over to place a kiss on my nose. When he lets out a breath, I inhale. The scent of him makes the muscles in my back relax as I breathe him in.

"I didn't mean to fall asleep," I say. But the words have me stifling another yawn.

His lips turn up on one side. "Am I exhausting you?"

Shaking my head, I smile as I turn on my side to face him— pulling the covers over me as I do. He reaches out to tuck them around me before running his hand over my arm and gripping my hip through the blanket.

"Will you be there Saturday?"

He nods, smirking at me. "If there's a club function, I'll be there."

"Don't you have a job?"

"This is my job."

"So you get paid?"

His eyes fall to my lips, that smirk still on his face. "You're just full of questions tonight."

"Are you avoiding the answer?" I quirk a brow at him.

"No."

"No you aren't avoiding the answer or no you don't get paid?"

He meets my gaze. "No. I'm not avoiding. Yes. I get paid. But in experience, not money. This is something I want, so I took the time off to make sure I could give the club the one hundred percent they're owed."

"How do you pay your bills?"

"With money," he quips. I roll my eyes in exasperation.

"But if you don't work..."

"I'm not poor, babe. I have money." A deep sadness shines in his eyes, but he quickly blinks it away, replacing it with a smile. "You ready for your big date?"

I let out a groan at the reminder. "You really know how to ruin the moment."

"We were having a moment? I wasn't aware." He winks. I melt. *Again...*

When his phone vibrates in his jeans, I find myself frowning. I don't want him to leave. I'm enjoying his company. Our simple conversation. The teasing banter. The scent of him. But he doesn't return my regretful look. He simply raises a brow in curiosity when he notices mine.

"Yeah," he says into the phone. His voice alert, his body stiffening in preparation for a command. "I'll be there." It's similar to the same line he always gives. Then just as expected, the moment he hangs up, he moves to leave.

"Don't forget Drake wants you there at ten. Not a minute later." He's fighting his laughter. I'm struggling with the urge to throw something at him. He's such a...*smartass.* But then as if it fell from the sky, a thought hits me. Not only is Saturday my chance to make Jud jealous, but Cook too.

Beaming at him, I sit up and watch as he pulls his cut over his shoulders. "Oh, I'll be there. With bells on."

"Bells, huh?" He grins, sliding his phone into the inside pocket of his vest. "Want to make sure everyone knows you're there?"

"Trust me, *Cook.*" I sneer his name. "I won't need bells to alert anyone to my presence. I plan to stop the whole show when I arrive."

"Showstopper...that's gonna be tough. You'd be surprised how many women go unnoticed when there's a parking lot full of Harleys. But hey..." He points his finger at me, his look serious. "If anybody can do it, it's you, gorgeous." Then he laughs. The bastard *laughs.*

"Patronizing asshole," I mutter through my smile. "We'll see who's laughing Saturday."

"Well hopefully it won't be at your expense." I narrow my eyes on him, but he's undeterred. "But if that happens to be the case, which it likely will, I'll happily break the jaw of any man who laughs at you."

"No one is going to laugh at me," I snap. He lets out another chuckle, but has the grace to try and hide it. "Will they smile? Look at me with lust-filled eyes? Drop their jaws when I step out of my car? Probably so."

"Conceited much?"

"Not at all." My tone is defensive. "I just know how all men think." My admission doesn't sit well with Cook. And I know his next comment will be in an attempt to bring me back down to size.

"So what? You think you're just gonna show up and render everybody speechless?" Having already predicted his snarky remark, it's easy for me to appear wounded. For a moment, he looks a little apologetic. *Perfect.*

"You know," I start to say, making a show of studying my nails, "if the image of your eyes rolling in the back of your head while you came balls deep inside me, weren't permanently indented in my brain, I might consider your little comment an insult."

Shaking his head, he lets out a laugh—licking his bottom lip as he drops his head. Then, peeking up at me from beneath his lashes, he smirks. "Is that how you wanna play this?"

"Play what?" Feigning innocence, I lean back against the headboard. Propped up against the pillows like a queen. "I'm just saying that since you are clearly so affected by me, then maybe you should double check your armor on Saturday. You wouldn't want to find any chinks in it," I whisper.

Crossing his arms, he gives me his best, confident smile. "Oh, game face on, baby. This is one jaw you won't drop. Remember..." His voice dips, "I've already seen that sexy little body you hide behind your clothes. Tasted it. Touched it. *Fucked it.*" He lets the words hang in the air a moment before shrugging, as if seeing me naked wasn't very impressive. Although his eyes tell a different story. "Not much left to the imagination."

It takes me a moment to calm my heavy breathing and spiked heart rate. When I finally do, I meet his challenging stare. "I better not see even a ghost of a smile on your lips."

"Don't worry, gorgeous. You won't." He stalks over to me. Slow. Predatory. When he closes the distance, he leans down— bringing his face close to mine. "That tight cunt of yours might have the power to distract me when I'm inside it, but my game will be on point come Saturday." His nose brushes against mine. I hold my breath, refusing to inhale his intoxicating scent. "You can bet your sweet little ass on it."

Surely he doesn't mean...

He grins at my reaction. Somehow, I feel like he can read my thoughts. But he doesn't answer. He leaves me wondering. Nervous. A little scared. Pretty wet. And a whole lot of horny.

10
EAGLES ROAD CAPTAIN DRAKE

Emily swore it wasn't too much. But despite how sexy the vixen staring back at me in the mirror looks, I can't help but feel a little self-conscious. It doesn't even look like me. I look...*hot.*

Conceited much?

Cook's words have me shaking my head in disgust. I've never been vain my entire life. Then again, I've never looked like this either.

I woke early in order to have enough time to hot roll my hair. The process is slow and grueling due to its heaviness and length, but the result couldn't have come out better. It now falls in thick, brown waves down my back and over my shoulders.

My makeup is dark and sultry. I went heavy on my eyes, putting multiple coats of black mascara on my lashes and using a smoky grey shadow for my lids. The gold flecks seem to shine brighter now in my hazel eyes. I opted out of blush and used clear gloss instead of lipstick. But my face and hair are nothing compared to the outfit I splurged on.

The black, leather corset, is tight across my stomach, but the peak-a-boo lacing opens wider as it nears my breasts—exposing their sides and giving a whole new meaning to cleavage. The built in, padded cups lift them higher and make them appear a couple sizes bigger than they actually are. The straps over my shoulders tie into the back which is laced the same as the front, exposing most of my back.

The website I'd ordered the black leather stiletto pants from, promised to give me the same "painted on" look as Sandy in the final scene of Grease. They didn't disappoint. It took me a while to get into them, and I'll probably have to cut them off, but they fit me like a glove--accentuating my curves and slimming my legs.

They sit low on my hips, leaving exposed skin between them and the corset. Thankfully, work and minimal food has kept my stomach flat and toned, despite the fact that I haven't been to the gym in weeks. I've also managed to maintain the dark golden tan I've had since spring.

Since I'd used up all my extra funds on the outfit, I couldn't afford new shoes. But when I mentioned to Emily that I'd be wearing a pair of black flats, she screamed at me. Then she overnighted me a pair of black booties with a four inch, spiked heel that are to die for.

I pull my eyes away from my reflection and check the time. If I didn't leave now, I'd be late. Grabbing a small, red clutch I'd found in my closet, I stuff powder, gloss, some cash, a few hair ties and a bunch of bobby pins inside. With one final glance in the mirror, I snap a quick selfie, send it to Emily and shove my phone inside my bag. This is it. Show stopping time. Time to remind Jud of what he lost. But truth is, it's Cook's reaction I'm looking forward to most.

It's ten a.m. sharp when I near Pops' crowded parking lot. I'm so overwhelmed by the number of people and bikes that I nearly run over the guy who's directing traffic. He comes to my window and I roll it down, not missing the onceover he gives me as he peers inside my car.

"You here for the poker run?" he asks, sweat dripping from his face and onto my door.

"Yes. I'm meeting Drake."

"Who?"

"Um," I struggle to remember his title. "Eagles Captain Drake?"

"Oh yeah." He studies me a moment, a confused look on his face. "You his girl?"

I let out a nervous laugh. "No. I'm just riding with him today."

"Lucky fucker," he mumbles, then points to the back of the lot near the dumpsters. "There's a few spots left over there. We reserve them for the MC affiliates in cages, but I'll make an exception for you."

I have no idea what any of that means. I assume a cage is a car, but why am I an exception? Isn't Drake in an MC? Or is that an RC? Is there a difference? Confused, I simply thank him and pull in the direction he points.

Maneuvering between the endless rows of bikes is challenging, but I manage to wedge my car in a tight spot next to a dumpster. Nervously, I check my reflection and take a breath. Hoping Emily has responded with some words of encouragement, I look at my phone. Sure enough, I have a message. Actually, I have two. The first is from her.

Holy shit. Now I want to fuck you.

It's a definite self-esteem booster. I want to send a reply, but I'm too anxious to read the message from Cook that was sent one minute ago at 10:01.

Your tardiness is gonna earn you a spanking from CAPTAIN Drake

My lip curls in disgust as I hurriedly type out a reply.

Jealous?

The correct response was "Only you get to touch me."

His message makes me laugh, and I'm thankful for the pack of bikes entering the lot that prevent me from getting out just yet. I want to tease him a little more.

Does that mean you're going to deliver his spanking?

A few minutes pass and so does the line of bikes. It's now 10:09, and I give up on waiting for his comment. But as I shove the phone in my clutch, it vibrates with a notification. I nearly break my hand trying to retrieve it.

Are you trying to be funny or just piss me off?

I'm trying to get a spanking.

Only seconds pass before I receive his next message.

Consider it done.

Heat floods me. I'm wet with desire. His words have me wanting to ask him to join me in the bathroom for a quick repeat of the first time we met. It wouldn't take long. If a text message can get me this worked up, I'll be halfway to an orgasm when he looks at me. Then a single swipe of his tongue will be all it takes.

With that in mind, I exit the car. My movements are fluid, calculated and determined as I stride across the parking lot toward the entrance of the bar. He's going to touch me tonight. He's going to eat me. Fuck me. Spank me. The erotic thought makes me feel wanted. Sexy. Like the vixen I saw staring back at me in the mirror.

I'm transfixed as I pull open the door. I forget why I'm here. My goal. The plan. Drake. And when I realize where I am. Who I am. I discover that I've done just as I said I would. I've stopped the show.

There's a crowd of men and women surrounding me. Someone was talking when I walked in. There was only one voice, but even it faded. Now all I hear is the sound of breathing as every set of eyes in the place is focused on me. But I only notice one.

Blue crystals of promise stare back at me from the bar. They hold me. Paralyze me. But from a distance, I can still see his mouth. Lips parted. Breathing heavy. Stunned in silenced. *Rendered speechless.*

A throat clears, and I follow the sound to Ronnie who steps from the crowd. His wrists crossed at his waist. A beer bottle dangling from his ringed fingers. "You looking for me, sugar? I sure as hell hope so." A low rumble of laughter sounds around the crowd.

I respond with a nervous laugh. "Sorry. Didn't mean to stop the show." I let my eyes slide to Cook for a second and find him recovered and now smirking.

"I'm glad you did," Ronnie says, eliciting another round of laughter from the group. I scan the crowd for Drake, but come up empty. Feeling a little lost and a lot embarrassed, I offer another quick apology to the group and try to shrink inside myself as I move to stand next to Cook.

The speech resumes. I try to listen, but I can't focus. I can feel Cook's eyes burning into me. Looking up, I find him smiling. Then his head dips to my ear.

"Well played, gorgeous," he whispers, and I have to bite my cheek to keep from laughing. Beaming up at him, I follow the slight jerk of his head. I'm still smiling when I notice Jud glaring back at me. He looks livid. And I'm surprised when he doesn't drag his finger across his throat to express how much he wants to kill me. I shoot him a wink.

When I feel Cook stiffen beside me, I look at him in confusion. He tries to cover up his reaction with a smirk, but it's clear something is under his skin. Then hands are on my hips and I'm being pulled flush against a body. Lips are at my ear. I'm holding my breath in fear—knowing who it is. Unable to not cringe when I hear his voice.

"Hey beautiful."

Drake.

"Sorry I'm late," Drake says, once the crowd starts to disperse. "Ronnie had me doin' some shit out back." I cautiously sniff the air as I turn to face him, relieved to find that he smells much better today. And he may have even showered, although his clothes look just as dingy and dirty as they did the other night.

"Damn, girl." I allow him to twirl me like a ballerina in a jewelry box. "You fine as hell." Drake's compliment doesn't have the same effect as Cook's reaction, but I thank him anyway.

Taking a deep breath, now that I know it's safe, I force myself to focus on the positive. This is a day of firsts for me. First date

97

since Jud. First ride on a bike. First time I've hung out with bikers—sober.

"So…" I beam at Drake, making myself notice something good about him. *His pants are nice.* "What we riding?"

"It's over here." Grabbing my hand, he pulls me out of the bar and through the cluster of motorcycles—passing Jud on the way. I don't give him a second glance as we stop at a bike next to his. It's has definitely seen better days. The fender is dented. The seat is ripped in some places and patched with duct tape. And the headlight is held in place with a bungee cord.

"She may not be pretty, but she's mine."

"It's…" I search for the right words, catching Jud watching us from a few feet away. He's fuming. Ignoring Clarissa as she rambles on about something. "I love it," I say, turning back to Drake and offering him a smile.

He shoots me a smirk, handing me a helmet that looks about as beat up as the bike. "Knew you would."

Noticing my struggle to fasten the strap, Drake invades my personal space to assist me. I stare at the few scraggly hairs on his chin to avoid his gaze. After the helmet is secure, he gives me a heated look—his eyes glancing from mine to my lips and back. He wants a kiss. I'd rather hurl.

The rumbling sound of pipes draw his attention away from me. Everyone is mounting their bikes, firing their engines and pulling out. I clamber on the back of Drake's bike once he's on, gripping his shoulders for support.

"This your first ride?" he asks, glancing at my death grip on his shoulder. I nod nervously, but don't try to hide my smile of excitement. Despite how much I don't enjoy being on a bike with *him*, I can't deny the thrill of riding.

"Don't worry, beautiful." He winks at me. "I won't let you fall off." He turns the key and the bike makes a terrible noise. He tries it again. And again. And again. Then tells me it's cold natured. I'm not sure how that applies, considering it's nearly eighty degrees. But I shrug anyway.

"So where are we going?"

His hand comes to rest on my knee as he turns to face me. "We got five stops to make then we come back here. At each stop, you get a card. Whoever has the best poker hand at the end of the day, wins the fifty-fifty drawing."

"Fifty-fifty?"

"Yeah. The ride is to raise money for St. Jude. The split is about a thousand dollars. Maybe I'll win." He shoots me a grin. Hell, maybe he will win. Then he can afford to fix his bike.

Looking out at the pack, I notice there are several small groups gathered across the lot. Each group wears a different patch. The group we're in consists of six people—Drake and Jud being the only two I recognize.

I scan the crowd again and find Cook near the front of the line. He's so sexy and confident on his big, black bike that looks like something Batman would ride. His hands rest high on the handlebars, his feet pushing the bike back and forth a few inches as he waits patiently for the ride to start.

Then, just as Drake tries to crank the bike again, Cook turns and looks at me. When the engine fails to turn over, for the fifth time, he throws his head back on a laugh. I give him the finger, wishing I could see his eyes that are hidden behind his dark glasses. He shakes his head as he lifts one foot from the ground and shifts into gear, then pulls out.

Finally, Drake manages to get the bike started. But we continue to sit and wait until every other group has pulled out, before falling in behind them.

The ride doesn't go as well as I'd hoped it would. When Drake's bike wasn't back firing, he was swerving all over the road. Either he was new at riding, or he just sucked at it. By the time we reach the first stop a few miles away, I feel like I need a Dramamine and a Xanax.

I stand around the parking lot while Drake and a few other guys tinker with his bike. I do my best to comb out my hair with my fingers while I wait.

It's hot. I'm starting to sweat. And I desperately need a mirror. When Drake still hasn't made a move to go inside after about fifteen minutes, I interrupt his conversation.

"Drake?" He looks up at me from his squatted position. "Is it okay if I go inside?" His head turns toward the bar, then back at me. A woman with a clipboard starts toward us and he stands quickly.

Tucking a strand of hair behind my ear, he grins. "Yeah, babe. Go ahead. I'll be in shortly."

I turn on my heel, looking back over my shoulder in time to see Drake pointing at me as he speaks to the woman. Maybe she's his wife, and we'll have to cut this date short. Wishful thinking, I suppose.

Inside, the bar is crowded, loud and smoky. I maneuver through the mass of people and find the bathroom in the back. There's a line, so I lean against the wall and wait.

The women are laughing and talking—ignoring me completely. I wonder if Kat is here. At least I'd then I'd have someone to talk to. Even Delilah's company would be nice. I feel like an outsider. A loner. I thought this would be more exciting.

"Why the sad face?" I smile at the voice, turning to find Cook standing behind me. His sexy voice and scent is enough to lift my mood. But the sight of him makes me downright happy.

"I have to pee," I say, not wanting to give him any reason to tease me. Second to Jud, he's the one person I don't want aware of how out of place I feel.

"Where's ya boy?"

I roll my eyes, wanting to smack that grin off his face. "Busy."

"Are you Carmen?" My head jerks at the sound of my name to find the lady with the clipboard. She smiles up at Cook a moment, then slides her gaze back to me.

"I am."

"I need you to sign this waiver." She thrusts the clipboard in my hand. I scan the page as she talks to Cook—asking him how he's been. He's cordial, but I can feel his eyes on me.

After briefly reading the liability form that states the club isn't responsible in the event of death or injury, I scribble my signature at the bottom and pass it back. She raises an expectant eyebrow at me. "It's twenty dollars," she says, holding out her hand.

"Oh, okay." I dig in my purse for some cash, but Cook beats me to it. He hands her a twenty, mumbling something under his breath. She snatches the bill from him, quickly waves to us and leaves.

"You didn't have to do that," I say, locating the money in my purse and offering it to him. He dismisses it with a shrug.

"I'll get it back later." There's a hardness in his voice, and I wonder if he's going to make me pay for it in another way. My body heats at the thought. "Have fun today, gorgeous," he says, pushing off the wall.

I reach out and grab his wrist. "Is Kat here?"

He nods. "I'll let her know you're lookin' for her." He looks down at my hand that still holds his wrist. Immediately I release him. I don't know why his mood changed so quickly. But I don't think it's because of anything I've done. Then, as if to prove it, he winks at me and smiles—erasing all the tension from his face.

I watch him walk away—moving through the crowd like a shadow. He arrives at Ronnie's side and stands next to him, clasping his hands at his waist and remaining silent. Ronnie motions with his fingers and Cook's head dips so he can hear him. He says something, then both their eyes find me. I quickly look away—thankful the bathroom is now open so I can disappear inside.

The hours I spent on my hair this morning were a waste. After the humidity and the ride, it's a frizzy tangled mess. Having no other option, I pile it on my head in a messy bun. Then I touch up my makeup and contemplate using the bathroom. But after a quick deliberation, I decide against it. Fearing I won't be able to get my pants back up.

I open the door to find Kat beaming at me on the other side. "Hey there, hot mama." She gives me a onceover and whistles, smacking her gum in my ear when she pulls me in for a hug.

"Damn, I'm glad you're here," I admit. "I don't know any of these people."

"Well, I'll just have to introduce you at the next stop." She grabs my hand and starts pulling me toward a pool table. "Did you get a card?" I shake my head. "Draw one."

There are only a few cards left scattered across the table. I pick up the first one I see. It's an ace of spades. Kat lets out a whoop, and takes the card. *I guess I did something right...* A man writes something on a piece of paper then hands it to me. It has my name next to Drake's in parenthesis.

"Keep that. You'll need it at every stop," Kat says, and I wonder why she's in such a hurry. It's then that I notice the bar is almost empty. "See you in a few!" She blows me a kiss and sprints across the lot toward the front. I head to Drake's bike to find it already running. He greets me with a whistle.

"Ready to ride, beautiful?"

Hell, I reckon.

Over the next four stops, I find myself having fun. Kat has been kind enough to help me with my plan—promising to line up some future dates with several of Jud's brothers. I'd made my one rule clear: the date had to happen wherever Jud was. Considering the bar seemed to be the one and only hangout spot for all of them, she agreed that she'd set all the dates up there.

I was worried some of the guys might question why or prefer something a little different—a more intimate setting, if you will. She ignored my concern and simply said she'd handle it. I trusted she would.

Kat also introduces me to a bunch of girls whose names I'll never remember. They're friendly enough, but I can tell they're a little cautious of me. At least they're kind enough to allow me to hang inside their circle. Although, I'm pretty sure it's only because I'm with Kat.

Drake never goes inside the bars. Instead, he stays near his bike with several other guys. I don't mind it. Actually, I prefer it. I seem to have more fun when he's not smothering me.

I see Cook every now and then, but he doesn't speak. In his defense, he's always doing something—taking out trash. Emptying ashtrays. Getting beer. Standing next to Ronnie. Looking hot and sexy and edible.

At the last stop, I'd asked Kat who Ronnie was. The question had our entire table of women growing quiet and looking at me in disbelief. "He's the president of the Devil's Renegades, the most prominent MC in this area. And he's one of the founding members."

She'd said it almost reverently. Now I understood why he'd been so popular the first night I'd met him. It was a show of respect for everyone to greet him when they arrived. I couldn't deny that it made me feel good that someone so important had treated me so good.

On the final stop before going back to Pops, Drake finally came inside. This place was bigger—the main area lined with tables set for eating. As part of the ride, we were served BBQ for dinner. Which I'm pretty sure is the only reason Drake came in.

I'm sitting at a table with him and his club. The only people from the Eagles who aren't sitting with us are Jud and Clarissa. Fine by me. They might spoil my appetite.

The food is delicious, and it has nothing to do with me being as hungry as a hostage. When I'm finished, every one of my fingers is covered in BBQ sauce.

"Do you know where the napkins are?" I ask Drake, who's too busy stuffing his face to even look up at me.

"Ask a Prospect." This has a few people at the table laughing, but I hardly see what's so funny. Although I've felt like I've been in the dark about every conversation they've had. Not that I minded. It's usually about parts and bikes and people I don't even know.

I stand and look around, frowning when I don't see Brett, the prospect from Drake's club. Then my eyes land on Cook. He's a prospect. And he's not doing anything but standing there looking too damn good. So I make my way over.

The moment I'm in front of him—sticky BBQ fingers in the air, he smiles. "Hello, gorgeous."

"Hey. I was told you have napkins?"

His brows draw together. "Why would I have napkins?"

"Well, I asked Drake for some napkins and he said ask a prospect. You're a prospect, so…"

He gives me an amused look. "Did he call me a prospect?" He sounds almost hopeful.

"No. He just said to ask one."

"He did, huh?" he mutters, looking over the top of my head toward Drake with a flash of possessiveness in his eyes.

"Cook," I snap, bringing his attention back to me. He beams at my annoyance. "Do you have napkins or not? Look at my fingers." I wiggle my fingers in front of his face. He grabs my wrist. His smile turning wicked—he's up to no good.

"Let me see if I can help you out."

"Thank you. Who knew napkins…" My voice trails off when he pushes my index finger between his lips. All I can do is stand and stare and drip as he sucks the sauce from my fingers one by one. The heat of his mouth and the swirl of his tongue has me doing the one thing he promised me I would do—*remember.*

The soreness lasted for only a day, but every now and then when I move just right, I can still feel how tender I am from what he'd done to me. But now, in this moment, I can feel the ache deep inside me. It's as fresh as it was the morning after. Or maybe it's not from what he did, but a longing for him to do it again.

When he's sucked my fingers clean on my left hand, he moves to my right. He's just as thorough. Licking. Sucking. Teasing. Reminding… His fiery blue gaze holds mine. Promising me more delicious torture very soon.

He gives my pinky a light nibble before pulling it from his mouth. "There," he says, his voice dark. "Make sure you tell your friend the prospect didn't disappoint."

I shake my head. "I'm not telling him what you did," I whisper, my breath coming in quick pants.

"Fine." He shrugs. "I'll tell him myself."

Then Drake is next to me, slinging his arm over my shoulders and narrowing his eyes on Cook. "Everything okay, beautiful?" Cook smirks at that.

"Fine," I squeak. "Everything's fine." There's a silent stare down for a few moments—Drake giving Cook a look of warning. Cook wearing a satisfied smile.

"She's with me," Drake growls, but Cook only widens his smile.

"I can see that." Cook's looking at me as he speaks—a twinkle of mischief in his eyes. I want to set the record straight. Tell Drake I'm not really *with* him. But I can't find my voice.

"You bout ready to get out of here, Carmen?" I nod, unable to pull my eyes from Cook. "Let's go. I gotta make an appearance at Pops, then you'll have me all to yourself."

Cooks smile doesn't falter, but his eyes darken. Mine widen slightly.

Leaving with Drake was not part of the plan. I don't want to leave and chance the rumor that I'm a snooty bitch who blew off her date, but there's no way I'm spending an extra second with him if I don't have to. I'll just have to fake an illness to get out of it. Shouldn't be too hard considering I'm already feeling queasy with Drake so close.

I shoot Cook a pleading look over my shoulder as Drake all but drags me away. Sensing my turmoil, he shows a little compassion and gives me a small nod of reassurance. Then he winks, and my anxiety vanishes. I don't know what he'll do. Or how he'll fix it. I just know he will.

I bet my sweet little ass on it.

11
MR. BIG MOUTH

We're back at Pops. I'm sitting at the bar, drinking one of Kat's special margaritas, which is much needed and well deserved. This plan for revenge is more exhausting than I'd thought. Or maybe it's the double shift I worked last night. Or the fact that I've only had six hours of sleep in two days. Or it could be these damn booties that feel like the soles are made out of sharp rocks.

"You look as tired as I feel," Ronnie says, sliding me a buttery nipple shot. I thank him, clink my glass to his and throw it back. It tastes scrumptious.

"Trust me." I motion for Kat to give us another. "I feel it too."

He grabs my hand in his and gives it a squeeze. "Plan seems to be working." I look at him. He answers my unspoken question with a shrug. "Cook didn't want to tell me. I made him."

I laugh at that, unable to imagine Cook doing anything he didn't want to do. "What all did he tell you?"

"Just that you're going to get back at Jud by making him think you're sleepin' with his brothers."

"Making him *think* I'm sleeping with them?" That was something I didn't want anyone but me and Cook to know. If it ever got out...

"You think I'm stupid enough to believe you actually would?" He gives me an expectant look.

I sigh and shake my head. "No. I guess not."

Kat hands us the drinks, but when I try to pay, Ronnie smacks my hand. "I don't let women buy me drinks. How'd you do on the poker run?" I pull my paper from my purse and show him. "Damn...Full house. Not bad."

I shrug. "I don't know much about poker."

"I do. That's a good hand. You'll probably win. Highest hand I've heard of is Cook's. He has a straight."

"Yeah, Drake seemed pretty excited about it. After I got a pair, he suggested we split it if either of us won. But I don't know what he has."

"That's cause he didn't play," Ronnie says, disapproval evident in his tone. "I bet he would've if he'd have known you paid for him to." I frown in confusion. "My bad. Cook paid for it," he adds on a grunt.

"No...I only paid for me. Well, Cook paid for me. But I was going to." Ronnie points a finger to my paper on the bar. I read the print beneath it. Fifteen dollars for one rider. Twenty for two. *Cheap bastard.*

Embarrassed for Drake and myself for coming here with him, I force a smile. "No big deal. It's for a good cause. I don't mind paying. He was nice enough to let me ride with him."

"So you still gonna split it with him if you win?" Ronnie asks, amused by my attempt to defend Drake.

"Nah. I'm going to donate it back."

He raises a brow at me. "Really? That's a lot of money. Probably more than you make in a week." Now it's my turn to raise a brow. He smirks. "Cook told me about that too. You know, you workin' to pay for your own place and shit."

"How very big mouthed of him," I mutter. Ronnie laughs. "Anyway." I take a sip of my drink. "That is a lot of money, but St. Jude needs it more than me."

I feel him looking at me as I stare down at the outfit I'd splurged on. How selfish would I be to take something from someone who really needed it? If I could afford to buy slutty clothes, I could do without taking from charity.

"Well let's hope you win. Or at least someone with a heart like yours does." He spins on his stool to face the gathering crowd as they get ready to announce the winners. I tuck my legs beneath me and turn too, leaning my back against the bar.

"Would you give it back?" I ask, wondering if doing that was common. I couldn't imagine anyone who wouldn't. Other than Drake, of course.

"I would. I have. And any man who wears my patch will."

"Because you'd make them?" I shoot him a smile, but his look is solemn.

"No." He angles his head to look at me. "They'd do it because it's the right thing to do."

There's something about Ronnie, Cook and the few other Devil's Renegades I've seen, that set them apart from everyone else. They're good people. Better people. I'm sitting next to the most important man in the bar, yet he acts as if he's just another biker. He's unselfish. Quiet. Kind. He wears that aura of power well, but I've yet to see him use it to his advantage.

"Listen up!" the emcee yells out across the bar, dragging my thoughts back to the present. "Time for the fifty-fifty."

I guess hearing the words drew him out of whatever hole he climbed in, but Drake comes to stand beside me for the first time since we arrived back at Pops. He'd disappeared the moment we walked in, saying he had to meet with his guys out back, but that he'd find me later.

"You got this in the bag, beautiful," he says, laying his arm across the bar behind me as he leans against it.

"Beer, Drake?" Kat asks, her tone bored, as if she had to ask even though she already knew the answer.

"I'll let you know in a minute," he says, pointing down at my paper—insinuating that he'll buy one if I win. But even if I wanted to be a jerk and keep the money, I damn sure wouldn't split it with him. Now I wish I hadn't defended him at all.

"Carmen?" Kat looks to me, and I nod.

"What you drinkin'?" Drake asks, peeking over in my glass as I drain the last of it. Ronnie bristles beside me but doesn't say anything. Kat, on the other hand, let's his ass have it.

"If you'd have bought the motherfucker you'd know, you cheap shit." I bite my cheek to keep from laughing. Ronnie doesn't bother holding his in. It's deep and raspy. Comforting. I feel my body angle closer to his and further from Drake's.

"Why you gotta give me hell, Kat?"

"Because you deserve it. She was nice enough to hang out with your ugly ass today and you won't even buy the girl a drink. I bet you made her pay for her ride today, too."

Before Drake can respond, one of his brothers steps in. "I got her drink," he says, putting some money on the bar. "And get Drake a beer too, will ya?" He looks over at me and smiles. He's not too bad. At least he looks clean and seems kind.

I nod my thanks to him. When I notice a patch on his cut that reads *Secretary,* I bat my eyelashes. Maybe he could be the next brother I "fuck."

"Cook's got a straight!" The emcee's comment has me searching for him. He's easy to spot—standing in the crowd next to the event organizers table. He wears a blank expression. His back straight. Shoulders square. Standing with his hands crossed in front of him. It's not an intimidating stance, it's respectful.

"Full house over here!" Drake yells, causing me to jump. Cook's lips turn up when he sees me.

Nervous and wobbly, I walk over—cringing with every step. *Damn shoes.* I smile the best I can, hissing through my teeth the entire way.

Cook's eyes narrow and his head turns a fraction when he notices my discomfort. Discreetly, I point to my shoes—knowing he's the only one paying close enough attention to notice. He eyes drop to my feet a moment before he smirks back up at me.

"Anybody got a better hand than a boat?" the emcee asks, as I hand him my paper. He asks twice more, making me stand center stage while he does.

Every eye is on me. Even Jud, who for the first time today doesn't look at me like he wants to rip my head off. It's not a particularly friendly look, but it's not quite a glare either.

"Congrats, honey. Looks like you're the big winner." He hands me a wad of cash. "That's nearly twelve hundred dollars."

I thank him and turn to the two women wearing St. Jude T-shirts. They came as volunteers to help with the event and receive the donations. Not wanting to draw any more attention to myself, I lean in so only they can hear me.

"I'd like to donate my winnings back."

They accept the money then pull me in for a hug. It's as discreet as I'd hoped, until the emcee notices and blabs his big mouth over the microphone.

"How about that, folks. She's donated it back. Let's give a round of applause to Miss…"

"Carmen," Cook says next to me. There's a sparkle of awe in his eyes as he pins me with his gaze. "Her name is Carmen."

"Well let's give it up for Miss Carmen. She's just donated her winnings that totaled over twelve hundred dollars back to St Jude…" The emcee continues to rattle on as everyone claps. I'm mortified as I try not to hobble back to the bar. I feel Cook's hand touch my back a couple times, guiding me through the crowd.

I breathe out a sigh of relief when I finally take a seat on my stool. Ronnie offers me my drink, and I greedily accept it.

"You'll be drinkin' free for a while," Kat says. "I think everyone here bought you a drink after that." Her eyes roll in annoyance. "Well, almost everyone."

"Speaking of Drake, where is he?" I ask, looking around for him—my eyes falling on the word PROSPECT as Cook disappears back into the crowd. "I'm about to head home and I wanted to say bye."

"He's busy." Ronnie doesn't look at me when he speaks. "I'll tell him for you." Something in his tone has me narrowing my eyes. I have a feeling he had something to do with Drake being busy. I also feel a deep relief at knowing I won't have to see him again.

"Thanks, Ronnie. See you next time?" I frown, realizing I don't know when that will be. Kat had promised to help me get some dates with Jud's brothers, but how soon would that be?

Then I feel a tap on my shoulder and turn to find the guy who bought me a drink earlier with his hand outstretched. I take it and give him my best smile.

"Eagles Secretary Juice. Can I walk you out?"

12
MR. DELICIOUS SAVES THE DATE DAY

I literally fall through the door of my apartment. Kicking off my shoes, I contemplate throwing them in the trash. But decide against it considering they were a gift.

Tiptoeing across the floor, I head into the kitchen where I grab a full bottle of wine from the fridge. Throwing myself down on my chaise, I prop my feet up and check my phone. Sure enough, Jud doesn't disappoint.

Drake is desperate. He'll fuck anything.

Not surprised that he wants to fuck you.

I bet you're fucking Ronnie too.

Stay the hell away from me, Carmen. And my club.

I laugh as I look down at Juice's number in my hand. He'd asked me to bike night next Thursday. I graciously accepted knowing Jud would be there. And somewhere, lurking in the shadows, would be Cook.

I start to call Emily and give her the rundown about my night, but am too exhausted to give her the details she demands. I'd rather sleep. But when I hear the loud rumble of pipes on my street, my pulse picks up and sleep becomes the last thing on my mind.

I should fix my hair. Brush my teeth. Takes these damn pants off that are glued to my body. After sweating in the heat all day, I'm sure I probably don't smell the best either. Doing a quick underarm check, I find that my 24-hour Degree has held strong. But I doubt my soap has the power to mask sweat odor inside my leather pants.

My feet feel stone bruised from sole to heel. Just standing on them is killing me. Dropping to my knees, I start to crawl toward the bathroom—confident I have plenty of time to make it there before Cook catches me in the embarrassing position. But I'm not even out of the living room when his voice sounds from behind me.

"What are you doin'?"

He must have ninja powers. It was only seconds ago when I heard his bike. Now he's standing in my living room, looking down at me in amusement.

"My feet hurt." I turn my head to look up at him. He's staring at my feet.

"What the hell kinda shoes were you wearin'?"

"Cheap ones, apparently." Damn Emily. She'd probably bought them from some stripper clothing site.

Wrapping an arm around my waist, Cook scoops me up in his arms and carries me back to the chaise. He sits with me in his lap, then grabs my foot in his hand, causing me to fall back against the pillows.

"Damn, Carmen." He frowns as he studies my foot.

"Do they look bad?" I crane my neck to see.

"No but they smell bad."

"Do not!" I jerk my foot out of his hand.

Laughing, he reaches out and grabs it again. "I'm kidding."

"Jerk," I mutter, crossing my arms over my chest.

He stops laughing, but keeps a smile on his face. He studies my foot a moment longer, then presses his thumbs into the heel. My body tenses and I let out a whimper. He doesn't ease the pressure, but watches me thoughtfully. Slowly, the pain begins to ebb. The relief that follows is orgasmic.

"Holy fuck."

His brow quirks. "Look at you. Cussin' and shit. I must be doin' something right."

"I'll say whatever you want if it means you won't stop." He chuckles, and then it's silent for a while.

I relax further into the pillows, allowing my eyes to flutter closed. When I pull in a deep breath, my lip curls and I can't help but giggle.

"What's so funny?" Cook asks, a smile in his voice.

"My feet really do stink." Another giggle erupts and I shake my head. "Or it may be other parts of me I smell. By the way..." I crack open one eye to look at him, "leather pants in summer are a bad idea."

He gives me a fiery glance. "Seeing you in them is worth it, gorgeous." He drags his gaze down my legs.

"The correct response was, 'you don't smell bad at all.'" Throwing his own words back at him wasn't such a good idea. Now, all I can think about is that spanking he promised me. And by the look in his eyes, he's thinking about it too.

He grabs my other foot, causing me to hiss when he presses his thumbs against the sorest part. But just like before, the pain soon turns to pleasure. Only this time, I'm feeling it in places other than my feet.

"You're tired tonight." It's not a question, but I find myself answering regardless.

"It's been a long week."

He nods. "That's right, so get your mind outta the gutter, dirty girl." My face scrunches in confusion. "You're so transparent, babe. Your body language gives you away."

So I'm breathing a little heavier. Licking my lips. Giving my thighs the occasional rub together in search of release. Letting my thoughts run wild. I can do that and still control myself. I think.

"I'm not that tired." *Or not.*

"Your eyes tell a different story."

"I know what I want."

His lips tilt a little, but he doesn't smile. "So what do you want?" *Like I'd say it out loud.*

I could tell him though. I could end this crazy day on a good note. Go to bed sated and get better sleep than I've had since the last time he was here. Only this time, I can sleep as long as I want, considering I'm off tomorrow.

"I want to take a shower," I admit, images of him showering with me flashing through my mind. But he shakes his head.

"Not an option."

"Why?"

"Because when you pull those pants off, I won't be able to wait." *Oh... okay then.* He releases my foot and motions with his finger. "Come here, Carmen."

"I—"

"Come. Here." His tone is full of authority. The sound of it shoots straight to my sex—prompting me to sit up and face him. "Lay down." Confused, I start to lie back, but he grabs my wrist. "Across my lap." A wave of heat hits me. I can feel my cheeks burning red as I stare at him wide eyed.

This is what I want. What I begged for. But I didn't expect it to be a play by play scene. I'd imagined something a little subtler—us in bed. Him fucking me. Then flipping me to my stomach in a surprise attack. Not this.

My mouth opens and closes. My mind screams at me to tell him no. But if my vagina had legs, she'd walk across his lap, lay down and beg for it. I don't know what to do. I look down at his lap, then back at his face. He tilts his head a fraction and studies me.

"You're wasting your time trying to figure out what to do," he says, his rich tone confident. His smile cocky. "All you're doing is delaying the inevitable."

I start. "Inevitable? Hardly."

His brows raise in amusement. "You think so?"

"I think I can walk away if I want to."

"But you won't."

He's right, but for some reason I feel the need to argue. "I might."

He, on the other hand, isn't in the mood to argue. "I won't tell you again, Carmen." Inside, I'm doing a little victory dance. If he pulled me over his lap, I can always say I didn't go willingly. It will likely lessen the embarrassment when I think about this in the future.

Then he grins, and doubt begins to creep in. "I know what you're thinking. But it ain't gonna work, gorgeous. So make a decision. You gonna let your pride stop you from getting what you want? Or are you gonna bring your pretty little ass over to me? Because if you don't in the next thirty seconds, I'm not gonna drag you across my lap. I'm gonna get up and leave."

When I tell this story in the future, this is the part where I'll be sure to say, "And that's how I got my first spanking from Cook." The bastard likes toying with me. If I were more of a woman, I'd tell him to eat shit and make him leave. But I'm not. I'm a quivering, horny hussie with no dignity.

"I hate you," I mutter, crawling to my knees. He just grins as I position myself across his thighs. He grips my hips and crosses his right ankle over his left knee—lifting my ass higher in the air.

"For the record," he says, dragging his fingers down my back. Then his hand slides over the tight leather of my ass, gripping a handful. Instinctively, I lift my hips to him. Begging for contact. "I wouldn't have left."

I want to call him an asshole. A jerk. Bastard. Peckerhead. The list is endless. But when he raises his hand then brings it down hard on the lower part of my ass, all I can do is moan. His hand is strong. The force behind his swing powerful. But the ache where he hits me resonates through my backside and drives pleasure straight to my core.

"I've been thinking about doing this all day," Cook says, delivering a harsh slap a little lower. I spread my legs in offering. Hoping he'll hit me there. "Greedy, girl." He ignores my invitation and spanks me higher this time. It's not as pleasurable as the others, and I grunt in disapproval.

"I bet your pussy is fuckin' soaked." He cups my sex and growls, then slaps my ass hard. Instinctively, I try to wiggle away, but he holds me steady. "Did you wear this to make me jealous?"

"No!" I cry, bucking my hips against his thigh.

"Who the fuck did you wear it for then?"

"I..." *Shit. My brain won't work.* "I don't know."

His hand lands hard between my legs and my back bows. My breath catches in my throat.

My heart stutters. *Ohdearlord that felt good.* "Is your pussy wet for me, gorgeous?" His voice is low, smooth as satin. He's going from one extreme to the other—confusing the hell out of me.

"Yes," I breathe.

"Yes what?"

"Yes I'm wet for you."

"Stand up." His command has me scrambling to my feet. If they're sore, it doesn't register. I'm too busy trying to hump the air. He motions to my pants. "Take em' off." It's almost a whisper.

It's a struggle, but I manage to remove the painted-on pants. I must have looked like an idiot, especially when I stumbled and he had to reach out and steady me, but he never cracked a smile. He just stared up at me with that powerful, dominant look of his I was coming to love more than his smile.

Standing in nothing but a tiny, black thong and my corset, I wait for his next command. But it never comes. After his eyes eat me up from my toes to my head, he loops his finger inside my panties and tugs me forward.

"You're gonna stand right here," he says, positioning me between his knees. "You're not gonna close your eyes. You're not gonna talk. You're gonna watch me finger fuck your pussy until you come all over my hand." *Holy mother of mayonnaise...* "Understand?"

I nod vigorously. "Y-yes."

"Good." He leans forward and presses his lips to the bared flesh just above my panty line. Then he grips the thin string at my hips, and pulls them slowly down my legs.

His nose is mere centimeters from my sex. But I don't care that I've been sweating all day. In leather pants. In the middle of summer. Why don't I care? Because he sure as fuck don't. When he inhales, he growls deep in his throat and his eyes turn to blue lava.

He trails his fingers back up the inside of my legs—tapping my thigh to get me to spread a little wider. Of course, I oblige. Then I watch as first one finger dips inside me, and then two. Pumping in and out. Coated in my arousal.

My eyes close and he pulls his fingers from inside me and reaches between my legs to smack my ass. The force of the blow has me stumbling a step forward. He grips my ass cheek in his hand and pulls me back.

"I said, *watch*." His words send a shiver down my spine as I drop my head and do as he says. Then he's fingering me again. Using his thumb to circle my clit as he fucks me harder. I reach out and grip his shoulders, unable to hold myself up with the force of his thrusts.

I feel my insides tighten and still, waiting in anticipation for the joy to ensue. Seconds later, a supernova of pleasure explodes inside me. Dirty words fill my ears. The scent of my orgasm fills my nostrils. All while Cook's fingers fill me. Milking every last drop of my desire.

When it's over, I feel numb. I'm not even sure my legs are still holding me up. I just want to sleep. Every muscle exhausted. Every limb weighted.

With a little guidance, I fall into Cook's lap. My arms wrap around his neck as I rest my cheek on his shoulder and breath him in. He smells like sweat. It's manly and just as intoxicating as the clean, cologne scent I'm used to.

"You need me to set an alarm for you?" he asks, his voice soft.

"Uh-uh."

"You don't have to work tomorrow?"

"Uh-uh."

He smiles against my cheek then kisses me there before repositioning us slightly until my chest is flat against his. I tuck my arms beneath me and curl further into him. His fingers are at my back, unlacing the corset. I could tell him there's a zipper on the side, but I'm afraid once he takes it off, he'll want me to move. If he continues to unlace it, I'll be asleep by the time he's finished.

I drift in and out every few seconds, wanting to prolong the joy I feel from being close to him. Being taken care of. I've never missed this kind of intimacy because I've never had it. Jud never cared for me like this. But Cook has since the beginning. Now that he's shown me how it feels to be worshipped, I don't know how I'd ever go without it.

13
EAGLES SECRETARY JUICE

I slept like a rock that night. I don't even remember going to bed. But when I woke up, I was naked and alone. The only reminder I had of Cook being there was the lingering scent of him on my skin. And the swirling of butterflies in my belly every time I looked at my chaise—where place he'd spanked me. And the spot on the carpet just in front of it—where I'd stood while he fingered me.

I haven't heard from Mr. Delicious since Saturday night, and now it's Thursday. The first few days were easy. I was still mildly embarrassed by what he'd done to me. But since I woke up yesterday morning, I've been struggling with the urge to call or text him. As I get dressed for my date with Juice tonight, I find I'm more excited about seeing Cook than I am anything else.

My last date outfit was pretty slutty, so tonight I'm going for something a little classier. The dark orange romper is still pretty revealing with its plunging neckline and super short length, but the golden tassels that dangle from the cinched waist and long, silhouette sleeves add a hint of sophistication to the sexiness. And to hell with those stinky, uncomfortable shoes. Gladiator flats that lace up my calves are just as sexy and a hell of a lot comfier.

I style my hair into a perfectly messy bun, put on my gold watch, a few bracelets and favorite diamond studs. For even more class, I'm wearing black-framed glasses.

Stupid me didn't bother to check the weather. And by the time I walk through the door of the bar, I'm soaked.

The chilly air inside has me crossing my arms to cover my hard nipples. Cursing myself for not wearing a bra, I force a smile and take a seat at the bar to wait on Juice.

"Is that Michael Kors?" Kat asks, eyeing my clothes.

"Y-yes." I clamp my jaw shut in an attempt to stop my teeth from chattering.

"Love it. Gotta borrow it. This will warm you up."

I take the glass from Kat with a nod of thanks and toss back the whiskey. It burns all the way to my toes. But as promised, I feel warmer. "Juice here yet?" She smacks her gum and grins, as I feel a tap on my shoulder.

Juice stands behind me wearing a crooked smile, his bottom lip filled with tobacco that instantly has the air smelling like wintergreen. Wiry hair is scattered across his jaw. Obviously the guy can't grow a beard, but I have to give him credit for trying. *At least he doesn't smell like bologna.*

"Almost didn't recognize you with those glasses," he says, pointing to my face.

"They're new."

"Juice!" I tense at the sound of Jud's voice as he yells from across the room. "It's your shot!"

Juice glances over the top of my head. "He's pissed cause I asked you here."

I raise an eyebrow. "Do you want me to leave?" He drags his eyes to my exposed chest then down to my legs before shaking his head.

"Nope. He'll get over it."

"So you don't care that he's mad?"

"Not even a little."

I beam. "Great! Let's shoot some pool."

This date is about as bad as the last one. I'm holding Juice's spit bottle—*eww*—while he shoots pool. Clarissa is a few chairs down from me, making sure to give Jud a kiss every time he makes a shot. And pool balls aren't the only thing Jud's shooting. He's been sending me daggers and sneers every chance he gets.

There is one upside to this date, though. In the corner of the room, standing tall and cocky, is Mr. Delicious. Where Jud's glances are hateful, Cook's are appreciative—when he's not laughing at me. Like the time I almost dropped Juice's damn spit bottle in my lap. Or when I curl my lip in disgust when he hands it back to me after spitting in it.

"I need a beer," Juice says, leaning on the table as he pulls a wad of crinkled up dollars from his pocket. "You thirsty, babe?" I suppress the urge to vomit as he gurgles the words, motioning for his bottle. I shake my head. "Jud?"

"I can get my own shit, Juice. I don't need your puppy to fetch it for me." He cuts his eyes to me as I take the money from Juice who shrugs.

"Suit yourself." Juice rubs his thumb over my cheek, his look apologetic. "He's probably afraid you'll poison it," he says so only I can hear.

"He's probably right," I deadpan, although my words are loud enough for everyone to hear.

"Shit!" Jud says. His tone slightly panicked as he looks down at his phone. "We need to step outside." He shoots Juice a pointed look. "Now." After all this time, Jud finally did something good for me. He allowed me a temporary reprieve from Mr. Spitbottle.

Patting a reluctant Juice on the shoulder, I give him my best smile. "Go ahead. I'll be at the bar."

"It might be a minute."

"I'll still be here. Promise."

He relaxes and alarms go off inside my head. He's probably hoping this party will last long after we leave the bar. He shouldn't hope. Not even a little bit.

Avoiding Cook, I go to the opposite side of the bar to order the drinks. Kat's smiling when she walks up. "Well...how's it going?"

I narrow my eyes at her. "You know good and damn well how it's going." Her laugh is infectious and I can't help but smile back at her. "He's outside right now."

"Why?"

"I don't know. They got a call or message or some shit. Anyway, he wants a beer. And I need something really strong." The idea of drinking anything liquid while holding Juice's...bottle...repulsed me a few moments ago. But now that I'm free of the thing, I'm afraid I can't make it through the night without a little help.

The dirty money in my hand isn't enough to buy me a drink, so I tell Kat I'll pay the difference.

"You will not pay. You have a tab, remember? I think you have like ten drinks in the hole."

"And I'll probably need them all tonight," I grumble.

"No way. You still have a few more dates I've already lined up. Pace yourself. You're gonna need alcohol for all of them."

"Are you serious?" I stare at her in open mouthed. Disbelieving. "A few? And they've already agreed to go out with me?"

"I wouldn't consider this going out." She gestures to the room with her hand. "But yeah. They agreed."

Flabbergasted, I ask, "But...why?"

With an exasperated sigh, Kat leans her elbows on the bar. Face to face, she stares at me a moment. "Look around, doll. You see any women in here that's as hot as you?" I flush at her compliment, averting my gaze. "Better yet, do you see *any* women in here who are available?"

I scan the room, noticing only a handful—all of which wear a property patch. "It doesn't bother them that I'm dating all their brothers?"

"They're men," she answers simply. "And they all want a chance at you. Besides, you're a Patchwhore." Loudly smacking her gum, she winks. "They expect you to work your way up the ranks."

I should feel ashamed at such a title. Instead, I feel liberated. There's a sense of freedom that comes with the term Patchwhore. It almost makes it okay to do whatever and whoever I want. And it's pleasing to my morals to know that I'm only sleeping with one man. Despite what everyone else thinks.

"Well...thank you for helping me with this."

"Don't thank me just yet, doll," she says, straightening. "Juice is one of the hotter ones."

I have to stifle my groan. "On that note, I'm going to the bathroom. And I may be a while. Will you let him know if he comes back before I'm out?"

She gives me a knowing smile and points to an area behind her. "Use the employee bathroom. I got you covered. Hide for as long as you need to."

I duck under the drop door behind the bar and quickly make my way to the bathroom. It's cleaner than the public one but just as big. Besides the basic bathroom amenities, it has a small seating area with two chairs and a table. I take a seat in one of the chairs, searching for a stack of magazines and come up empty.

I wish I'd brought my cell phone inside with me. I'd left it in the car because I didn't have a way to carry it. Looking back, lugging it around all night would've been worth it. At least then I could occupy my mind with a game. Or Facebook. Or call Emily for some encouragement. Although I'm pretty sure it would come only after she stopped laughing at me.

Leaning my head back, I close my eyes and enjoy the silence. It only lasts a second before the door opens and loud music fills the room. When it closes the noise disappears. As does the oxygen in the room.

Mr. Delicious stands only feet from me. The room I thought was large only moments ago seems tiny with his big frame inside it taking up all the space. And air. Causing my chest to tighten. Heart to beat harder. *Panties to dampen.*

"Hello, gorgeous."

Okay, maybe my reaction isn't due to the lack of air but the overwhelming presence of this man. So ruggedly handsome. So sexy in leather. Has the smile of the Devil. Eyes like the ocean. *And there's not a spit bottle in sight.*

Focus, Carmen!

"I'm on a date."

"You're hiding in a bathroom."

"What's it to you?"

His eyes darken. "You're wearing glasses." He takes a step closer.

"And?" He takes another step.

"And you're *not* wearing panties." *How the hell does he know that?*

I shift in my seat, adjusting the frames on my head. He makes some kind of throaty noise. He's closed the distance. Standing over me. Staring down at me. Grabbing my arms and hauling me up. My back is to the wall. His hips have me pinned.

"Kiss me," he demands. I want to. Damn I want to. But I have a goal. A plan. I can't really remember exactly what it is, but I'm sure it doesn't entail this. Right here. Right now.

"Like I said," I breathe, refusing to meet his eyes. "I'm on a date."

His lips touch the corner of my lips. "I." Then they kiss the other corner. "Don't." Mine part in invitation, but he doesn't grant me the kiss I silently wish for. "Fucking." He trails his mouth to my chin. "Care." Across my jaw. Then he comes back, his lips hovering over mine. A hairsbreadth away. "I said, kiss me."

He smells so good. He looks good. That hardness against my belly feels good. But I bet he tastes even better. One kiss. I can allow myself one kiss. This isn't a real date anyway.

Mind made up, I press my lips to his. Then, like some crazy, starved animal, I attack. My hands in his hair. His tongue swirling with mine. I roll my hips against him. He responds by shoving his knee between my legs—giving me something to grind against. *Son of a bitch this escalated quickly.*

"I want you. Now," he says, pulling the straps of my romper down. I push it over my hips and it pools at my feet. He drinks in my naked body with fiery eyes as he unbuckles his jeans. "You've been swaying that sexy little ass all night." He pulls a condom from his cut and rips the package open with his teeth. "Teasing my fuckin' cock...makin' me rock hard." Sheathing his dick, he strokes it a few times. "We're gonna make this quick, gorgeous." I nod, gripping his shoulders. Ready for him to fuck me senseless. "And try to be quiet."

He presses the head of his cock against my entrance. Then he lifts me around his waist, impaling me as he does. I release a blissful cry and he growls into my mouth, smothering my cries with his kiss. He fucks me hard, pulling his mouth away from mine and replacing it with his hand. I scream against his palm.

"So tight...so fuckin' wet...this pussy belongs to me." His drive hardens. His thrust rougher as he stakes his claim. My eyes roll back in my head. "You like it hard don't you, dirty girl." I moan into his hand. "I need you coming on my cock, gorgeous. Soaking me with that sweet cunt."

His pace quickens. My body tenses. He said it would be quick, and he meant it. Pumping his hips faster. Pushing deeper. Mercilessly pounding inside me. He makes me come so hard I scream. I clench him tight, forcing him to bury his face in my neck to muffle his roar. It only adds to my euphoria.

I'm throbbing with wicked pleasure. Pulsing with fiery passion. Nobody could ever fuck me like this man does. Make me come so violently. So quick. Take me so savagely in a bathroom. While I'm on date. And have me not giving a single shit.

He silently dresses me. Kissing me back to the present, before righting himself. He keeps a hand on my hip as he tosses the used condom in the toilet a few feet away.

"I bet I look a hot mess," I say, my voice thick.

Smiling down at me, he kisses the tip of my nose. "Even ravaged, you're still the prettiest fuckin' thing I've ever seen."

"Flattery doesn't work on a true lady."

He laughs, his eyes a lighter blue now. "True ladies don't find themselves fucked in the bathroom of a bar."

I return his playful smile. "This one just did."

"Well, my lady," he bows slightly, "you have a date to get back to and I have a president who will be needing a beer in about thirty seconds."

"Seriously?" I give him a disbelieving stare. "You know down to the second?"

Flushing the toilet, he straightens his vest and grins at me. "I know what he needs, when he needs it, because I pay attention."

"Is that so?" I smirk. "Well you've been watching me all night. Does that mean you know what I need?"

"Yep." He shoots me a wink as he opens the door. "And you just got it."

14
EAGLES TREASURER LEFTY

My last date ended rather abruptly.

When I returned from getting screwed in the bathroom, I was notified by Kat that Juice and the entire club had to leave. He left his apologies too. All I cared about was that he hadn't left his spit bottle.

Now, one week later, I have another date. And once again, I find myself looking forward to seeing Mr. Delicious more than anything else.

Tonight, I'm meeting Eagles Treasurer, Lefty. We haven't been formally introduced, but when Kat described him, I remembered having seen him around. Well, I guess it's him. Unless there's another Eagle that's five foot two, wears glasses and has feet so big he literally flops when he walks. Kat told me to take one for the team and find out if what they say about men's feet is true. I told her to eat shit.

Already standing three inches taller than Lefty, I make sure to wear flats. And since his head is closer to my chest than my eyes, I decide to wear a top that shows zero cleavage. The three quarter length, plain black shirt might be unsexy, but the short, white jean shorts make up for it. And they make my tanned legs appear even darker.

Per her request, I shoot Emily a selfie for approval. She immediately calls.

"You look like a fucking tutor," she starts. "And not a hot, sexy tutor—one who looks like she's going to help a twelve-year-old kid with his math homework." *She doesn't realize my date looks like a twelve-year-old kid.* "Change. I demand it."

"I'm not changing. My outfit screams fun and flirty."

"It screams K-Mart. That's a shirt a mom would wear pushing a stroller. With a toddler on her hip. And a ponytail. To keep her kid's sticky little fingers out of her hair. We want long tresses begging to be pulled. Take that shit down."

"Fine," I huff, shaking out my hair. Hating her because she's probably right.

"Now put more makeup on. You're not slutty enough."

"The girl next door look is what I'm going for. It may not be slutty but it's still appealing."

"It's not appealing. This girl next door is ugly. Stop watching Taylor Swift music videos. They're messing with your head. You need more of a Nicki Minaj look."

I roll my eyes. "I'm trying to make Jud jealous. I don't have to be a slut to do that."

"Um...yeah. You kinda do."

"Whatever. I'm not changing."

"Well when I envision Cook fucking you in the bathroom later, you won't be wearing that. Just so you know." And she's found my Achilles heel.

"I'll text you back." Hanging up, I sprint to my closet and rummage through my outfits until I find something sexier.

I trade in my "mom" top for one of the sluttiest items I own. I'd bought it for the first frat party I attended my freshmen year. So not only is it sexy, it should trigger a memory for Jud.

The white vest has a tiny chain just below my breasts that connects the two sides—exposing most of my stomach, chest and plenty of side boob. I dig around until I find the extreme low-rise stiletto jeans. And since I'm going all out, I toss my flats and opt for my white heels that are probably something a stripper at Magic City would wear.

Darker eyes. Redder lips. A little tease to my hair. I snap a picture and get a bunch of emoji in response—all approving.

I don't care if Lefty's eyes only come to my belly button. If I'm getting fucked in a bathroom by Cook tonight, I'm going to look hot doing it.

"You smell really, really good."

I look down at Lefty and give him a tentative smile. "Thanks?"

"I mean, really good."

I hate Emily. I hate myself for listening to her. Lefty is a toucher. And he's taking advantage of all the bared places on my body. His feet might be big, but his fingers are tiny. And sticky. And I wish I had my mom clothes on.

Burying his face between my breasts again, he inhales. I put my hand on top of his head and push him away. "How about we sit down, hmm?"

I thought it would help. It didn't. Now my chair is impossibly close to his. His arm is around my waist. And he keeps trying to tickle me with his tiny hands. I've tried to laugh it off. But if he continues, I'm going to have to hurt his feelings.

Good news? Jud is affected. It helps that Clarissa isn't here tonight, but I don't care why. Instead of hateful looks, he's giving me lustful ones. He's remembering the last time I wore this top. When he tried to unhook it and couldn't, so I wore it during sex. Probably the best three minutes of his life. Unfortunately for me, it wasn't nearly as rewarding as the three minutes with Cook last week.

Speaking of Cook, he's here. Making me regret even considering having sex with him. This is all his fault. I'd be wearing a sensible, K-Mart shopping mom outfit if it weren't for him and his magic stick. So while he's getting his ten chuckles over my predicament, I'm imagining all the ways I could castrate him.

"I'm going to get a drink," I mumble, pulling out of Lefty's embrace. He starts to follow but I stop him by putting my finger in his forehead and pushing him back in his seat. When he finally arches his neck high enough to meet my eyes, I smile sweetly at him. "I got this, sweetie."

"Okay...*sweetie*." He winks. I struggle with the urge to put my heel through his throat.

I don't even care that the only open spot at the bar is the space between Cook and Ronnie. I throw myself between them and immediately start shaking my head at Kat. "I can't do this," I say, grabbing Ronnie's drink and downing the rest of it. It's so strong and burns so bad, I make a pirate sound through my teeth— prompting Kat, Ronnie and Cook to laugh.

"Shut up and give me one of whatever that was but make it a double. Triple."

"Come on, Carmen," Kat says, between her fits of laughter. "Lefty's a good guy. He's just a little strange."

"A little strange?" I scoff. "He asked if he could put his finger in my belly button." Another round of laughter. Another stolen drink. To hell with them all. "There's something really wrong with these guys. I've yet to find one that's even half-ass tolerable. Bologna...spit bottles...big feet, tiny fingers and a tickle fetish? Come on! They're supposed to be bikers. I may not know a lot about MC's, but I do know these guys aren't like any of the rest here."

"Well, sunshine, that's because they're not—"

"They're not used to a girl like you being interested in them," Cooks finishes. "You're much too classy." He grins at me, leaning against the bar like he owns the damn place.

Unable to come up with a snarky comeback, I narrow my eyes. "Shut up." Turning back to Kat who places a drink in front of me, I give her a pleading look. "Please, Kat. Help me out a little."

She shrugs, smacking her gum to cover her smile. "Sorry doll, my hands are tied. I promised him a night with you. If I go back on that, I'll lose my fifty bucks."

I gasp. "Fifty bucks?"

"Yeah. They pay me to get a date with you." She leans in and whispers, "They think I'm some kind of matchmaker."

"I'll give you a hundred bucks and my entire wardrobe to get me out of this. Just put some Visine in his beer. It's all I'm asking."

Shaking her head, she grins. "No can do. I'm a woman of my word. But you…," she points her finger at me. "You can leave. Anytime you want."

"No," I snap. "I'm not leaving. Have you noticed how Jud's been looking at me? It's killing him seeing me here. But if Lefty suddenly gets sick, then *he'll* leave."

The body next to me bristles and I glance up at Cook. He's looking toward Lefty, but when he notices me watching him, he shoots me a toothy smile. I roll my eyes.

"Drink, Carmen." Kat thrusts the drink at me. "After this one, you might actually enjoy the tickling."

I take my drink and back away, pointing my finger at her. "I hate you." I motion to Ronnie and Cook. "All of you."

My drink is so potent; I'm surprised it doesn't melt my cup. Despite its strength, I manage to suck down half of it before I make it back to my seat. But before I can sit, Lefty is on his feet.

"Let's dance," he says, taking my massive hand in his and pulling me toward the dance floor.

I refuse to look at the laughing faces by the bar as I rest my hands on his shoulders and allow him to put his on my hips. We haven't even made it through the first verse of the song before he's sliding them up my sides and under my vest.

"Lower your hands, Lefty." My warning is coupled with a glare. Grinning like an idiot, he takes my words out of context.

"If you say so." Slowly, he slides them to my hips, then around to cup my ass. I slap his hands away, ready to unleash my wrath when I hear Ronnie's voice ring out across the room.

"Load up!"

"Awe man," Lefty groans, looking over his shoulder at the men filing out before shooting me a hopeful expression. "Wanna go to dinner sometime?"

Despite his awkwardness. Wandering hands. Huge feet and annoying demeanor, Lefty really isn't that bad. So I decide to let him down easy.

I give him a sweet smile and pat the top of his head before saying, "Not a chance in hell."

15
THE WARNING

It's late. Or early, depending on how you look at it. It's still three a.m. I've been in a deep sleep for about two hours when a noise wakes me. Fear creeps up my spine. I hold my breath and fight the urge to cower under my covers. Eyes wide, I stare into the darkness.

My mouth opens to scream when a large figure appears in my bedroom door. Then it speaks, and fear becomes desire.

"It's me, gorgeous."

I can't answer. My throat feels thick. I try to swallow, but I have a sudden case of dry mouth. And a bad case of breath.

"You know," he starts, and I squint through the darkness trying to make him out. "Lefty's harmless. I'm pretty sure the guy wouldn't know what to do with a woman if he had one."

My eyes start to adjust and I pull in a shaky breath at how large and intimidating he looks. And delicious. Very, very delicious.

"But when that *other* motherfucker looked at you like a man possessed, like you were still his. Like he wanted to fuck you. All I saw was red. Do you know why, Carmen?" I shake my head. My ears straining. Praying to hear that unmistakable sound of him removing his belt. Then his cut. Shirt. Boots. Jeans.

"Because me and you, we have a deal." He stalks toward me slowly, still fully dressed. I suppress a whimper. Wanting to beg him to get naked and in my bed. "They can look. Stare. It's impossible not to." His fingers curl around the covers, pulling them slowly away from me. "But all of this belongs to me." *Oh…I'm going to come from just his voice.*

"And if they even think about touching you…I'll break their fingers. If they even think about what you taste like…I'll break their jaw. And if they *ever* think about fucking you…fucking what's mine…I'll break their neck." Okay. Point made. It's yours. *Now touch it. Taste it. Fuck it before I implode.*

He drags two fingers across the bottom of my foot. Up the inside of my leg. Thigh. Pausing to press against the wet heat between my legs. "So you remember that on your next *date.*" Slipping his hand inside my panties, he drags them between my folds. I'm a shuddering, breathless, horny mess.

"Remember who this tight cunt belongs to." He trails upward, over the top of my shirt. His hand gently squeezing one breast until my nipple hardens to a painful peak, before moving to the other and doing the same.

"Who these belong to." *Oh for shit's sake.* I'll remember. His last reminder left a lingering tenderness inside me for days. And it was so much sweeter than this. No need for words now. I like a more physical approach.

My chest expands as I pull in a deep, shuddering breath. He moves his still damp fingers to my lips where he traces them softly—coating them with my arousal. "Be careful, gorgeous. Tread lightly. Those sexy little outfits are gonna get you in trouble." He removes his fingers. I'm panting. Wet. So aroused, he could breathe on my clit and I'd come.

"Next time," he says, pausing to push those two digits between his lips, "I might not be so forgiving." Then he winks. He turns. He walks out. I sit in a sexually-induced fog, confused, wanting and feeling empty as I wait for his return—that never comes.

16
EAGLES ENFORCER CLINT

"No!" Emily gasps, her disbelief as evident as mine. "He didn't!"

"Oh yeah." I blow on my coffee. "He did." I chance a sip, burning the tip of my tongue.

"I'm driving over. You kill him and I'll help dispose of the body."

It's seven in the morning. It's hasn't been four hours since my visitor left. It's too early to plot someone's death. But I'm contemplating making an exception.

"Do you have a date already lined up for next week?"

"Yep. Thursday night. His name is Clint. He's the enforcer."

"Oooo. Enforcer. Sounds hot."

"Yeah, he's really not."

"So how are you going to deal with Cook?"

I've considered this. Death still isn't off the table. But I'm giving my mind the week off and letting my body decide what it wants. And after last night, there's only one solution to the problem.

"I'm going to dress like a K-Mart mom."

"Um…" Kat wrinkles her nose as she takes in my mom top and Capri pants. "Cute outfit?"

"Don't ask," I grumble, taking the drink she offers. I'm quickly becoming an alcoholic. Before long, I'll be spending Thursday nights in an AA meeting instead of the bar.

"Clint's here. He's probably waiting for the sexy Carmen to show up, but he'll catch on soon."

I shake my head and scan the bar, finding Cook watching me from across the room. He smirks. *Smug bastard.*

I hadn't heard from him since he left me a heated catastrophe a week ago. Since then, I've been an ass to everyone I've encountered. Sexual frustration will do that do you. And it's affected my job. My lack in tips this past week has left me scraping to make rent. I should make him pay it.

"Cheer up, buttercup." *Are you fucking kidding me?*

Clint grins next to me. His stupid line has me wanting to choke the life out of him. I know my thoughts are a little extreme, but I can't help it. When my vagina isn't happy, I'm not happy.

I give him a smile that doesn't reach my eyes. "Sorry. Long week."

He shrugs as he takes a seat. "I get it."

Clint is in his mid-thirties. A little overweight. His round face is kind and boyish making him appear younger than he is. But he smells nice. Doesn't dip. Has normal sized feet and his hands are calloused, rough and not the least bit sticky. Compared to the other Eagles I've met, he's a dime.

"Can I ask you a question?"

"Of course," he says, smiling warmly at me.

"Kat." I cringe on the outside as Cook ambles up next to me. But on the inside, I'm on fire. "Ronnie needs a beer."

Noticing Cook, Clint stands to shake his hand. Cook straightens and returns the gesture with a nod. He slides his gaze to me a moment before his signature smile claims his face.

"What you two getting into tonight?"

"Few drinks. Maybe some pool. Not too much going on here," Clint says with a chuckle. It's then that I notice Jud isn't around. Actually, none of the Eagles are here. The bar is pretty scarce tonight.

"You know," I start, spinning on my stool as I mirror Cook's grin. He gives me a suspicious look. I ignore it and turn to Clint. "It really is boring here. You want to go for a ride? Maybe grab something to eat?" My stomach wakes up at the mention of food. Too anxious about seeing Mr. Not-So-Delicious, I'd forgotten to eat.

"Really?" Clint looks over my shoulder, to who I'm sure is Kat— the matchmaker—before settling his gaze back on me.

"Sure." I flip Cook the finger so only he can see as I beam at Clint. "Why not?"

"Okay. Let me make a quick call and we'll go."

"Sounds perfect."

He's barely out of hearing distance when Cook starts in on me. "What are you doing?"

"Not getting laid by you, obviously," I spit, a little shocked at my outburst. Though he tries to hide it, Cook is a little impressed.

"Someone's feisty."

"Someone's pissed. We had a deal, remember? And you didn't hold up your end of the bargain."

He winks. "So greedy."

I give him a nasty look. "Says Mr. So-selfish."

"Hope that stool is comfortable, gorgeous." He grabs Ronnie's beer, lowering his mouth to my ear. "Because you're not going anywhere."

I'm still stewing when Clint returns. "You ready?"

"Beyond ready," I snap, glaring at Cook who's a little too confident. If he thinks I'm not leaving, he's as bat shit crazy as Lefty.

"Something goin' on with you and Cook?" Clint asks once we're outside.

"Hell no," I lie. "I just have little tolerance for arrogance."

He laughs. "Cook? Arrogant? He's the humblest guy I know."

"You've known him for a while?"

"Years." I'm somewhat confused by his answer. Did he know Cook before he became a Prospect? While he fastens my helmet, I make a mental note to find out more once we get where we're going.

Straddling the bike, he motions for me to climb on. I do so gracefully—relieved to see there's no duct tape holding the damn thing together.

"Shit."

"What is it?" I ask, watching as he flips a couple switches and presses a few buttons.

"It won't crank."

"Maybe it's the battery? Can you jump it off?" My tone is a little desperate. "My car is here…." I trail off when Clint curses under his breath.

"What?"

"Someone stole my fuckin' battery." *That son of a bitch.*

I didn't bother going back inside the bar. I didn't even tell Clint I was leaving. When he went inside, I got in my car. When I got home, I took my key out from under the mat and dead bolted my door.

A bottle of wine, call to Emily and three hours later, I give in and check my phone that's been vibrating like crazy with messages. The first few are from Kat.

You okay?

Worried about you.

Please don't make me send the Calvary.

I type out a quick reply.

I'm fine. Home. If you send the Calvary, make sure they have food

Two messages are from Jud.

You fucking Clint now too?

Whore.

Classic, dick.

And there's one message from Cook. I start to delete it, but I'm buzzed. A little curious. And too hopeful that it's a promise to fuck me crazy.

I'll be there at midnight.

I should tell him to piss off.

Kick rocks.

Eat a dick.

Instead, I unlock the door.

"I hate you," I whisper, my breath catching in my throat as he pounds into me from behind.

"Your cunt tells a different story." He delivers a hard thrust that has my toes curling. "My thighs are fuckin' soaked." Another brutal drive. "You've come on my tongue. My fingers. Twice on my cock. And I haven't been here twenty minutes."

He's right.

The moment he pushed open the door of my bedroom, everything inside me awakened. I was already naked. His clothes were off in a matter of seconds. He didn't even kiss me—he dove right between my legs. He fucked me with his tongue. His fingers.

When he said he'd missed the taste of my pussy, I came.

He growled about how he had to stretch me with his fingers because my cunt was too tight for his cock, and I came.

Then he fucked me so hard he had to tell me to breathe. And on that breath, I came.

He slowed. He caressed. He trailed kisses down my spine. He said, "I've missed you, gorgeous. So fuckin' much." I'm still reeling from that one. Even as another starts to build.

My body is limp. Face in the mattress. Ass in the air. His hands grip my hips, holding me up. My orgasm consumes me. Voice lost. Breath gone. Heart still. I can't even fist my fingers in the sheets. I just ride the wave—trusting he'll keep me from drowning.

I feel him stiffen. Make a strangled noise. My flesh is hypersensitive and I shiver when he pulses inside me. Breathes down my back. Kisses my neck. As attentive as always, he pulls out of me slowly, covering me as the bed dips and he stands.

Moments later he returns, pulling me from unconsciousness and into his arms. "Don't ever make me wait that long again," I say, my voice hoarse, not sounding like my own. He smiles against my ear. "You nearly killed me."

"The wait nearly killed you?" he asks amused.

I shake my head. Well, I try to. "No. All the coming after my dry spell almost killed me."

"I apologize. From now on every date will end with me." In the few moments of silence, I'm dozing again. But his voice wakes me. "I gotta leave soon, gorgeous."

"Deuces," I mutter.

His light laugh has me smiling. "You only want me for my cock."

"And you only want me for yourself."

"So true." He kisses my temple. "See you soon, selfish, greedy, gorgeous girl."

"Wait." His lips still in my hair at my demand. "Did you steal Clint's battery?"

I feel his grin at my ear. In my toes. Then he whispers, "What do you think?"

17

EAGLES VICE PRESIDENT ZACK

The next day I'm holding my schedule in my hand, begging my co-working Jeannie to cover a shift for me. I'd asked for Thursdays off, but my manager didn't seem to care. He'd scheduled me anyway for the evening shift. And I have a date that night with Eagles VP Zack, who Kat promises is normal.

"I'd do it for you," I say, hoping guilt will convince her.

She lets out a loud sigh. "Fine. But are you ever gonna tell me why you need Thursdays off?"

"It's for a family thing," I lie. "Thanks Jeannie. You're the best." I clock out and head to my car, calling Kat on the way to get the details on this "western themed" party she'd texted me about, that just so happens to be on the same night as my date with Zack.

She tells me it's a tribute to John Wayne on the thirty-seventh anniversary of his death. I'm apprehensive at first. This party doesn't sound like a club function at all. There's no point in meeting Zack there if Jud wouldn't be there for me to rub it in his face. But my reluctance fades when she informs me one of the clubs is hosting it as a way to raise money.

The wait for Thursday is killing me. The week is long and boring. And not hearing from Cook seems to make the time pass that much slower. I think I need to add a clause to our deal that says he has to come over every night. Regardless if I have a date or not.

I'm sure his response would be something like, "Greedy girl." Not that I mind. Actually, I find it kind of hot when he calls me "girl."

Finally, Thursday arrives. I'm more than ready to shake my ass to some George Straight, make Jud blow steam out of his ears, then come home and wait for Cook to fuck me so hard I pass out.

It's nearly eight when I arrive at Pops. The crowd of men outside the door doesn't bother to keep their lewd comments to themselves as they gaze lustfully at me in my western outfit--cut-off jean shorts, flannel shirt unbuttoned enough to show a generous amount of cleavage and cowboy boots.

I brush past them nervously—offering a tight smile as I quickly make my way inside.

"Howdy, ma'am," a young guy standing just inside the door drawls. I laugh at how in character he is. He must be a member of the club hosting the party.

"Howdy."

"Malfunctional Prospect, Lyle. Nice to meet you."

I take his hand and nod. "Carmen."

Tightening his grip, he pulls me closer to him and dips his head. "I swear I don't usually sound like that. It's just another way for the club to make an ass out of me."

I meet his friendly gaze and smile. Intrigued, I ask, "Why would they want to make an ass out of you?"

"It's all part of prospecting. Allowing them to take my pride helps to prove my loyalty."

He pulls back, and I can see the reflection of said loyalty in his eyes. I want to know more. Maybe by learning this Prospect's reasons, I can better understand another Prospect I know.

"But why pride? You can't prove yourself in some other way?" *Like robbing a liquor store or stealing a car….*

"Pride is a real man's greatest gift to give. I have no self-respect when it comes to my club. Because it's not about me. It's about brotherhood."

"Prospect!" someone yells, causing me to jump. He just smiles—as finely attuned to the outburst as Cook.

"Nice to meet you, Carmen. Have fun tonight."

I smile back. "You too."

My face falls as a burly man who is seething with anger approaches. I spin on my heel and fight through the crowd to the bar. Looking back over my shoulder, I can see the man yelling in the Prospect's face. I have the urge to defend him. He wasn't doing anything wrong.

"Don't feel bad for him," Zack says, turning on his stool to greet me. He motions to the empty one next to it. "We all have to go through it. One day, he'll be doing the same thing to another guy."

144

I sidle up next to him, forcing myself not to look back at the door. "Just seems like it sucks."

Zack laughs. "Oh, it does. But it's worth it." He winks, and although it doesn't light a fire inside me like Cook's winks do, there's something warm about it.

Zack isn't by any means hot, but he's nice looking. Early-thirties. Medium height. Square jaw covered in thick, dark hair. Gray eyes that always seem to smile and have yet to look at me like I'm a piece of meat. Instead, they have a kind, respectful gleam in them. Appreciative, but not lecherous or dirty. It seems the further I move up in the rankings, the more normal the Eagles get. *I bet their President is a real winner...*

"Would you like a drink?" he asks, motioning with his hand to get Kat's attention. She immediately comes over—snapping her towel in the air between us.

"Look at this feisty cowgirl!"

"Hey Kat. Margarita?"

"You got it!"

Conversation with Zack is easy. Simple. He asks about school and seems impressed that I'm studying engineering. He works for a pipeline company, and even hands me his business card—promising me an interview with his employer once I've graduated.

Thirty minutes, two margaritas and a few buttery nipple shots—my new favorite—later, he asks me to dance.

I find myself comparing him to Cook who I've been nonchalantly scanning the room for since I got here. I've yet to see him, but as I dance with Zack, I can't help but wish it was his arms holding me.

Where Cook is a hard wall of muscle, Zack is softer. Cook towers over me, Zack only has me by a couple inches. Zack's hands lay respectfully on my hips. Cook's linger on my ass. Lower back. Between my thighs...

"Jud can't keep his eyes off of you," Zack says, bringing me back to the present. I find Jud sitting at a nearby table ignoring the guy talking to him as he shoots daggers at me. *So much for those lusty looks...* "He won't say anything, though. Clarissa would kill him."

I peel my eyes from Jud just as Clarissa climbs in his lap. "Wouldn't want that to happen," I mutter. Zack smiles, but doesn't comment. "It doesn't bother you to dance with me knowing I used to be with him? I mean, he is your brother."

He studies Jud a moment before meeting my eyes. "Drake asked him in front of all of us did he care if the two of you went out. Jud said no. Swore it. Gave his word. So we took it. Plus, he named Clarissa as his property. She wears his patch." His eyes drop to mine. "Can't claim but one ol' lady, babe." I give him a tight smile and ignore that gleam in his eyes. The one that suggests maybe I could be his ol' lady.

Hell no.

145

We finish out the song, then return to the bar—his hand not possessive, but supportive in the middle of my back.

I take a seat, and he doesn't follow. I spin on my stool and find him standing with his hand outstretched. The hand that receives it is all too familiar to me. Then I hear his voice.

"Good seeing you again, Zack. How's that new Street Glide treating you?"

Zack answers, but I'm too busy playing Cook's words on a loop inside my head. So deep. So manly. So damn panty wetting. The things this man does to me. Dressed in his white T-shirt and ripped jeans. That damn leather vest. Cocky grin. Throaty voice. *Oh, he's going to fuck me tonight.*

After what feels like years have passed, he finally notices me. His smile touches his cool, blue eyes. They're not blazing or amused. They're just...blue. He doesn't look jealous or possessive. He doesn't even give me a warning glare about my outfit. He just looks...satisfied. Like he knows something I don't.

"I see you got a seat next to the prettiest girl in the bar," he says, still looking at me.

Zack lets out a chuckle. "Yeah." As if he's afraid Cook might ask to sit down, he takes his seat. Cook's lips twitch in amusement. "She's definitely something." I flash a shy grin at Zack who sits a little closer to me now than he did before.

"Well you should get a seat closer to the dance floor. Competition is about to start."

"Competition?" I ask Cook, who nods slowly—something secretive lurking in his gaze. *What the hell is he up to?*

"Something the clubs come up with to help raise money. Just another opportunity for them to make an ass out of us." He quirks a brow at me. *Had he been listening to my conversation with the Prospect at the door? Did someone tell him about it? Wait. Is he...*

"Are you in this competition?" He nods again. I giggle for some reason. "What kind of competition is it?" Before I can get my answer, Ronnie calls him from a few feet away.

"Come on, Prospect. I got some money to win." I wave to Ronnie, but he's already heading toward the stage—laughing and shaking his head.

"See you soon, gorgeous," Cook says, winking at me before giving Zack a nod—a flash of victory in his eyes. "Have fun...Zack." I watch as he struts away. Swaying that sexy ass of his through the crowd in confident, powerful strides.

What the hell was *that* about? Why do I feel like he's up to no good? And why did he just look at Zack like that? Is he that confident he's going to win the competition?

"Let's get closer," I say, grabbing my fourth margarita of the night from the bar and hopping down from my stool. I don't wait for Zack as I lift my drink high in the air and maneuver through the throng of people that has gathered around the dance floor.

Several men are on the stage. Cook stands tall and proud and composed in the center. I recognize two of the other six men as Eagles Prospect, Brett, and Malfuctional Prospect, Lyle.

There's only one available seat and it's next to Ronnie. Not wanting to be rude to Zack, I stand with the rest of the people who couldn't find a seat and wait—my eyes fixed on Cook. *A week is just too long.*

"Carmen?" I nod to a waitress holding a tray filled with empty beer bottles and ashtrays. "Zack told me to tell you he has to step out a minute, but that he'll be back shortly."

I frown. "Is everything alright?"

Shrugging, she grabs another couple bottles from a table next to us. "Don't know. Didn't say." Noticing my look, she flashes me a smile. "I'm sure it's fine." She leans in and lowers her voice. "You didn't hear this from me, but I heard Ronnie say like, way earlier, that he was gonna send some guys with a trailer somewhere. Guess a bike broke down or somethin'. Funny how he waited till now to send someone though. Don't you think?"

She lifts her chin at someone on the stage—beaming at them. I feel a wave of jealously crash through me, but find it's one of the other guys looking at her. Not Cook, who has his back turned and is speaking with the man holding the microphone.

The chair next to Ronnie is still empty. And I'm not surprised when he motions for me to take it. Sliding in next to him, I bump my shoulder with his. "Did you intentionally sabotage my date?"

He winks. "Maybe."

"Why?" It's not that I care, but what's it to him?

"Tell you what, sugar," he says, resting his arm on the back of my chair. "If I win, I'll half it with you." He touches his beer bottle to my glass and drinks, leaving my question unanswered as the emcee calls to everyone in the room.

"Listen up, folks." The noise dies down instantly. "Malfunctional MC's Lake Charles chapter is celebrating their five-year anniversary." People shout and clap, including Ronnie who stands. When he does, everyone else follows suit.

A man wearing a patch that names him President of Malfunctional MC, steps up to give Ronnie a hug. I guess Ronnie's show of respect means something.

We take our seats and the emcee starts again. "The cover charge you paid today will go to show your support. So, on behalf of the MC, I want to thank you for coming out."

Cover charge? I didn't pay... Is that why the Prospect was getting yelled at? I look for him on the stage, but I find Cook first. And he's watching me. I narrow my eyes playfully—silently accusing him of being a part of the plan to sabotage my date. *Again.* He just smirks.

"To show how much we appreciate you being here, we're gonna provide you with a little entertainment...free of charge." He motions to the men on the stage. "Every man on this stage is trying to prove himself to the club. Each one is

147

from a different club or chapter. We're gonna see who has what it takes. Who wants it the most. Who's gonna earn braggin' rights for their club."

The crowd cheers for their favorite—calling out the name of the man representing their club. I hear several people yell for Cook who stares out at the crowd. His expression stoic. *Game face...*

"In memory of the legendary John Wayne, we're gonna do this..." The emcee's voice drops. "Cowboy style."

"You know anything about line dancin', sugar?" Ronnie asks, leaning close enough for me to hear him over the emcee who's going over the rules.

I smirk. "I'm from Georgia, baby. You can't be a sweet peach if you don't know how to line dance."

He raises a brow and grins. "So I should double my bet?"

"I'm not the one dancing." I nod my head in Cook's direction. "You need to worry about if your boy up there is any good. He's the one with something to prove."

"What about two-steppin'? You any good at that?"

I roll my eyes. "Again, I'm from Georgia. *Again*...I'm not the one dancing. You think he's got a chance?"

Ronnie just shrugs. "I guess we'll see."

"Hey," I start, the lightbulb going off in my head. "Are they two-stepping? Do you want me to be his *partner?*"

He throws his head back on a laugh at my twisted-up face, then tugs a strand of my hair. "You catch on quick."

I stare at him in disbelief as Cook approaches—crooking his finger at me. "Come on, gorgeous," he says, smiling like we've already won. "Let's see if those boots are just for show."

"Slimy bastards," I mumble, grinning like crazy. I shoot Ronnie a look over my shoulder. "If we lose, it's his fault."

Ronnie's eyes move to Cook—sparkling with pride and confidence. "He won't lose. He doesn't know how."

18
I'M NOT YOUR PROSPECT

I'm on edge. Palms sweaty. I pull my hand from Cooks to wipe it on my shorts. He smirks down at me, his demeanor cool and calm. I give him a nervous smile. I don't want to disappoint him. I don't want Ronnie to lose his money. *I wish I had time for about five more shots.*

Cook leads us to a corner away from everyone else who is clustered together in the middle of the dance floor. "Why are we way over here?" I ask, anxiously fidgeting with the strings on my cutoffs.

"Because we're gonna dance around them."

"What?" I squeak, my heartrate speeding. "I-I only know square two-step. Two to one corner...two to the other corner...two—" He places a finger over my lips shushing me.

"Can you spin?" I nod. "Stay loose?" I nod again. "Hold my hand?" I put my hand in his. "Then you'll be fine."

"What if—"

"You'll. Be. Fine. You look beautiful. You smell delicious. And I'm going to fuck you while you're on your knees, wearing nothing but those boots tonight. So let's get this shit over with. Because if I win, I get the rest of the night off." He winks at me.

I just stand here, mouth open like an idiot and mutter, "Oh. Uh. Okay."

"Relax." He grips my hip possessively. My body immediately relaxes into him. "Good girl." *Son of a bitch.*

"Round one!" the emcee announces. "Who likes tequila?" The crowd roars. "Who likes it when tequila makes her clothes fall off?" Everyone cheers louder as Joe Nichols' *Tequila Makes Her Clothes Fall Off* begins to play. Cook raises a brow.

"Fitting, don't you think?" I have a snarky come back, but we're moving before I can say it.

He leads us around the dancefloor—pushing my body in the direction he wants me to move. It only takes a few steps for me to follow his fluid movements. Even though I'm moving backward, completely unaware of where I'm going, I trust that he's leading me in the right direction.

We turn. Twist. Our strides in sync with one another. He spins me. Twirls me. That big body of his floating smoothly across the floor. He's graceful. Every motion confident and precise. I feel light as a feather. He feels like steel under my touch. He's relaxed but focused. Every time he spins me I laugh. And it's the only time he smiles.

As the song comes to an end, he twirls me once more, then kisses my hand. When the emcee asks the crowd to give it up for the Devil's Renegades Prospect, he steps back and extends his hand—giving all the praise to me. I beam like an idiot.

Two couples are voted out and we move on to round two. I bounce on my heels as we wait for the song. Cook is just as composed as always. He gives Ronnie, who appears to be as excited as me, a cool nod. But when he drops his eyes to mine, they're heated.

"You're fuckin' killing me in those shorts."

My smile is so big, the corner of my eyes crinkle. "I thought you liked my boots."

"I like it all," he growls—that beastly stare causing my breath to hitch.

"Let me ask you somethin', man." The emcee comes to stand next to us, propping his arm on Cook's shoulder as he speaks into the microphone. "Is she country?" Catcalls ring out among the crowd. "Cause Jason Aldean says she's country." The song starts and the emcee steps away. Then we're dancing.

Either he's trying to get the other competitors to quit, or he's enjoying this as much as I am, but Cook steps it up this round. Spinning me. Turning us both. Our bodies moving faster across the floor—keeping perfect time with the rhythm of the song.

He ends the round by dipping me so low my head comes dangerously close to the floor. I laugh—unable to feel anything but giddy. I don't know if it's the dance or him that has me so high. But I'm loving it. Ronnie is loving it. The crowd is loving it. Cook is...well he's just being Cook. Humble and quiet.

"How are you not sweaty or winded?" I pant, wiping my forehead with the back of my hand. *Eww...*

"I've been conserving my energy."

"For what?"

"For something else." His tone is clipped.

I give him a knowing look—figuring his mind is in the gutter. *"For when I'm balls deep inside you, baby."* I laugh at my terrible impression of him. But he's not smiling. He's focused on something behind me.

"No." His eyes are dark, but not in that hot sexy way. I mean, they're still hot and sexy, but he looks...*pissed*. "For when I break that motherfucker's legs." My spine stiffens at his words. I try to turn my body so I can see who he's talking about, but his grip tightens on me. "Don't."

"Alright, Prospect," Ronnie calls, oblivious to the rage building inside Cook. "One more round." Cook nods, but Ronnie isn't convinced. "Hey!" Both our heads jerk to where he's now standing. "Fuck him. I gotta lot of money ridin' on this. Don't fuck it up." *Maybe he's not oblivious...*

"Who is he talking about?" I ask, although something tells me it's Jud. I swear I can feel his beady little eyes firing rockets at my back.

"Nobody, gorgeous." There's not a trace of anger on Cook's face when he stares down at me again. He's smiling. Happy. The flames now dying embers in his eyes. "Let's win this so we can get out of here." He drags his gaze down my body. "I'm ready to feel those boots on my shoulders." Dropping his head to my ear, he nips it. "While I'm balls deep inside you."

I miss the emcee's announcement. I'm on my second turn before I even realize what song is playing—"Ticks" by Brad Paisley. I want Cook to check me for ticks. *I'm ready to feel those boots on my shoulders.* I'm ready to feel his shoulders under my boots. His hands under my clothes. My body under his body. Or vice versa. I'd happily ride him. *Like a cowgirl.*

The song ends. I don't want to let him go. He pulls away from me, but holds my hand as he shows me off to the crowd. They cheer. We won. Ronnie is collecting his money. Cook is thanking people. I'm breathless and it has nothing to do with the eighty million turns I just performed. It's *him*. The one who is going to fuck me in my boots.

"Girl you *killed* it!" Kat screams, wrapping me in her arms. Tearing me away from Cook's hand. *Good thing... I don't think I could've let go on my own.* "Shot. We need a shot." I allow her to pull me to the bar. Cook shoots me his I'll-see-you-soon-don't-worry-you're-still-getting-fucked smile as I'm dragged away.

I'm congratulated by numerous people. Stopped by several who hug me. I don't know any of them, but I graciously accept their embrace and kind words. By the time we finally get to the bar, I'm more than thankful for the chilled shots Kat made earlier.

"Someone had faith in me."

She smiles. "Girl I knew the two of you would win. You looked good. Cook looked *damn* good."

"I know, right," I snort, tossing back my second buttery nipple. *You could drink these things for breakfast.*

"Having fun, *patchwhore*?" Jud's words and presence are enough to sour the sweet drink.

"Woah. Take it down a notch, dude," Kat says to as he takes a seat in the empty stool beside me.

I hold my hand up. "No it's okay, Kat." I give a seething Jud my best smile. "Actually I am."

He shakes his head in disgust. Looking at me like I'm trash. His gaze is so angry. So hateful. So menacing. He actually makes me feel like trash. "You're a nasty, classless bitch, Carmen. And the worst fucking decision I ever made."

Ouch.

That one hurt. And despite my attempt, I can't hide my flinch. Jud's words have cut me before. But this time, the wound is deep enough to bleed.

"There a problem here?"

Cook's voice is like stitches. His presence my pain relief. He soothes me instantly—making Jud's brutal attack about as effective as a puppy licking me in the face. Cook wields just that much damn power over my emotions. He has the ability to make me forget bad shit. Think about only good shit. Deliciously stimulating, sexy, seductive, panty melting good shit.

Body tight. Muscles flexing. Jaw clenched. Eyes full of evil. He's leveling Jud with a look that has everyone around us tensing in anticipation. I want him to fuck me with that look. It'd likely kill me, but it'd be so worth it.

"I asked you if there was a problem," he repeats, his anger unmistakable. *I'm going to fuck him so hard tonight.*

"No problem." Jud glares at me, no doubt blaming me for Cook's interference. Hell I didn't ask him to intervene. But I can't deny that I'm glad he did. "I was just congratulating her on the big win." He smiles at Cook. "Good job to you too...*Prospect*."

Something shifts in the room. The air seems charged. People breathe a little shallower. I don't know what happened, but there's something about the way Jud addressed Cook that doesn't feel right.

Cook is smiling, but it's not his happy smile. It doesn't quite reach his eyes. "Thanks, Jud. I appreciate that."

Jud smirks, shoots me one last ugly look, then gets up from his stool. Then everything happens so fast, I'd have missed it if I didn't have front row seats.

Jud's legs are kicked out from under him. His ass lands in the stool and his back is pressed hard against the bar. Cook's hand is at his throat—his fingers squeezing hard enough to cause Jud's face to redden.

I stare at Cook open mouthed. I've never seen him so livid. Rage emanates from him. Thick veins bulge from his neck and the arm attached to Jud's throat. He looks...scary. Creepy clown, girl from The Ring, Texas Chainsaw Massacre scary. And when he speaks, a chill runs up my spine.

"I'm *not* your fuckin' Prospect."

He didn't roar. He didn't yell. He just spoke. But the conviction in his words...if Jud didn't know that Cook wasn't his Prospect before, he knows now.

So do I. And every other human in the greater Lake Charles area. That speech was like the thunder of God—giving even the nonbelievers faith.

After allowing Jud a few more seconds to absorb his words, he releases him. Jud gasps and chokes. I want to take advantage of his vulnerable state and throat punch him. But Cook is watching me—gaze feral. I'm licking my lips. I'm promising all sorts of dirty things to him in my head. He just defended my honor. *Well...* Kinda. Whatever.

He looks hungry again.

Hungry for me. So I'll let him indulge. Give him a taste of who he wants. Who he's had. And who he can get any fucking time he wants.

The classless bitch.

The bad decision.

Me.

The patchwhore.

19
THE SLEEPOVER...

I stand beside Cook, watching as the Eagles half carry, half drag Jud out the back door. Once he's out of sight, Cook turns to leave. I silently follow him. But when Ronnie pulls Cook to the side, I step past them and continue to my car. I don't wait for him to come out. I know he won't be far behind me. Sure enough, I see his headlight in my rearview as I pull up to my apartment.

As calmly as I can, I walk up the stairs. When I'm unlocking the door, I hear him on the first floor. I go to my room. Turn on the lamp. Sit on the bed. Two breaths later, he walks through my bedroom door—hanging his cut on the doorknob as he passes. Never slowing stride, he reaches behind him and pulls his T-shirt over his head.

My eyes are graced with the greatness that is his chest. Skin stretched tight over ripped, corded muscles that appear to be flexed, though he's completely at ease. He straddles my legs, giving my shoulder a gentle push until I fall back on the bed. Then his hands fist my shirt and pull—sending buttons flying across the room.

I let in a deep breath causing my stomach to concave. He traces the outline of my ribs with a finger. "Do I scare you, Carmen?"

I shake my head. "No." Another deep, uneven breath. He circles my belly button with a feathered touch.

"Do you know why I did what I did tonight?" His eyes move to my chest—watching the rise and fall of my breasts that threaten to spill out of my bra. It's difficult for me to think with him looking at me like that. Talking to me in that low, dirty voice. But somehow I manage to speak.

"Because he called you a Prospect," I breathe, goosebumps breaking out across my flesh from his stare.

"But do you know *why* it bothered me so much?" His knuckles brush the top of my breasts.

A strange noise escapes my lips. Something between a moan and a growl of frustration. "Because you aren't his fucking Prospect." Those lips that I want on my face and nipples twitch.

"But I am a Prospect. So how can I get away with doing that to a patch holder?"

If this is a guessing game, I don't want to play. If he wants me to know why, he should just tell me. Either way, he needs to get on with it so we can fuck. Boots on shoulders. Important shit.

"Cook?"

His eyes drag over my breasts, up my neck and finally to my face. "Yes, gorgeous?"

"I don't care. Prospect. Patch holder. You. J…"

He silences me with a rough kiss. Bruising my lips as he claims me with his mouth. "Don't say his name," he growls, soothing his attack by licking my swollen lips. "Don't say that motherfucker's name." *Motherfucker who?* I don't know anything. Anyone. I'm molten beneath him. That kiss turned me into liquid fire.

"Say *my* name." The demand is given against my neck where those heated lips are trailing a wet path to my breasts.

"Cook." *Mr. Delicious. Prospect. Founder of the Orgasm Giving Foundation.*

"So fuckin' sexy," he murmurs, his breath cooling my skin that's damp from his mouth. Jerking down the cups of my bra, he releases my breasts before devouring one with his mouth—sucking hard then soothing with his tongue before moving to the next and doing the same.

I writhe beneath him. My legs pinned. My nails in his back. Scarring his flawless skin. They move to fist in his hair as he slides down my body. Kissing and nibbling at my stomach while he makes quick work of my shorts.

He pulls them down my legs, moving to kneel on the floor between them. Then my shorts are gone. Panties ripped. His face between my thighs. And *finally…*my boots on his shoulders.

He savagely eats me. Tongue and lips touching me everywhere. Hands knead my ass forcing me further into his face. I buck against him, riding his face hard.

Hips are gyrating. Boots digging. Fingers tugging. Spiraling. Wandering. Tripping and fumbling in a crazy, offbeat pattern that is nothing compared to the synchronized dancing couple from earlier.

"Ahhh…" I cry out in relief when his tongue flicks my clit with just the right amount of pressure. He works the spot hard, lashing the swollen nub over and over until I can't breathe. My back arches. White light flashes behind my closed lids.

I'm still coming. Still not breathing. Body still twitching when the world flips. Or maybe it's just me who flips. I open my eyes. I'm on my knees. Ass in the air as I'm pulled free of my tattered shirt. With a snap of his fingers, my bra is stripped from me. The only thing I'm wearing is my boots. *Fuck you…on your knees…nothing but your boots.*

He's a man of his word. My legs are spread wider. He's pushing inside me. I'm full of him. He's gripping my hips. Kissing my spine. Telling me I taste sweet. Feel incredible. Tight. Wet. So soft. "Fuckin' perfect."

My real-life book boyfriend.

But the way he fucks me doesn't compare to any hero in any book I've ever read. That's all him—Cook. Tender and tough. Rough and gentle. Hard and soft. One extreme to another. The combination of all things I crave wrapped up and delivered with a pretty bow on top. Just. For. Me.

"Carmen."

Yes.

Carmen.

He said my name.

Growled it.

He's thrusting hard. His hands everywhere. I can feel his cock everywhere. The tips of his fingers bruise my hips. *I want more.* I tell him. He drives harder. Takes my breath. He's fucking me like he hates me. I've never wanted to be hated more than I do in this moment. *Hate me, Devil's Renegade Prospect, Cook. Please hate me.*

"You're fuckin' soaked."

I mumble a few unintelligible words that are a mixture of "shut the hell up" and "thank you."

"Love fuckin' you like this…sweet, little ass…wet, pretty pussy…them noises you make…you drive me crazy."

His filthy talk. Voracious drive. Unrelenting, shameless, unspoken demand to consume my mind and body. All of it is too much. It's just too much feel good for one person. I'm going to come. It's going to be earth shattering. The build alone has me sweating. Moaning. Quivering. Begging for something that will likely kill me.

"Please…I can't…"

He delivers another hard thrust, as his fingers trail a delicate path down my spine. "Can't what?" *Can't think when you talk in the sweet, yet gritty tone, fuck me like a savage and caress me like a rose.*

"I need…"

"Tell me what you need, gorgeous."

I let out a cry of frustration. "I don't know!" This is too intense. I can't handle it anymore. My body won't comply. I want to let go but I can't. My mind is waiting on something. A touch? A lick? A kiss?

"Come." *A word...*

I break. Shatter. Combust. Explode. It's Nirvana. Beautiful, irrefutable, uncultivated bliss. From my toes to my ears, my body sings. Every heartbeat. Every breath. Every shudder sends another tingling wave of pleasure through me. The Earth is no more. The end has come. I'm in heaven. It's the only reasonable explanation I have for feeling this damn good.

I want unlimited refills on whatever drug he slipped me. Then I'm going to get a Pez dispenser and pop them suckers all day long. Sex cannot be this good. He gave me ruffies. Or Mickey. Or Molly. Whatever the kids are calling it these days.

"You alive?" Cook asks, pushing my hair back from my face.

"Did you drug me?"

He breathes a laugh. "Not this time."

"Are we in heaven?"

"Don't think so."

"Is my ass still in the air?"

"My cock's growin' harder by the second at the sight of it."

I roll to my back in fear that he might want a round two. I need to catch my breath. Take a nap. *Allow my vagina some time to recuperate.*

Chancing a look, I find him propped on his elbow wearing nothing but his boxers. *Man, he's pretty.* I bet if I snapped a picture of him in this moment, I could sell it for thousands.

"You're not leaving?"

His eyebrows raise in amusement. "I can if you want me to."

"No. You just always do."

He gives me a warm, apologetic smile. "No plans tonight." It's then I notice how tired his eyes are. He looks like he hasn't slept in days.

"You can stay the night." I avert my gaze—my fingers fidgeting with my hair. "I mean. If you want to."

"Maybe." It's not a yes, but when I look up, he's smirking. And he just winked, so maybe it is a yes.

"I've got to..." My voice trails off and I flush with embarrassment and point to the bathroom. He grins and I feel my cheeks darken further.

Clambering off the bed, I quickly dart into the bathroom, grabbing a clean T-shirt from my unfolded basket of laundry on the way. *Don't know why you're so shy, Carmen. You've had your ass in the air since you got home.*

After I use the bathroom—turning on the sink so he doesn't overhear me peeing—I pull off my boots and socks. *Damn...what is up with my stinky feet?* Disgusted, I toss the sweaty socks in the hamper. Then cover them with a clean towel to try and mask the scent. *Don't want Mr. Delicious finding them.*

I brush my teeth, and since he's already seen me at my worst, I scrub the makeup from my face. Slipping on the t-shirt, I check my reflection. Then I realize I haven't stopped smiling since I got out of bed. *Is it because there's a single, hot man in there? Or because I flew with angels not too long ago?*

Biting my cheek to contain my smile, I walk back to the bedroom. I relax my jaw and grin at the sight of him sleeping. He's under my covers. His head on one of my pillows. He's staying the night. I do a quick victory dance because he can't see me with his eyes closed.

Careful not to wake him, I climb in beside his sleeping form and cut off the lamp. Then his big arm is around my waist. He pulls me until my back is against his chest. And he whispers, "Goodnight, gorgeous."

I melt. Sigh. Swoon. Get a fluttery feeling in my belly. What a good night indeed.

20
...AND THE MORNING AFTER

He's still here. His big, warm frame curled around mine. If my body wasn't sparking from teeth to toes from his heated embrace, I might be inclined to pinch myself. Afraid if I move too quickly he'll wake up and leave, I slither from beneath his arm like a snake.

I feel good this morning. Lighter. Happy. There's a bounce in my step. Flush in my cheeks. Eyes bright. Smile wide. And I'm totally rocking the "just fucked" look. My hair is a tangled mess. The T-shirt I slept in wrinkled and a few sizes too big. Lips still a little swollen.

He should stay over every night.

Famished, I skip from the bathroom to the kitchen—pausing to peek in on Mr. Delicious who is still sleeping. In my bed. Because he stayed the night. *Happy dance!*

My cupboards are pretty bare. Actually, they're very bare. The only food I have in my house is instant oatmeal. And there just so happens to be three packages. *It's a sign...*

He's a big guy, so I'll fix two for him, one for me and feed him with my fingers. A little reverse role play for when he sucked the BBQ sauce from mine.

"Get a grip, girl," I mutter, when the thought of what our children will look like flashes through my mind. "You're still planning your wedding." I giggle at my ridiculous conversation with myself.

I know him being here has me in a good mood. But this feeling of greatness is a mixture of several different things. The sex. The dancing. The image of Jud turning blue that is now permanently indented in my brain. And they all have one common denominator:

Cook.

Holding two steaming bowls of oatmeal, I return to the bedroom and find Cook on his back. One arm resting above his head. The other across his chest. Suddenly I don't want oatmeal. I want to eat him for breakfast. But he looks so peaceful. After a few more long moments of staring, I begrudgingly decide to let him be and turn around, figuring sleeping in is not something he's allowed to enjoy often.

"Where you goin'?" His deep voice is thick with sleep. The raspy tone instantly makes my nipples hard.

Oatmeal still in hand, I turn to face the chiseled god. "Good morning," I whisper, drinking in his long form. That sleepy, sexy smile. Those heavy lidded, bright blue eyes. Chest bare. Thick legs spread wide beneath the covers.

"Mornin'."

"I made you oatmeal."

"I see that."

I stand. He stares. I should give him the oatmeal. Cold oatmeal sucks. Then his phone vibrates. *I hate that damn thing...*

"You're up early," he says to the caller, his body still fully reclined. His gaze still on me. "It'll take me an hour to get there. An hour back. I should be there by two."

Two? It's only ten. An hour there makes eleven. And hour back twelve. Is he spending those extra two hours with me?

"She's good." *Who? Me.* "I'm staring at her." *Yep. Me.* "No. She'll figure it out soon enough." I hear a laugh I know belongs to Ronnie. Cook's smile widens. *Figure out what?* "See you then." He hangs up and I fire the question at him the moment he tosses his phone to the side.

"Nothing, babe. Not important." His eyes heat. "Not right now." He's right. In this moment, it's not important. Neither is his cold oatmeal. I have something better in mind for us. *Something else he can eat for breakfast.*

"Do you have today off too?" He shakes his head. "You have to go somewhere?" He nods. I smile playfully. "You don't *gotta* go to work...work. Work. Work. Work. Work. Work."

Smirking he raises a brow. "You gonna let your body do the work?" I'm surprised he knows the song. I'm even more surprised at how turned on I am by the possibility of doing the work. *Work. Work. Work...*

With courage I didn't know I possessed, I cross the room to him. I'm trying to go for sexy, but it's hard considering I forgot to put the damn bowls down. I

160

quickly set them on my night stand, take a breath and step on the bed—straddling his hips before sitting on top of him. I let out a little whimper at the feel of his rock solid cock pressed hard against my sex.

"Good morning," he teases, those kissable lips turning up on one side.

"Someone's *cocky* this morning." My silly remark makes him laugh. The joke is on me though because I can feel that laugh *there*.

"So, gorgeous. Can you make it clap, no hands for me?"

"Well Mr. Song Quoter, you'd be surprised at what I can do."

"Well Ms. Cock Tease, I do love a good surprise."

Dragging my fingers down his chest softly, I grind my hips against him. My courage is fueled when his mouth snaps shut to stifle his groan. "If you weren't so demanding and impatient every time we had sex, you might already know what I'm capable of."

"Fuck," he says. I quirk a brow. "We *fuck*." Regaining his control, he gives me a teasing smile. "Still can't say it, can you..."

I shrug, scraping my fingernails across his nipple. "I could. But I like when you correct me."

He's yet to touch me, but I see his hands twitching to give me just what I want. "Do you like when I tell you what to do?" *Yes. Hell yes.* Fuck *yes.*

"I always comply, don't I?"

"And you never disappoint."

"So what do you want me to do?" I meet his gaze. Shit he's hot. I'm pretty sure he can feel how wet I am through the covers.

"I want your sweet pussy on my face, and my cock in that smart little mouth." My body shudders. Breath hitches. Oh how I want to taste him. *Have him taste me.*

Something buzzes against my leg. I close my eyes and groan, collapsing on his chest. "I fucking hate that fucking thing. Phone...fucking phone." He chuckles, wrapping one arm around my back to hold me in place as he searches for the phone with the other.

"Yeah?" His hand moves under my shirt—rubbing my back in soft, calming strokes. It's sweet and intimate and killing my sex drive. "I did." I can't hear the caller because his phone is wedged between the pillow and his ear. Dammit.

He begins to answer a series of questions, or so I assume. Bored, I silently play along. "October twentieth." *Eleven days before Halloween.* "Lacey, Lawrence and Laken." *Kid names that begin with the letter L.* "All of them." *How many of my orgasms Cook's responsible for.* "Cheese." *Smile!* His hand stills a moment, then continues. "I don't know, but I'll find out." *Maybe we can Google it. Together.*

"I gotta go, gorgeous." *...Oh...he's talking to me.*

"Were you answering questions?" I ask, unmoving.

"Yes."

"Why?"

"Because I was asked."

I roll my eyes. "Well I have some questions for you too."

"Ask away, but you'll have to do it while I'm getting dressed."

Poking my lip out to pout, I tilt my head back on his chest and look up at him. "You can't wait five minutes?"

He smiles, smoothing my hair off my forehead. "Okay, gorgeous. Five minutes."

Beaming, I sit up so I'm straddling him once again. But the moment I gain my balance, he grabs my hips and repositions me until I'm sitting on the bed beside him. I hiss at the contact when his fingers cover the bruises he left last night. His brow furrows. I distract him with rapid fire questions so he won't ask what's wrong.

"Did Ronnie wait until the last minute to send Zack to get that bike because he wanted me to dance with you?"

"You'll have to ask him that."

"Did you have something to do with it?"

He drops his gaze back to where he grabbed me. "I don't have any control over the Eagles or what they do."

"Did you eavesdrop on my conversation with the Prospect at the door? Lyle?"

"Eavesdropping is rude." He quirks a brow. *I didn't eavesdrop just now...I tried, but I didn't actually do it.*

Fidgeting with the hem of my shirt, I lower my gaze. I might be stepping over some boundaries, but I have to know. "Was Jud calling you a Prospect the only reason you got mad at him?" Silence stretches on until I'm forced to meet his eyes. When I do, he's thoughtful.

"He deserved worse."

"That's not an answer."

"It's the only one I can give."

I stare at him a moment before whispering, "Why?"

"Me being a Prospect complicates things. There are some things I can get away with. Others I can't."

"So defending my honor is one of those *other* things?" I smirk, but his expression is guarded.

"It wouldn't be if you belonged to me." *Is he simply explaining this to me? Or is he hinting that he wants me to be his?*

The latter has my stomach somersaulting. Heart skipping. Voice barely audible. "But I don't...belong to you."

He smiles then. A hint of sadness flashes in his eyes, but it disappears just as quickly. "No, gorgeous. You don't."

The mood has shifted. There's a crackle in the air between us. To avoid saying something I might regret, or listening to my heart instead of my head— again—I attempt to lighten the conversation. "But my body does."

Blue eyes take in my naked legs and bare feet. "And what a body it is." I flush, fighting the urge to tuck my legs under my shirt.

"It's been six minutes," I say, trying and succeeding to pull his attention away from my lower half. He smoothly climbs out of bed giving me a great view of his back. I lean against the pillows, crossing my arms behind my head as I watch him dress. "If I had known you were going to be so easy to convince, I'd have asked you to stay longer."

Pulling his cut over his shoulders, he leans down and brushes his lips against my cheek. He smiles. Winks. Speaks. I'm melting again.

"For you, gorgeous, I'd have stayed all fuckin' day."

21
SHE'S THAT GIRL: THE CLUBWHORE

There will be no dating this week. Starting tomorrow, I'll be working from six in the morning until ten at night for the next seven days. I'd agreed to cover the shift months ago when an employee asked off for vacation. I needed the extra money. I still do. But now that the week is here, I'm dreading it.

Since today is the last day I'll have off for a while, I spend it cleaning my apartment. I also make sure to call Emily and fill her in on last night. She is only interested in the sex—no longer caring about Jud or his reaction. When I finish giving her all the dirty details, she tells me she has to get off the phone so she could masturbate.

I also call my mom and dad to check in. They're remodeling the kitchen, so I'm able to keep the conversation more focused on that than on me. They still ask how things are going, and I simply them them "fine," before asking about the new countertops.

By ten o'clock, I'm tired enough to sleep. But as I lay in bed, my thoughts drift to him. When will I see him again? Will I have to wait until my next date? That would be nearly two weeks. Does our arrangement only count after I go on a date? And how long will this deal between us last?

Figuring that last one is a question that deserves an answer, I grab my phone and call him. He answers after three and a half rings—not that I'm counting.

"Hello, Carmen." *Butterflies…his voice gives me butterflies.*

"Hello yourself."

"Your ears must've been burning."

"Why? Were you talking about me?" Grinning, I sit up—suddenly hit with a burst of energy.

"I was."

After a moment, I ask, "Well…what were you saying?"

"I was just telling Delilah about your hot dates with the Eagles." My face falls at the mention of her name. Then my stomach flips when she yells hello to me.

"Tell her I said hi," I say, my voice barely above a whisper. He repeats my message, laughing at something she says. Meanwhile, I'm dying.

I shouldn't be so affected by hearing the two of them together. They're probably at the bar. Hanging out. While I'm here. It shouldn't hurt, but damn it does. We have a deal. A monogamous understanding. He's never given me any reason to doubt his commitment before. And as far as I know, he's done nothing wrong tonight. So why do I feel betrayed? And the most alone I've felt in my life?

He says something, but it doesn't register. He follows it up with another laugh, and I catch the words "another one, babe." I guess they are at the bar. *Is he buying her drinks? Drinking himself? I've never seen him drink…*

"Hey, Cook? I better go. I've got to pull a double tomorrow, so I need to get some sleep." His voice is muffled a moment as if he covered up the phone, but I hear him clearly when he speaks again.

"You okay, babe?" *Babe?* Why not gorgeous? Why didn't he call me gorgeous when he answered? He said "Carmen." *Why does that make me want to cry?*

"Hello?"

"Hey! I'm okay. Good. Great," I say quickly, my hands fidgeting like crazy.

"Did you need something?"

Shaking my head, I squeeze my eyes shut. *Don't cry. Don't cry. Don't cry.* "No." I pinch my nose to keep from sniffling. "Just wanted to say hi. I'll let you go."

He's silent a moment before giving me a simple, "Okay."

"Bye!" I stab at the screen—taking all my frustration out on the big red "End" circle.

Falling back, I cover my face in my hands. I'm being ridiculous. He's a biker. This is his life. I'm not his priority, I'm his fuck buddy. He's my fuck buddy. So why the *fuck* are my feelings so hurt?

My eyes burn with unshed tears I refuse to let fall as I curl into my pillows and mentally list all the things in my life that have me feeling blue.

My one and only friend is back home, five hundred miles away, surrounded with other friends and her family. In the house next to where she's probably sleeping this very moment, are my loving, caring parents. They all have someone close to them. Me? I'm alone.

I'm three states away. The closest thing I have to a friend is a bartender who's never even been to my house. I'm having sex with a man whose last name I don't even know. And he's hanging out with *that girl.* The Clubwhore who claims she *used* to get paid to have sex with men. But she probably still does. Once a whore always a whore. Right?

My job sucks.

My feet stink.

My ex is a tool.

The burn in my eyes becomes even more intense. And because I can't afford Kleenex, I have to press my shirt into the corners to keep the tears from falling.

I wish I had ice cream. I wish I had cable. I wish this was a romance novel. I wish my Prince Charming would show up and save his damsel-in-distress. And because I'm a pathetic, attention-starved, dramatic, hopeless romantic, I get up and unlock the door so he doesn't have to break in.

22
THE PROPOSAL

He didn't show.

I fell asleep. With my door unlocked. Granting access for any serial murderer or rapist to come in and do their worst. The risk was for nothing. Filled with disappointment, my day started shitty. And by noon, it got even shittier.

We ran out of waffle batter. At Waffle House. People were pissed. And because Waffle House has such a strict health code, we couldn't even go to the store and purchase more. It was a disaster, to say the least.

My shift ended at ten that night—sixteen straight hours of hell. Apparently Waffle House isn't as strict about their labor policy as they are about their health code. I wasn't even offered a lunch break.

Tired, hungry, overworked and underpaid, I head home. Halfway there, I receive a text from Kat—tempting me with something I cannot refuse.

We cooked steaks tonight at the bar. Come by when you get off!

Twenty minutes later, I'm pulling open the door at Pops. My mouth waters and my stomach lets out a low growl the moment the scent of grilled meat hits me. The place is just as packed now as it is on Thursday. It's a little surprising considering it's after eleven on a Monday night. Then I notice a banner that reads, "Congratulations Eagles Brett!" And standing next to that banner is Cook. Just...being.

He'd unintentionally hurt my feelings last night. Unknowingly, he'd left me prey to every evil vulture on the streets—all because I'd left my door unlocked for him. This morning, I'd decided I was going to hate him for the rest of my life. But as the deliciously stimulating, smug bastard watches me with a cocky smirk, I find myself struggling with the decision to hate him.

He's just too handsome with his sturdy jaw and perfectly symmetrical nose. Too damn cute with his boyish grin and messy hair. Too friggin' sexy with his bedroom eyes and muscled body. Too much of a biker-bad-boy with his cut, ripped jeans and ringed fingers. And of course, he's coming over.

"Hello gorgeous," he says, taking in my Waffle House uniform. "Judging by your scowl, I'm guessing you're mad at me."

"Mad? I'm not mad." I say quickly, averting my eyes so he doesn't see the truth there. If I admit I'm upset, it might make me look needy. Or pathetic. I'm both. But he doesn't need to know that. "Why would I be mad?" Shrugging, I fidget with the hem of my shirt and study my feet. "I'm a little tired. Pretty hungry. But mad?" I shake my head, pressing my lips into a thin line as I raise my chin to meet his gaze. "I'm not mad."

"You're not a very good liar, either." His lips curve on one side. His arms are crossed over his chest. His stance wide. Confident. Powerful. My mind hates him. My vagina wants to grow legs again.

"Come," he says, grabbing my hand. My legs quiver at his one-word demand. "I'll get you a plate."

Leaving me with no other option, not that I would take it if he had, I follow him to the corner of the bar that's usually reserved for Ronnie. And even though Ronnie isn't here, his stool, along with the four next to it, are vacant.

"Hey doll," Kat says, walking through the swinging door that leads to the kitchen. "Consider yourself privileged. Only a select few get to sit in that chair."

"Where is Ronnie?" I ask, feeling honored to be one of the "select few." And a little guilty for not choosing one of the other four seats.

"Outside." She jerks her head toward the back door, her eyes narrowing slightly on me. "You look like hell." I shoot her a look but it falters when she sets a plate holding the biggest damn ribeye I've ever seen, right in front of me. "I can't pronounce it for shit, but I got you this too." She pulls a bottle from beneath the bar. I nearly weep at the sight of it.

"Pinot Noir," I whisper.

"Yeah. That shit. I tried it...ugh." She makes a face as she pours me a generous amount.

"You have no idea how much I needed this." Turning up the glass, I devour nearly half of it. Kat dutifully refills it before leaving to tend to someone else. Three bites into my steak, I notice Cook has yet to take his eyes off of me. "Didn't anyone ever tell you that it's rude to stare?"

The question is simple. It doesn't require him to tilt his head a little and study me as if there's some underlying meaning to my words. But he does.

"I wanted to come over last night," he says, his voice low and deep and throaty and driving me friggin' crazy.

I let out a small laugh, keeping my eyes on my food. "You did, did you?"

"But I got tied up."

He's so funny. I release another breath of laughter and meet his gaze. Of course he's amused. "That," I say, lifting my glass to him. "I believe."

His stupid, stupid smile widens. "Figured you got the wrong idea. I guess I was right."

"Wrong idea?" I shake my head, eyes wide with innocence. "Whatever do you mean?"

"I mean you thought I was fuckin' Delilah."

Time for more wine.

Thankful to Kat for leaving the bottle, I refill my glass. When I spin on my stool to face him he's leaning against the bar—ankles crossed. Arms still crossed. Muscles flexing. Too damn close. Too damn hot. Too damn delicious.

"Did you sleep with her?" It was meant to sound bitchy. My tone was more of a whimper.

"No." For the first time tonight, he's not smiling. Grinning or smirking. He's serious. "We have a deal. An understanding. You're only fuckin' me, and I only want to fuck you."

For a moment, I think about crying. Letting him take me in his arms. Tell me it's okay. Rub my hair and listen to my sob story. Then take me home. Lay me down. Make love to me. Spend the night, and wake me up with breakfast in bed. I'm thinking a donut around his cock. *It'd have to be a big donut...*

Instead, I shrug and refuse to acknowledge the tingling I feel in my spine at his admission. "I don't care if you did or not."

"Well just so we're clear, I didn't. I wouldn't." His gaze narrows on me—burning with possession. "And I'd sure as fuck care if you gave that pussy to someone else. I'm hungry for you, Carmen. Fuckin' starved. And when I get a taste of something I like, I don't share it."

Out of all those sexy, panty-dropping words, only two registered. Hungry and starved. My belly growls loudly—roaring and grumbling and it's so shocking, all I can do is sit here and listen. I should get a "mood killing" award. The moment is lost. Cook's smile is back. *I guess he heard it too.*

"Seems I'm not the only one who's hungry." His eyes drop to where my grease stained shirt covers my belly. "Eat. We'll talk later." Then like a shadow, he disappears into the crowd.

I'm beginning to think this particular spot that I'm sitting in comes with an unspoken warning—stay the hell away. Because even though I've seen familiar faces pass by, not one person has stopped to talk to me. They simply smile and move along, allowing me to consume my meal in silence. I'll have to remember to thank Ronnie later.

"Hey!" someone yells. "Listen up!" I crane my neck to find the voice calling for attention. A man steps on the stage, taking the microphone offered to him by the D.J. Squinting my eyes to get a better view, I make out Lou—President of the Eagles.

"Can you hear me in the back?" Lou asks over the mic. Several people behind me yell back a confirmation. "Got an announcement to make."

I watch in curiosity as Jud joins him on the stage. The sound of the back door closing pulls my attention away from the front. Ronnie walks in, pausing to speak with Kat. Cook is right behind him. I can feel his heated stare warming my body even before our eyes meet. But the moment they do, heat vanishes and an uneasy feeling engulfs me. Something is wrong.

Cook is emotionless. Pinning me with a grave look. Watching me. Studying me. That blank stare confirming I'm right: something is wrong. And whatever it is, is happening in this moment.

He refuses to look away from me even as him and Ronnie close the distance. I try to hold his gaze. Stare at him until he gives me a flicker of emotion. Search his eyes for some explanation. But Jud's voice over the microphone demands my attention.

"I wanted to share this with all of you tonight, because you are my family." He holds his hand out and Clarissa slips hers inside it. She looks confused as he pulls her on stage.

A knot forms in my stomach, slowly making its way up my chest. "Clarissa," Jud says, pausing to look deep into her eyes. That knot climbs a little higher— tightening around my heart. "I love you. More than anything." I can't breathe. Or maybe I can, but I'm just scared to. Too afraid of what I might say if my lungs fill with air.

"You have my heart. My patch." When he reaches in his pocket, my world stops spinning. He drops to a knee and my heart stills. Holding up a box, he smiles. She covers her mouth with her hand. My soul shatters. Then he says, "Now I want you to wear my ring."

The thunderous applause is deafening. Cat calls and whistles shriek through the room. But it sounds far away to my ears. Champagne and beer is shaken and spewed. Everyone participates in the celebration. But I'm numb to the cool liquid that soaks my clothes and hair. There's a crowd of people around me. The horde moves slowly toward the stage. But they're just a blur in my eyes. All I can see is *them*.

Clarissa—her legs folded around Jud's hips.

Jud—his arms around Clarissa's waist.

The perfect couple.

Too caught up in one another to care about the people around them. Their moment is intimate. Their love palpable. Connection unbreakable. Hearts beating as one. Souls merging. Bodies touching. Lost in the others' gaze. Smiling. Crying. Eyes reiterating what they both know. What everyone in the room knows. What I know.

They're happy.
Jud's happy.
Happier than I've ever seen him.
Happier than he ever was with me.

20
INTO THE BLACK

Someone steps in front of me, blocking my view of the stage. I instantly feel protected from the crowd. Safe in his shadow. He's more than just a man in a cut. He's a presence. A sense of calm. A safety net. Breathing deep, I inhale the scent of his cologne and leather that powers through the heavy cigarette smoke and champagne odor. I'm searching for the calm it always brings me. Instead, I feel the burn building behind my eyes.

He lifts my chin with his finger. Immediately I'm pulled to those crystal blues that shine with empathy and regret. "Hey gorgeous," Cook whispers, his touch soft as he trails his thumb over my quivering lip.

"I want to go home." My voice is weak. Barely audible.

His look softens even more as he nods. "Okay."

Tucking my hand in his, he gently pulls me through the crowd. I keep my head down. Eyes on the floor. I should hold my head high. Smile through the pain. Appear unaffected. Pretend that it doesn't hurt. But I can't. Not this time.

The night is warm. Humid. The air sticky and thick. Yet I can't shake this cold feeling. A shiver starts at my neck, runs down my spine and shoots straight to my toes. I shudder on every breath. Blood flows through my veins like cool molasses--chilling me all the way to my core.

Cook opens the passenger door of my car and I climb in. I avoid looking at him. Not wanting to see it again—the pity. Remorse. That penetrating gaze that speaks to me when he knows words will fall on deaf ears. The one that says he's sorry. That I'll be okay. Time will heal. It'll get easier.

I thought that once. That I was healed. That it had gotten easier. I'd distracted myself. Got over him. Chose revenge over heartache. For the past couple of months, I've felt like I was really going to be okay. Now I'm not so sure.

The passing cars on the interstate become a blur. Tears pour down my cheeks. Each one coming in quick succession. Every single drop shed for a different reason. Representing a different time. A memory. Our first date. Kiss. The first time he made love to me. The night he told me I was his. That there would never be another. For him, there was only me.

A sob escapes my lips. I press my hand over my mouth to stifle it. But another starts to build. Tears begin to fall faster. I blink furiously in an attempt to clear my vision. Swipe my cheeks with the back of my hands. Fight against the unrelenting wave of sadness.

"Just let it out, gorgeous." Cook's hand finds mine. It's big and warm. Then he's kissing my fingers. Lips soft and smooth. His voice whispering over my knuckles. "I got you. Let it go."

Maybe I was waiting on his permission. Trying to hold in everything because I feared he'd somehow feel responsible for me. Inclined to take care of me. But the promise and conviction in his words—*I got you*—has me doing as he says.

My elbow on the door, face buried in one hand, holding Cook's in the other, I let go. Gut wrenching sobs wrack me. Stealing my breath. Shaking my body. The car is filled with miserable cries. Whimpers of pain. Cook's reassuring words, which make me cry harder. Wail louder. Hurt deeper.

The car stops. Hands are under my arms. Lifting and pulling me across the console and into his lap. His arm is around my waist. His lips in my hair. My head on his chest. His hand on my cheek, holding me there.

"I feel--" My breath catches. "I f-feel so c-cold," I cry, hiccupping another sob. "On the in-inside." I curl further into him. His grip tightens around me as he kisses my hair.

"I know, gorgeous. I know." But he can't know. A man as confident as he is could never have been as broken as I feel. Yet his words still soothe me.

His embrace is comforting. Unhurried. Patient. He rubs me. Holds me. Absorbs my pain. Carries my burden. My sobs soon weaken to sniffles. Deep shudders are diminished to light trembles. Tears flow instead of pour. The pounding ache in my chest is still there, though. Never dulling. A constant reminder.

"I'm sorry," I whisper into his shirt.

He tilts my head back, burning me with the intensity of his stare. "Hush." His command is soft but firm.

"I just don't know what to do." My nostrils flare and my lips tremble as I feel another wave of sadness building. This time for a completely different reason. "I want…" I clench my teeth trying to stop it. "I need…" I pull in a deep staccato breath. Guilt eats away at me. And no matter how hard I try, I can't say it. I can't tell him how much I need him. It's selfish and unfair.

His thumb brushing my cheek. Catching a tear. His gaze softens as it follows the trail of his fingers across my jaw. "Say it, gorgeous," he coaxes. "I said I got you. And I meant it."

My chest tightens. I'm overwhelmed with emotions. I can feel myself starting to lose it again. I fight it long enough to tell him the only truth I know. "It hurts, Cook." His brow creases with concern. "It hurts so b-bad." I cling to him. Weeping. Lost. Scared of what I'm feeling. Afraid I'll never recover.

His phone vibrates against my hip. "Please," I whimper. Begging. Unashamed. Too frightened at the thought of him leaving me to care. "Please don't go." My hands fist in his shirt.

"Shhh," he soothes. "I'm right here." He shifts us before somehow managing to open the door and climb out gracefully with me in his arms. "I'm not leaving."

His kindness has me crying harder. I'm so conflicted. Unsure of what it is I'm really feeling. Jud hurt me, but Cook's compassion is just as devastating. I don't understand it. Can't figure it out. The confusion pulls at me. Tears me in half. Shreds me. Rips away my sanity.

"Hush now." He starts up the stairs. Carrying me as if I'm weightless. I pull in deep breaths. Using the comfort of his arms, his scent and the steady beat of his heart to calm me. "Good girl," he praises, unlocking the door and pushing inside.

He steadies me on my feet in the bathroom. After gently prying my arms from him, he grips my hands. His eyes are suddenly level with mine. They're a vivid blue. Assertive. Demanding my attention.

"You trust me don't you, gorgeous?" My lip trembles as I manage something similar to a yes. "You believed me when I told you I wasn't leaving, didn't you?" I nod. "Then calm down. Let me take care of you."

I stand silent as he leaves me to turn on the shower. Almost immediately, steam fills the small bathroom. The thick heat helps to clear my stuffy head—allowing me to take deeper breaths in an attempt to calm down. But the ache in my chest is nearly unbearable. The pain is intense. I keep seeing Jud's face. His smile. The way he looked at Clarissa. The love he obviously had for her.

Cook peels away my soiled clothes, exposing my naked body. I wish he could do the same with my heart. Peel away the bruised layers. Strip away everything tainted by Jud until there's nothing left but raw muscle. But I know that even there, in the deepest depths of my heart, lies corrosion.

Taking my hand, Cook leads me under the steaming spray. I close my eyes and let the water pour over me as he takes his time washing my hair. My body.

Cleansing me from the outside in. Every touch removing another layer of bad, replacing it with something good.

Then, on a sudden epiphany, I realize my turmoil might have stem from Jud's proposal, but it's not the reason for it.

I don't want to be Clarissa. I'm not envious that it was her, not me, on that stage. What hurt wasn't seeing Jud so happy, it was watching his life move forward while mine stayed still. It pained me to see the man who deserved nothing, gain so much. He was engaged. Had moved on. Was focused on his future. And I was still living in the past—devoting my entire life to making him pay for what he'd done to me.

At one time, Jud was my everything. But that ended a long time ago. Even before we officially broke up. I suffered through the loneliness. Endured the heartache. Channeled all my energy into rage. I was committed to hurting him, when my priority should've been moving on.

Now, during the blackest moment of my distress, is Cook. Appearing like a beacon of light. Reminding me that I'm not alone. That something good has been standing in front of me for months. But I've been too consumed by the past to really acknowledge him as an essential part of my life.

Every time I think about us becoming more, I push away the idea. Claiming I'm not ready. That I'm still mending my broken heart. Piecing my soul back together. Telling myself that I couldn't put my faith in someone again. Trust again. *Love* again. It's too soon to feel this way about anyone. Then again, Cook's not just anyone.

He's the man who makes me feel like a woman. Wanted. Special. Beautiful. Sexy. He's the guy who calls me gorgeous. Cooks for me. Washes my hair to make me feel better and holds it when I'm sick. He kisses away my tears. Tells me he's got me. Carries me when I can't walk. Rubs my feet when they hurt— even when they stink.

He's responsible for that feeling of happiness that makes me light headed. Buzz with excitement. Smile with giddiness. He is the reason I get that tingle in my spine. Twinkle in my eye. Flutter in my belly. Everything that makes me feel alive comes from this man.

His caress becomes distracting. When his hands innocently caress my breasts, heat pools in my belly. I shiver as they move lower. Feathering across my thighs. Between my legs. Replacing my sadness with desire. But it's not enough. I need more.

"I want you to make it stop," I say, pulling my eyes up to meet his. He struggles to understand something I can't explain. "Please..." My voice drops to a whisper. "I don't want to think about him. I only want you."

Realization starts to unravel in his mind. He knows like I know, he's the only one who has the power to make me forget everything that isn't him. He claims me. Owns me. Makes me feel wanted. Worshipped. Adored. *Loved.*

"Say it, gorgeous," he whispers, his eyes roaming my face. Fingers ghosting up my arms to my neck.

I shake my head. "I don't want you to fuck me." There is no flash of understanding in his expression. He's known exactly what I've wanted since I asked.

"I know, baby." His voice reflects the pain in his eyes. "But I need to hear you say it."

I'm not sure why he looks so tortured. Sounds so pained. Is it because he's afraid I'll read deeper into it than what it really is? If so, I don't care. The pain can't be any worse than it is now. So I'll ask him. Accept what he gives. And I'll have no expectations for more when it's over.

"I want you to make love to me."

He studies my eyes. My lips. The hollow of my throat. Then he dips his mouth to mine—kissing me softly. His touch tender as he pulls me closer. Kisses me deeper. Unhurried. Lazy but passionate.

His mouth moves down my throat, licking the water there. Saying, "You're beautiful," between kisses. Whispering, "So precious," as he kisses his way down my belly. His breath fanning across my wet sex as he breathes, "So sweet," before parting my lips with his tongue and gently sucking my clit.

I lean against the shower wall, my toes curling into the hard tub. My fingers knotting in his hair as I lose myself to his touch. Feeling the pain fade into delicious pleasure. His fingers explore me. Widening me as his tongue and lips continue to softly tease my aching clit.

My legs shake as he places lingering kisses up my body until he's standing. I arch my head back to meet his face, finding his lips parted. Eyes burning with an emotion I've never seen in them. Instantly, I'm lost.

Both of us dripping wet, he carries me from the shower to my bed—covering me with his big body. My legs part and he fits perfectly between them. Linking our hands, he holds them above my head as he slowly pushes inside me. Filling me with all of him. Searing me with his gaze.

He rocks his hips to a steady rhythm. Pumping in and out. Long, deep strides. Inch by inch. Breath by breath. Heartbeat by heartbeat, he claims my body. Owns my mind. Absorbs my thoughts. Repairs my heart.

Tears leak from my eyes and he kisses them away. My mind is at war. My body coiled tight with tension. Still he makes love to me. Catches my cries with his mouth. Lets me come apart beneath him—wordlessly promising to catch me when I fall.

"I'm so confused," I cry, wishing I had some explanation as to what's happening to me. Why only moments ago, I was crying because a man I once loved hurt me. Now I'm crying over this man. Over a feeling I just can't convince myself is real.

"I know, gorgeous." The defeat in his words is palpable. He seems resigned. Yet he doesn't stop. He doesn't leave. He doesn't run from the inevitable truth that is slowly revealing itself in my mind—a truth he's already aware of.

It's not just about the sex anymore with us. It hasn't been for a long time. It's not about Jud. Broken hearts. Betrayal. Wounds or scars.

It's about one man. One woman. And this one defining moment that changes absolutely everything.

24
CHANGE ISN'T ALWAYS A GOOD THING

My alarm wakes me early—notifying me of a new day. While the arms holding me remind me of that moment that changed everything.

Last night Cook chose me. He'd left his club behind to take me home. Ignored them when they called. Made love to me like I was his. Treasured me as if I was the most precious thing on earth. Worshipped me. Cared for me. Treated me to a level of intimacy I'd never experienced. Our connection was so deep, so beautiful, so captivating that I felt him in my soul.

I slept wrapped in his arms. Limbs flaccid. Body sated. Dreaming of nothing. Even in my sleep, my subconscious mind couldn't create a fantasy more beguiling than my own reality. But as enthralling as it is, it's even more terrifying. Because truth is, I don't know anything about this man.

I don't know his story. Though I have my suspicions, he's yet to tell me the reason behind that sadness he tries so well to hide. So I have to ask myself, do I really want to have feelings for a man who keeps himself such a mystery? Who deflects every time I ask him something personal? Who's more dedicated to a club than most people are to their marriages? Who makes me feel like I'm the most important person in the world one moment, only to leave me in an instant without even an explanation? How many mornings would I wake up cold and alone before he found me worthy enough to stay?

As if he can sense my thoughts, Cook tightens his hold on me. He pulls me further back into the warmth of his chest. Soft lips ghost across my shoulder, heating me from the outside in. I melt deeper into his embrace. Breathing in his scent. Delighting in his presence. Wondering...what if?

What if last night was the start of something new between us? What if it was his way to prove I do mean more to him? What if from now own he stayed more? What if we ended every night together? Started every day together? What if he found me worthier than his club? Worthier of his time? What if he opened up to me? Revealed his secrets? Talked about his past? Would that stop me from ignoring my feelings and make me realize I am undeniably in love with him?

The sound of his phone ringing has me holding my breath. Hoping he doesn't answer. He'd ignored it last night. Would he now? He answers with his signature, "Yeah," and that single word slashes my thoughts with a blade so sharp, I feel its cut in the depths of my soul. Reality crashes around me. Shaking me from my fantasy. Reminding me why I'm so terrified of giving my heart to this man.

Last night he'd put me first, but obviously that was a one-time thing. Now, I feel stupid for over analyzing it. He simply hadn't answered because he knew he couldn't leave me in that state. It didn't mean he shared the same deep feelings for me. It was just a reflection of the kind of man he is. I'm sure he'd have done the same for Kat or Delilah.

The insight is sobering. I lock my heart back in its iron cage. Drown the feelings I'd let surface only moments ago. What we have may be more than sex, but it's not as powerful as I'd thought. At least not on his part. And I refuse to care that deeply about someone who cares so much more about something else.

Rolling me to my back, Cook looks down at me. Studying me with blue eyes that are filled with sympathy. But there is no regret. "I have to go, gorgeous," he says. Not a hint of apology in his tone for putting me second. And that's just as it should be. Because he doesn't owe me anything.

What happened last night changes nothing. It's not his fault I let my thoughts run away from me. He'd given me no reason to believe we had something more. He's been the same man since the moment I met him. It's me who's different. But I have no problem reverting back to that girl he met months ago. Only this time, I'm not living my life for anyone but me.

25
BY THE LIGHT OF THE REFRIGERATOR

The day is long. The night even longer. I haven't heard from Cook since this morning. Not that I expected to. Actually, I'm thankful for his silence. It validates my decision to suppress my feelings toward him.

I'm dead tired and hungry as hell by the time I make it home. It takes every ounce of energy I have to drag my ass up the two flights to my apartment. Inside, I head straight to my refrigerator, holding my breath as I open it up. Butter, ketchup and wine. It's what's for dinner. With all the drama from last night, I hadn't thought to go to the store and buy groceries today. Now, I'll be going to bed hungry.

Closing the door, I press my head against it and stand in the darkness. When life hands you lemons, you make lemonade. When life hands you wine, you drink until you're too drunk to care that you're hungry.

Too lazy to walk to the bedroom, I kick off my shoes and fall back on the chaise. Emily had been blowing up my phone all day, insisting that I call her ASAP and tell her about last night. You'd think I wouldn't want to relive it. Instead, I'm anxious to fill my best friend in on what happened. And share with her my relief at finally having the weight of the past off my shoulders.

An hour and a bottle of wine later, I'm struggling to keep my eyes open. With a quick goodbye and a promise to talk more soon, I end the call. Immediately after, I set my alarm before I forget. Making sure to give myself an extra fifteen minutes so I could swing through a drive-thru for breakfast on my way to work.

I still need to shower. Brush my teeth. Change out of my uniform. Sleep on something that won't leave me stiff and sore all day tomorrow. But after working all day yesterday, being so emotionally drained last night and work day, I'm too tired to move.

So I curl up on the couch and close my eyes, allowing myself just a minute of rest--knowing good and damn well I won't have the energy or the will to get up.

It's before five when I slap the button on my alarm and stumble from bed. Fumbling my way through the dark half asleep, I find the bathroom and cut the light on. The sight of my reflection snaps me out of my current state and fully wakes me.

Instead of my uniform, I'm wearing a faded LSU T-shirt. My hair is mussed from sleep and wild around my face—no longer in a bun on top of my head. Then I realize I woke up in my bed. Not on the chaise. *Cook...*

He'd broken into my house. Again. Carried me to bed. Undressed me. Even put my phone on the charger. Those feelings I'd stifled yesterday begin to stir. Leaving me with a warm feeling in my chest and a smile on my face. *Second place is looking better and better.*

Thirty minutes later, I'm dressed and on my way out when I notice a note hanging on the refrigerator. Cautiously, I move toward it. As I do, I find notes on my cabinets, too. Even the one where I stash all my wine. When the writing comes into focus, that smile I've been wearing all morning widens.

If you're looking for food, you won't find any here.
On the cabinet next to the refrigerator:
Or here.
Another cabinet:
None here.
When I make it to the wine cabinet, I laugh.
But if you're looking for wine...We have white wine. Red wine. Sweet wine. Old wine. New wine. Nasty wine. Pretty good wine. Cheap wine. More cheap wine. What the fuck is "goat" wine?

Glancing at the clock, I see I've already wasted five of my extra fifteen minutes. Leaving the notes, because I'll probably need something to smile about when I get home tonight, I sprint toward the door. My blast of energy is fueled by the thought of a biscuit loaded with bacon and cheese. It's there I find another note. This one doesn't make me laugh, though. It makes me swoon.

Have a great day, gorgeous. Dinner is on me tonight.
-The Prospect

I find myself glancing at the clock all day. Every time I look, it seems time slows down. It's not the anticipation of the end of my shift that has me so

181

anxious, it's seeing Cook. Even though he was at my house last night, I didn't see him. Smell him. Feel him. I guess the truth is, I miss him.

By the time I pull up at my apartment, my heart is pounding in my chest. I'm excited. A little nervous. Butterflies swarm in my belly. The eagerness to feel his touch is profound. But when I scan the parking lot for Cook's bike, I come up empty.

My good mood crashes. I'm left feeling bereft and alone. His absence wouldn't affect me so much had I not anticipated his presence since I read his note this morning.

Tonight I will definitely be indulging in my guilty pleasure—wine. Not only will it help take the edge off, but I'll be having it for dinner, too. *If I can ever make it up these friggin' stairs.*

Breathless, I fall into my apartment and head straight to the refrigerator. When I pull open the door, I gape at what I see. Then blink a few times to make sure it's real. Wonder if I'm dreaming as I stare into the light. I'm surprised angels aren't here singing about this miracle.

I have food.

Tons.

The shelves are filled with everything from meat to mayo. Opening the freezer, I find it full too. A breathy sigh escapes me when I see the one thing I love more than wine.

"Ice cream," I breathe, pulling out the frozen container. I grab a spoon and rip the lid off, take a bite and let out a moan. "Delicious."

Delicious.

Mr. Delicious.

The hair on the back of my neck stands up. I swear I can feel his presence.

"Did you do this?" I ask, somehow knowing he's here. *I think...*

"Someone had to." *I think right.* He's here. Behind me. But seeing his handsome face doesn't bring me as much excitement as ice cream. So I don't bother turning around.

"Tell me something." I take another bite. "How do you keep getting in my house?"

"I have a key." Well that's enough to make me turn.

My eyes search the darkness for him. I make out his form on my chaise—his feet propped up as he reclines. *Damn, I've missed him.*

"I moved the key."

"I made a copy before you did."

It's weird. Stalkerish. A little creepy. I should care. I don't.

"Why do you need a key to my house?"

He stands. The ice cream in my mouth seems to melt a little faster. "Because we have a deal. And it's usually late before I get here."

Striding over to the island, he leans his elbows on it. The light from the still open freezer illuminates me, but he's in the shadows. "So you did it for convenience?"

"Maybe." Even in the dark, his smile is unmistakable. "You gonna offer me some of that?" He nods his head toward the carton in my hand. I shake mine. His grin widens.

Stabbing at my ice cream, I keep my eyes down and whisper, "Why did you do this for me?"

The silence stretches until I meet his gaze. "Because I can." After a moment, he smirks. "Is this the part where you tell me it's too much?"

I laugh, shaking my head. "Hell no." When my smile finally dies, I give him a sincere look. "It's tough sometimes, you know? Being on my own. No family close by. No friends. Hate kept me here. Pride won't let me go home."

"Time has a way of healing, gorgeous."

Unable to refrain, I smile. "How original."

His lips don't even twitch. "How true." His voice is small. Almost sad.

"Thank you for this, Cook. I'll pay you back."

"No, Carmen. You won't. It's my gift to you."

Then his grin returns. Eyes smiling. Mood playful. "You're too skinny. I like the women I fuck to be a little thicker."

"Well...since I'm the only woman you're..." I give him a pointed stare. "*Fucking*..." He laughs. "I can see why you did this."

I put the ice cream back in the freezer, shutting the door and leaving us in darkness. My breathing picks up when I turn back to face him. My body already responding to what I know is coming. "But how ever will I repay you?"

He calmly straightens before sauntering around the island toward me. Backing me against the counter, he presses his hips into me. He smells masculine. Heady. *Mouthwatering.*

"You don't have to repay me, gorgeous." His lips feather across my cheek. "But I can think of several ways for you to thank me."

Over the past few months, he's tasted me many times. But I've never had the opportunity to taste him. *Really* taste him. The idea has me licking my lips as I place my palms against his chest—pushing him a step back from me.

Wanting to see his face, I open the refrigerator door again. I notice his brow quirk the moment we're flooded in the fluorescent glow. "Looking for something?"

I shake my head. "I want you to see me...And I want to watch you."

"By the light of the refrigerator. How romantic," he teases, smirking down at me. But when I drop to my knees, the smirk wipes right off his face.

Taking my time, I loosen his belt. Unbuckle his jeans. Then he's in my hand. Thick. Hard. Long. Hot to touch. I'm dying to taste. And when I softly kiss the tip, he groans. I gaze up at him from beneath my lashes—separating my lips and swirling my tongue over the head of his cock.

Heavy blue eyes look down at me. His breath comes in short, shallow pants between parted lips. I open wider. Take him a little deeper. He's big, so I take it slow. Using my tongue to make up for not being able to take more of him. But he's not complaining. Although he is struggling with the lack of control. Hands clenching and unclenching as he watches me. Nostrils flaring. Chest heaving. Body rigid.

He tastes better than ice cream. Even better than wine. The power I have over him is thrilling. Toxic. Addictive. I see why he loves it so much. Why he doesn't want to give it up. Why he's fighting to let me continue. But as exciting as this moment is, it's not nearly as gripping as when he's running the show.

"Tell me what to do," I say, stroking my hand up and down his length.

"What you're doin' feels pretty fuckin' good, gorgeous." The hoarse whisper makes me want to shove my hand in my panties. I want him to talk more. Say something dirty. Force his cock down my throat. Treat me like a greedy little slut. I don't know where the urge comes from, but just the thought has me whimpering.

"Tell me," I beg, dropping my hands to my lap as I look up at him with wide eyes. His heavy, fully erect cock sits mere inches from my face. I have to bite my cheek to keep from licking it.

Recognition flickers in his gaze. His lids grow heavier with lust. I'm not sure how he so easily reads me, but the man knows my body. My mind. My wants. Especially when it comes to sex.

He slowly becomes the dominant, self-assured, nipple hardening, thigh clenching god he usually is. Tension fades from his face. Breath evens. Shoulders relax. Power exudes him. He radiates confidence. His eyes darken to a midnight blue. *Ohmylordhavemercy.*

"Take your hair down." His words are like velvet. Their texture sending goosebumps up my arms. I'm so stunned by their effect, it takes me a moment to get my muscles to comply.

Leaning back on my haunches, I pull the band from my hair and shake out the long locks. My heart is hammering. Sex dripping. Impatiently waiting for his next demand. "Sit up and put your hands behind your back." I nearly break my elbows jerking them behind me, surprised that I don't fall face first into his crotch as I sit up. If he wasn't in "dominant" mode, he would smile. *I wonder if I should refer to him as master...*

His hands slide up the sides of my neck and cup my cheeks. "I hope it's me you're thinking so hard about." *Oh if he only knew.* "Open your mouth, gorgeous. Let me give you something a little harder to think on." I'm salivating as my eyes move to his massive erection. Just standing there. Waiting to be tortured by my tongue.

Cook sweeps my hair into his hands, fisting it at the back of my head as he teases my lips with his cock. "Wider," he demands. My jaw opens to the point of pain. Saliva immediately begins to build in the corner of my mouth. "Good girl." *Son of a...*

He pushes inside, slowly working his cock in and out. It's thick. Filling. Gliding smoothly over my tongue. Between my lips. He thrusts deeper and I try to pull away. His grip on my hair tightens.

"Relax." Shallowing his strokes, he caresses my cheek with his free hand. His gentle touch instantly smothers the well of panic building in my chest. "I'm not going to hurt you. Understand?" I attempt a nod. "Trust me." I already trust him. Why else would I be in such a vulnerable position with a cock the size of a Lincoln in my mouth? One hard jerk of his hips could paralyze me.

"Loosen your throat muscles." *How the hell does one do that?*

I try it anyway, and surprisingly, it works. He thrusts deeper again and this time I don't feel like I'm choking to death. "Breathe through your nose." I do and he pushes further inside me.

My eyes water, but I don't move away. Because even through my cloudy vision, I can see his reaction.

As he rhythmically plunges in and out of my mouth, that control begins to slip. The muscle in his jaw ticks. There's a tiny wrinkle between his brows. His breathing matches my own. I feel his hand tighten in my hair. He picks up speed. Forcing me to take him. Fucking my mouth.

Desire shakes me. My fingers twitch to touch myself. To rub through the wetness pooling between my thighs. But I'd rather he touch me there. So I fist my hands. Focus on my breathing. On pleasing him. Sucking him. Keeping my jaw slack. Mouth wide.

My throat is numb. Eyes watery. Burning from keeping them open and on him. My knees hurt. Shoulders ache. Hair pulled tight to the point of pain. And I've never been hornier. Felt more alive. Been given such an impassioned stare. Suffered a more rewarding moment.

"I don't want to come in your mouth." His voice rumbles through me. I moan my protest. His hips jerk harder, silencing me. "I want to be deep inside you when I do. I want to fuck you harder than this." He pulls out, but allows me to kiss and lick him a moment. Pleasure him at my own pace. Then he tugs my hair, forcing me to my feet.

My head tilted back, eyes still on him, I wipe my mouth and chin with my hand before dropping it. He drags his thumb over my swollen lips. "This mouth..." I fist his cut in my hands, leaning my body into him. "Now I want to feel that sweet cunt." I grind my pelvis against his thigh. "I bet that motherfucker is so wet...."

Mr. Delicious is Mr. Mercurial tonight. He's been thoughtful. Funny. Subservient. Dominant. And the explosion of heat in his eyes gives way to the next phase:

Beast mode.

He spins us so he's behind me. I'm bent at the waist. Chest and stomach splayed across the island. Then his hand is out of my hair. Impatiently tearing at my pants. Forcing them to my knees. I hear the tear of a condom. A light smack to my bare ass.

"Legs spread," he says darkly. I widen them as much as I can with my pants at my knees. He drags his fingers between my thighs. "Fuck, Carmen." I shudder at his words. How he says my name. How clearly he's affected by me. My pussy. Arousal. Desire. For him.

"Ah!" I cry out as he surges inside me. Filling me as he had my mouth, but deeper. Harder. Just like he promised.

His hands are on my hips. Pulling me to him as he shoves inside me. Pounding me. His thighs hammering against mine. A wicked slapping sound filling the room. The city. Notifying everyone of what we're doing. They might think he was beating the hell out of me if my moans of pleasure weren't topping the chart on the Richter scale.

"Come, gorgeous. I need you coming right now." The build is teasing. Or confused. The impalement is too overwhelming. The drive overpowering. And he's too overanxious.

"No," I pant. "More. I want more."

"Greedy girl..." But he gives me more. I didn't know he had it in him. I thought he was giving me all he had. I was wrong. He barks out commands and I scramble to obey.

"On your elbows. Hollow your back. Lift that sweet little ass for me." All of this is said and done without him slowing stride, making it a little bit difficult and a whole lot worth it.

My feet are lifted from the floor. The moment they're in the air, the fuse inside me is lit. He's found that place deep within my walls that's elusive to everyone but him. "Still want more, gorgeous?" he asks, his tone just as sexy as it is playful.

I'd answer, but I'm too busy imploding. Dying a beautiful death. Floating to the heavens. Slicing through the clouds like butter. Coming up with ridiculous sayings in my head to try and describe the indescribable.

Sprawled across the island, I shudder when he stills inside me. It's like gasoline to a flame. Triggering the aftershocks of an orgasm I thought was over. I just lay here and let it crash through me. Immobile. High. Probably from those drugs he's been slipping me.

"I've worked all day," I mutter, once I find my voice. My sanity. Gravity. "Probably should've showered first." *I guess hindsight really is twenty-twenty.* Thirty minutes ago, it never occurred to me that I might smell like a goat.

"Waffles and Carmen. It's hotter than you think," he teases, his voice becoming more distant with every word. I hear the toilet flush then his voice again—lulling me to sleep. The voice. Not the toilet. "Besides. It's gonna take more than an eight hour shift to mask your sweet aroma."

"Sixteen."

"Hmm?" he asks, lifting my limp body into his arms.

"I worked a sixteen-hour shift." The reminder has me yawning as he carries me to my room. Pants at my ankles. Modesty out the window.

"Damn. You off tomorrow?"

"Nope." He sits me on the bed and before I can kick my shoes off, he's kneeling to remove them. "This was day three. I have two more left."

"Of sixteen-hour shifts?" His tone is incredulous.

"Yep." I fall back on the bed. Physically exhausted. Mentally drained. Completely sated.

Voice low and serious, he asks, "Do you need money, Carmen?" His kindness stirs something in my chest. I quickly dismiss it.

"I won't by the time the week is up."

He's silent as he removes my pants. Straddles me. Pulls my shirt over my head. Unclasps my bra. Frames my face with his hands. I can feel his heated stare, demanding I open my eyes and meet it. I do. And I don't like what I see.

"Don't feel sorry for me, Cook. Like I told you before, my independence means something to me. If I have to work my ass off to keep it, I will." Respect drowns the pity from his oceanic eyes. He's thoughtful a moment longer before he smiles.

"So no time for a date this week?" I shake my head, feeling a sense of relief knowing I won't have to do that anymore. Now that I've moved on from Jud, what's the point? "Cheer up, buttercup," Cook says, and I realize I'm frowning. "I got you something to remind you of what you're missing." He winks. My eyes narrow. "Just in case you get lonely."

Sliding gracefully from the bed, he tucks my legs under the covers then pulls them up to my neck. He kisses me sweetly, his big hand cupping my jaw. Straightening, he cuts off the lamp and turns to leave. "See you soon, gorgeous."

"Wait!" I call, struggling to sit up. Pausing mid-stride, he looks over his shoulder. "What did you get me?" I drop my head and fidget with the covers. "You know...in case I get lonely." My mind goes crazy with the possibilities--a puppy. Life size poster of him. Mixed tape full of his dirty talk to masturbate to.

But then I catch his smile. That shit-eating grin he wears when he's about to say something to piss me off. And as always, he manages to do just that.

"Bologna."

26
POPS' BARTENDER KAT

"Carmen please come," Kat begs, pausing to tell someone to "hang the fuck on." I glance at the clock behind the dishwasher. It's barely ten.

"What are you doing at the bar this early?" I ask, spraying off one of the millions of dirty plates from the morning rush.

"I'm not at the bar."

"Well who are you telling to hang on?"

"This bitch at McDonalds. One sec, Carmen."

I smirk, tucking the phone between my ear and shoulder as she continues to yell.

I've been on the phone with Kat for only a minute. In those sixty seconds, she's asked me three times if I'd be her date to a river party. It's for one of the guys in the MC I've never met or even heard of. The event is being held on a private piece of land on the Calcasieu river in Lake Charles. I'd declined her offer the first two times, but she just isn't getting the hint.

"You still there?"

"Still here."

"Hate this place," she mumbles. "But they have the best damn orange juice. Anyway, will you go?"

"I'm tired, Kat. Saturday is my first day off in a week and I just want to relax." Tired is an understatement. I've been dragging all day. I still have twelve hours to go. Then sixteen more tomorrow. Next time I get hard up for money, I'll prostitute.

"You *can* relax. I even bought you a lounge chair. Besides, you need some sun."

"I'm really not in the partying mood." Even as I say the words, I can feel the sun kissing my skin. Cold drink in my hand. Water lapping at my feet.

"Nobody is really partying. It's just a nice, quiet get together." I'm still on the fence. Sleep sounds just as appealing as a day in the sand. As if she can sense my apprehension, she sweetens the deal. "I'm makin' those margaritas you love."

I groan, thinking of how delicious one would be right now. At ten in the morning. "Can I think about it?"

"No. I want you there. And you've spent the past two months going on dates that I set up for you. After all the work I've put in, you owe me."

"You got paid. Fifty bucks a date, if I remember correctly."

She smacks her gum loudly. "That's beside the point. Please?" Her whine would be annoying if I didn't find it so humorous. And so unlike her.

Nervously chewing my lip, I try to find the courage to tell her I'm not particularly thrilled about seeing any of the Eagles. I may be over Jud and "the plan," but I'm not ready to hang out with him and his new fiancé. Or his estranged brothers.

"Kat...I really don't want to see Jud right now," I say, figuring it's the simplest explanation that doesn't require additional reasons.

"Don't worry. He won't be there. None of the Eagles will. It's a Devil's Renegades party. Only club members and property will be there. Oh, and a select chosen few which includes me. And I'm inviting you."

Without a moment's hesitation, I agree. I try and tell myself the reason for my sudden change of heart is that The Eagles' won't be there. But really, it's because Devil's Renegades Prospect Cook will be.

Forty-eight hours later, I'm stumbling down a steep slope with a chair, beach bag and sun hat in one hand and one side of a cooler in the other. When we finally make it to the river, a million freakin' years later, we find the sand bank filled with people.

Tents are scattered across the wide strip of land. Grills are smoking. Rock music blaring. Men laughing. Women sunbathing. Kids playing. *A nice, quiet get together my ass.*

"Who's party is this again?" I ask Kat as we head toward an unoccupied spot near the water.

"Glen. That's his place up there." She points in the direction of the cabin we'd seen on our way in. "He's another one of the original Devil's Renegades."

"Like Ronnie?"

"Yep." I collapse on the cooler, my arms and legs aching from carrying the damn thing, as she closes her eyes and pulls in a deep breath. "I've so needed this. I'm not even gonna socialize. If they wanna speak, they can come to me." Good thing. It would take her all day to greet everyone. Considering there's probably a hundred people here.

Shedding my sweaty tank, I stand and push my cutoffs down my legs. When Kat pulls her sundress off revealing a modest, black one piece, I fight the urge to cover myself. Feeling like a complete slut in my mint colored, bombshell bandeau top and matching cheeky bikini bottoms.

I'm digging for the crotchet tunic in the bottom of my beach bag when she notices me. "Oooh. Cute suit."

I glance at her over my shoulder. "You don't think it's too slutty?"

"Asks the patchwhore?" she teases, giving me a smirk. "Girl please. The only reason I'm wearin' this shit is because Glen is like a father to me. Respect thing, I guess. Besides, look around." She motions toward the women scattered across the beach. "You don't see anyone else shyin' away from showin' skin."

She's right. Most of the women wear tiny bikinis similar to mine. The only difference is the air of confidence surrounding them. Even though not everyone has the slimmest or most fit body, they walk with poise—head held high. Classy in their own way. It's admirable.

It doesn't take long for me to gain a certain level of confidence myself. Granted it could be Kat's margaritas, but soon, I'm lounging back in my chair. Sun on my skin. Feet in the water. Drink in my hand. Enjoying the company of two women who've joined us. Our chairs are partially submerged in the water in a semi-circle, facing the sun and beach.

The women are from a chapter out of Mississippi. I was intrigued to find out one is the infamous Dallas Knox-Carmical, owner of Knox Realty—the largest Real Estate agency in the south. My father has actually done business with her. But what was really fascinating was learning that she's also the wife of Devil's Renegades President, Luke Carmical aka LLC, Mississippi. *Small world.*

I'm mindlessly listening to their chatter about people I don't know when Red, the other ol' lady from Mississippi, mentions a name I know all too well. "Cook's body belongs on the cover of Men's Fitness magazine. Or GQ. He's like a younger version of Luke. But hotter."

"Hey!" Dallas, snaps. "Luke's still hot."

Red shakes her head. "Yeah, but not that hot. I mean…" She sighs. "Just *look* at him."

Their voices fade as I scan the beach in search of Cook. It'd only been three days since I last saw him or talked to him, yet it feels like weeks. When my eyes finally find him, I liquefy at the sight. Today, he's not a Prospect. No leather. No jeans. Just low slung, black swim trunks. Chiseled, bare chest. Muscular legs. Dark shades. Backwards hat. Drink in hand. And…*son of a bitch…*flip flops.

"...I could kill that bitch for doing that to him..." My attention snaps back to the conversation at Red's words.

"Doing what? Who?" I'm asking questions I have no business asking. But I'm too damn nosey to care.

"Laura. His ex. She fucked his brother. His *real* brother. Blood kin brother." My heart sinks as Red continues. "Then the dirty skank showed up at Cook's father's funeral with his brother, wearing his dead mother's engagement ring. Crying and making a scene. Going on and on about how he was just like a dad to her. Greedy bitch. She did it all for the money."

"Money?" I ask, unable to pull my eyes from Cook as he stops to speak to a few men.

"Yep. His dad was a wealthy man. You wouldn't know it by the way he lived. He was conservative. Believed in hard work. When he got sick, rumor had it Cook's older brother was to inherit everything. Laura smelled money. So she made sure to sink her teeth into the brother who would benefit the most."

"Lot of good it did her," Dallas mumbles.

Red laughs. "Karma's a bitch, ain't it?"

"What do you mean?"

Her eyes turn to me and I'm forced to pull my gaze from Cook to meet them. "He left it all to Cook." Her focus returns to the beach. I do the same—the muscles in my body relaxing when he's back in my sight.

"He saw how quick his oldest son was willing to betray his only brother. So he gave it to the one who was loyal. Who put family first. Even though Cook knew he wasn't getting anything, it was him who stayed by his father's side."

"While his sorry brother was fucking the girl he wanted to marry," Dallas adds, a hint of disgust in her voice.

"Surely he can't look any better than that?" Red motions with her hand toward Cook. "I mean come on...look at the guy. I'd fuck him if he didn't have a pot to piss in or a window to throw it out of. He's..."

"Delicious," I breathe, earning me looks from every girl in our circle.

"Shut the fuck up," Red whispers in shock, leaning up and pulling her sunglasses off her face to narrow her eyes on me. "Are you—"

Kat interrupts her before she can finish. "She's the one I was tellin' you about."

"You're the patchwhore?" Red's incredulity is almost offensive. Dallas scolds her, but she ignores it. "You're the same girl who's been fuckin' around with all those Eagles when you could've been fuckin' *that?*" She points to Cook. I shift under the scrutiny of her disbelieving glare.

"Well...I mean...it's...complicated?"

"Complicated?" she nearly shouts. "Okay." She shifts her chair to have a better view of me and leans forward—pulling a cigarette from her pack. "I'm going to ask you a series of yes or no questions—"

"Red!"

191

She swats Dallas' hand away, telling her to shut up under her breath. "Have you been with Cook?" I flush, looking to Kat for help. She dips her head inside the ice chest. *Coward.*

"I'm really not comfortable with this," I say, wringing my sweaty hands in my lap.

"I didn't ask if you were comfortable. It's a yes or no question."

"That's enough, Red. Leave her alone."

Red whips her head to Dallas, motioning with her finger between the two of them. "We're married. Stuck with the same dick for the rest of our lives. Now." She holds her hands up. "I'm not complaining. It's good dick. But I'm interested in that dick." Jutting her thumb toward Cook, she pauses to light her cigarette before turning back to me.

"Here's the deal, Carmen. Being an ol' lady is great. I love my husband. Wouldn't trade him for anything. Would kill a bitch if she looked at him wrong. But sometimes, I enjoy living vicariously through others. In this instance, it's you. So please, for the love of all that's holy, *please* tell me y'all are having sex."

Kat's laughing. Dallas has her head in her hands. I'm crimson. And Cook is watching us. His focus mainly on me. That crooked smile promising. That V making my mouth water. Those fingers making my sex water. I want him to fuck me *in* the water. And because I like her, despite her personal questions, I'll let Red watch.

"No Red," I say. "We don't have sex." Her body sags in disappointment. Lips drooping in a frown. Then I look at him. Shoot him my best playful smile. And say the words that will make Red's day—knowing good and well he can read my lips.

"We fuck."

I'm buzzing by the time the sun sets. But all the alcohol in Louisiana can't dull the ache I feel from my recent knowledge of Cook and his heartbreak. Not only was he cheated on by the woman he loved, but it was with his own brother. And on top of that, he'd lost his father during that time. If it's gut wrenching for me, I can only imagine how he must feel.

Throughout the day, we spoke a few times, but he mostly stayed around the men. Even though he's obviously off duty today, he still seems to be in Prospect mode—watching everyone around him. Alert. Quick to respond. Making sure to socialize. Staying close to Ronnie who looks like a completely different man in swim trunks and flip flops.

"Let's go dance by the fire," Red suggests, stumbling as she stands. She reaches out for Dallas's hand to pull her from her chair. The movement causing both of them to fall on their asses. I laugh, but it catches in my throat as I stand—swaying from the movement.

"I need to pee," I announce, contemplating wading into the water so I don't have to make the hike up the beach to the cabin.

"One dance. Then we'll all go."

I agree as she refills my drink. Together the four of us make our way to the massive fire pit. Laughing and singing along to Dierks Bentley's *Somewhere on a Beach*.

Three songs later, I'm fighting the urge to hold my crotch like a five-year-old and cross my legs. Everyone is too busy dancing, singing into imaginary microphones to pay much attention to me when I tell them I have to go. Like now.

I sprint toward the wooded trail, as fast as the deep sand will let me. Stumbling more than a few times, I finally make it to the clearing at the top of the slope.

I've made the trip to the small wooden cabin a few times, but this is my first time alone. Crashing through the door, I stutter an apology as I nearly knock someone over on my race to the bathroom. Finding it empty, I throw myself inside—already shedding my bottoms before the door closes behind me.

Relief can't begin to describe what I feel. Elbows on my knees, I steady my swimming head and try to control my breathing. Drinking Kat's potent margaritas all day without water or food is quickly catching up to me. Finishing off the rest in my cup, I promise no more alcohol after this. But even as I think it, my mouth waters for another.

Looking at my reflection, I notice how glassy my eyes look. My hair is a tangled, damp mess. My skin is pretty red—especially my shoulders. Thankfully, I already had a base tan. Judging by previous experiences, the redness will fade overnight to a golden brown.

Someone knocks on the door. "Jussa minute!" I slur, washing my hands quickly. I offer a tight smile to the girl as she brushes past me—just as anxious to get in here as I was a few minutes ago.

Laughter and chatter carry through the cabin as I slip out the front door. It's darker now—the moon casting an eerie glow on everything it touches. But in the thick woods that lead to the beach, there's not a hint of light anywhere.

I can hear the music and voices in the distance as I make my way down the trail. I try to follow them, but soon find myself fighting against thick underbrush rather than the cleared path. "Shit," I hiss, tripping over a stump. Branches pull at my hair. Twigs scratch my bare arms and legs. If I weren't so numb, it might actually be painful.

When I was seven, I'd wandered into the woods near my house. I'd gotten lost—separated from the older, neighborhood kids I'd followed. It was the most miserable three hours of my life. When my father finally found me, I was so terrified I wouldn't let go of him. Deciding my fear was punishment enough, he'd let me off the hook for doing something so careless. I'd vowed to never do it again. Until now, I'd kept my promise.

Panic starts to creep its way up my spine as I relive the nightmare. Then reality starts to set in. I'm lost in unfamiliar woods. In the dark. Nearly naked. Without alcohol. And I think I lost a flip flop. Worse. Case. Scenario.

"Carmen!" I freeze. Not so much at the sound of my name, but at who's saying it. "You out here?"

"H-here! Cook, I'm over here!" I try to move toward his voice, but only manage to tangle my leg around a briar vine. "Crapcrapcrap."

"Stay where you are. I'll come to you."

"I have no choice," I mutter. "I'm hung up on a mother-friggin'...something."

He chuckles. "Figured as much." *Cocky bastard...*

Standing in an awkward position, I try to remain still as I wait. But my impatience is growing by the second. "Could you hurry up?"

"Demanding little shit, aren't you?"

I smile. "Pretend I said please." Light blinds my eyes and I turn my head away—pulling my hair in the process. "Ouch."

"Only you could get lost on a trail you've walked five times today," he says, untangling my hair from the limb.

"It's easier in the light."

"Hush, gorgeous. Or speak without movin' your hands."

I ignore him. "I'm surprised the skeeters haven't carried me off."

"Skeeters?"

"Mo-skeeters. Whatever y'all call them here."

He lets out an amused laugh. "Skeeters and y'all. You're definitely buzzed."

"I am," I say on a sigh. Not quite drunk, but close.

He kneels down and I move my head, relieved to find I'm free. "It's Kat's fault. She made them damn margaritas. They made me have to pee. Now here I am. Damseling and distressing and nearly eaten by the forest." I can feel his smile.

"Hey Cook." I snort a laugh.

"Hey Carmen."

"What do you do when you get a skeeter on your peter?" He stands, knocking my legs out from under me as he cradles me to his chest. The quick motion winds me, and has me clinging to his neck.

Smiling down at me, he kisses my head then winks. "You knock it off."

I throw my head back on a laugh as he carries me back to the trail. "I'm surprised that you even know the song."

"I'm a vessel of knowledge, gorgeous. Haven't you figured that out?"

"Vessel of knowledge?" I roll my eyes. "Doubt that."

"Well I knew you were out here. Stranded in the woods. Tangled in briars. Drunk."

"Buzzed," I correct. "And you didn't know that. You just assumptioned it."

"Assumptioned...that's a new one. I'll catalogue it next to mo-skeeters." We're back on the path and he sets me on my feet. "But I didn't have to assume anything. You've refilled that red Solo cup of yours eight times today. You haven't eaten since you've been here. And the only water you had was what you accidentally swallowed in the river during your failed attempt at a back flip."

194

I narrow my eyes on his face. My hands still clinging to his arms. They're so smooth. And warm. And *big...* "Aren't you the observant one."

"Always."

"Did you watch erryone like that?" I sway just to feel his hands tighten at my waist. It works.

He shakes his head. "Not today. Today, I only had eyes for you." My heart flip flops.

Flip flops.

"I lost my flip flop."

He pulls something from the back of his pants and hands it to me. "Would you believe I knew that too?"

I snatch it from his hand, unable to contain my smile as I drop it to the ground and shove my foot in it. "Smartass. There any food left?"

"Afraid not, gorgeous. You gotta eat early around here."

"Aw man," I whine, poking my lip out on a pout. "Reckon how long till Kat's ready to go?"

"She was doin' a keg stand when I left to find you. My best guess is she's spending the night." He's silent a moment—watching me as I try to come up with a plan to eat and get home. "You bout ready?"

"Yeah...but she's my ride."

"Did you really think I'd let you leave with her after seeing you in this?" His gaze blazes fire from my nose to my toes. "Besides, you're mine after every date. Remember?"

"This wasn't a date."

"That's not what I was told."

"Same sex dates don't count."

"Are you telling me you don't want to leave with me?" His eyebrows rise in challenge.

I shake my head. Open my mouth. Close it. Then finally stutter an answer. "I mean, I...I um, didn't really say *that."*

"Then it's settled. You walking or you want me to carry you?" *Really?* Like he has to ask...

"I need to get my bag. It's got all my..." I trail off as he releases me, walks a few feet, grabs my bag and slings it over his shoulder—shooting me a cocky smirk.

"I see I was a preconceptconsectional." His brows draw together in confusion as he turns his head to study me.

"I don't know what to make of that. A couch on birth control? An idea about a couch on birth control?"

I dismiss him with a wave. "You know what I'm saying."

"No...clearly I don't. Your drunken slurs are gettin' pretty ridiculous."

"You're ridiculous," I fire back, taking his hand as he pulls me behind him. "Everyone knows couches can't take birth control. Well, one of them can," I add, feeling his eyes burn into me.

195

"I'm gonna have to talk to Kat about what she puts in those fuckin' margaritas," he mumbles. I giggle. Then I giggle some more.

A smile tugs at his lips as he looks over his shoulder at me. "What?"

"You know you want to ask."

He laughs. "No. I do not want to ask."

"If you say so." I shrug, tilting my head back to look at the trees. Stars. Moon. Anything but him.

"Fine." He stops suddenly, forcing me to collide into his back. Adjusting my bag on his shoulder, he looks down at me in amusement. "Tell me."

I grin, knowing I've got him. "Tell you what?"

He bites his lip and shakes his head, breathing out a laugh. He can't believe he's actually entertaining the idea. I can't believe he's doing it either. "Tell me what pieces of furniture can take birth control."

"One." I hold my finger up. "Only one."

"Stupidest fuckin' thing I've ever done," he mutters under his breath. His eyes thin to tiny slits as he looks at me. He's too intrigued not to ask. Too amused by my laughter not to find out. And too damn nosey to just let it go.

"Okay, gorgeous. What single, non-breathing, non-human, magical piece of furniture can take birth control?"

"A love seat!"

My answer has me laughing until I'm crying. He just shakes his head and smiles, mumbling something about how addictive I am...even when I'm ridiculous.

27
THE GREAT ESCAPE

Hands are all over me. Strong and soft and smooth. Rubbing and caressing and touching. And for the first time in…ever, I let out a very unsexy grunt of disapproval.

"No sex," I say, keeping my breaths deep and even. "Too tired."

"We fuck, gorgeous. And, don't worry, we're not doing it tonight."

"Then stop touching me." My words are barely a whisper. Sleep is so close. But his voice is so nice.

"Almost finished," Cook says, his tone nearly as low as mine.

"Are you masturbating?" I try to pry an eye open to catch him in the act, but I fail. His deep, throaty chuckle shakes me.

"Unfortunately no. Your skin is cooked. I'm just putting some lotion on it." Tender hands rub my shoulders.

"It puts the lotion on its skin."

"Silence of the Lambs?"

I frown. "No. Joe Dirt. He went in the hole. Guy sent down a basket. He was dressed like a woman. Petting a—"

"I know the movie, gorgeous." The bed dips and his hands are gone. My skin feels colder now without his heat. And it smells like aloe.

"I didn't know I had any aloe. Where was it?"

"In my bathroom," he says from a few feet away.

"You brought it with you?"

"No."

"Then how…" My eyes open and the unfamiliar surroundings are enough to distract me from sleep.

I'm lying on my back in a bed. A big one. The room is dimly lit, but still visible. It's huge. Pristine and masculine. The walls a dark navy. Furniture a distressed gray. Carpet thick and nearly as white as the down comforter under me.

A wall of windows is to my left covered by floor to ceiling gray curtains. In front of me is a massive flat screen mounted above a dresser. To the right is a bathroom. And leaning in the doorway, arms crossed over his chest, barefoot and shirtless is the master of the master bedroom.

"Where are we?" I ask, partially sitting up.

"Three miles from where we were."

"Is this your place?"

He nods, pushing off the door and sauntering toward me. "Thirsty?" He grabs a bottle of water from the nightstand and offers it to me.

"How long have I been asleep?" Turning the bottle up, I guzzle half of it. Clearly dehydrated. *Damn tequila. Damn Kat.*

"About an hour." *That long?*

"Why would you bring me here?"

"Because I didn't want you to puke in my truck." He smirks when I give him the finger. I don't remember the ride here, but I do remember that truck. It was nice. Clean. Smelled like leather and money. I'd have died if I puked in it.

"It seems we're making a routine of this. Me drinking too much. You coming to my rescue."

"Always damseling in distressing," he teases, opening a draw on his dresser. He walks toward me, carrying a plain, white T-shirt in his hand. It's then I notice my cover-up on the floor, but I'm still dressed in my swimsuit.

Breathing becomes nearly impossible when he stops in front of me. He's so overwhelming—deliciously so. He drapes the shirt over his shoulder, then his cool hands are on my wrists. He feels his way up my arms, his fingers ghosting across my skin that's now covered in goosebumps.

Gently, he turns me. His fingers trail down my back before unclipping my swimsuit top. My nipples harden the moment the fabric falls away from my body. Then lips are on my neck. Caressing my spine. Hands drift down my sides to my waist.

Hooking his fingers into my bikini bottoms, he drags them slowly down my legs. Kissing my hip. Thigh. Teeth lightly skim my right cheek in a playful bite, followed by another soothing peck from his full lips.

Grasping my elbows, he guides my arms over my head. His touch makes me feel drunk. I sway on my feet slightly, swooning at how his big hands pay attention to every part of me. Caressing even the tips of my fingers.

His scent engulfs me when he dresses me in his shirt. The signature, manly smell is my aphrodisiac. I want him to make love to me again. Or fuck me hard. Eat me like a starved animal. Feed me his cock and call me his, "good girl."

When he turns me to face him, his hands slide to my neck. His thumbs whispering across my throat. Circling the area where my pulse beats erratically against my skin.

There's something different about the way he looks at me. It's not that heated look of desire. That playful expression, cocky smirk or amused gaze. This look is reverent. Adoring. Warm and liquefying.

The loud rumble of pipes shatters the severity of the moment. Framing my face in his hands, he places a sweet kiss on my lips. My eyes flutter closed as he keeps his soft mouth pressed against mine for a few moments. When he breaks the kiss, I peek up at him from beneath my lashes to see him wearing a crooked smile.

"Get some sleep, gorgeous. I'll be back soon."

And like so many other times, he walks out. Leaving me feeling abandoned and alone once again.

My body shakes awake and I reach out to slap whoever is moving me. "Carmen," a voice whispers in my ear. I crack my eyes open.

Leaning over me is a very drunk, Kat. "Wake up!" I sit up quickly, scanning the room—looking for signs of trouble.

"What is it? What's wrong? Where's Cook?" I whisper shout the questions as I clamber out of bed, pushing past her and into the bathroom to splash cold water on my face.

"Cook's outside talkin' to Ronnie and Glen. Nothing's wrong, I just need you to drive me home."

"What?" I ask confused. "Who drove you here?"

"I did, but drivin' a few miles through the woods is one thing. No way can I drive on the interstate. Can you? Please?"

"Why are we whispering?"

"Because they don't know I'm here."

"Kat you're not making any sense. If you drove here, and Ronnie is here, Glen is here and Cook is here, how do they not know you're here."

She shakes her head, her dark hair wild around her face. She smells like tequila and pot. "I parked down the driveway. Ronnie would be disappointed if he knew I drove. Glen would just kill me."

"So why did you leave?"

Her eyes narrow as her lips curl in disgust. "Remember the chick with the resting bitch face?" I shake my head. Having no idea who she's talking about. "Yes you do," she breathes, exasperated.

"No, Kat. I don't."

"Maybe you'd already left. Anyway," she says, dismissing it with a wave. "She's stayin' at Glen's. Where I'm supposed to stay. But if I stay, I'm gonna kill her. So I need you to take me home."

"Just stay here."

"Can't." She pulls a flask from the back pocket of her shorts. "They'll find out I left. That I drove. I'll have to hear that shit for a year. Or die. Remember? I just told you Glen would kill me. Pay attention, Carmen."

"Let me get this straight." I cross my arms and watch as she takes a pull from the flask. "You drove here and weren't supposed to." She nods. "You snuck inside without anyone knowing." Thumbs up as she tilts back the flask again. "Now you want me to disappear into the night, drive you home and tell Cook what? That I had to go?"

"Exactly."

"Oh, okay." I grab her shoulders and whisper shout in her face. "Are you out of your fucking mind? I've been drinking too!"

"It's after three in the morning, Carmen. You left at like eight thirty. You're hardly drunk."

She's right. I'm not drunk. I was pretty buzzed before, but after a nap, rubdown by Cook, crazy intimate moment and an additional several hours of sleep, I'm sober. But this idea is crazy. So I find another tactic to talk some sense into her.

"Don't you think he'll come looking for me? Thinking I'm wandering in the woods? I don't have a car here, Kat."

She points her finger at me. "You're right. You should leave a note." Scrambling out of my grasp, she searches the nightstand for something to write on.

"I'm dreaming," I mutter. "I'm in a nightmare."

"Here." She thrusts the stationery and pencil in my hand. "Tell him what's going on. And that you'll make it up to him."

"So you don't care that he knows?"

"Who, Cook? Hell no. But it's not like I can talk to him right now. Ronnie and Glen are drunk. They'll be on that porch all night. Then they'll probably pass out on the couch. Which is why we need to leave now. Before they discover I'm here."

"This is ridiculous," I say, even as I scribble the note.

Hyped on adrenaline, excitement starts to build at the idea of doing something that feels so wrong. I pull my shorts out of my beach bag and tie my hair behind my head. Tiptoeing through the room, I follow Kat out a door that opens to a private balcony.

The unmistakable sound of Ronnie's laugh fills the quiet night. Like a mouse, we creep down a flight of stairs to the ground level. Keeping off the gravel, we break into a jog—the only light coming from the bright moon. I see we're near some water, but am regretfully too scared of getting caught to turn and look at the house I'm escaping.

A few hundred yards later, past the tree line and out of sight, we arrive at Kat's car. I'm breathless behind the wheel. Laughing like a teenager. Feeling triumphant as I turn the key. Then I'm screaming when the headlights shine on a figure standing in front of us.

Cook's here. *Of course.* Holding my note in his hand. Looking unimpressed. Amused. And not the least bit winded. He walks over to the driver side window—rapping his knuckles on the glass. I glare at Kat who pretends to be passed out as I roll down the window.

"Cook...had to run. Kat needed ride. Didn't want her to die. I'll make it up to you. Signed, squiggly line." I roll my eyes as he drops down so he's at my level. "The next time you mention someone dying, maybe you should be a little clearer on your meaning."

"It's Kat's fault," I grumble, blaming her for the second time tonight. She doesn't even flinch next to me.

"You said you'd make it up to me. How?" Slowly, I turn my gaze to him. He's smiling like a Cheshire cat.

"What do you want?"

"This is some pretty valuable info I have here."

"How so?"

"Kat's life's at stake. Remember? I'd hate to tell Ronnie, or Glen what she did."

"Whatever you want, she'll do it," Kat says. I shoot her a disbelieving stare. She only shrugs. "Sometimes you gotta take one for the team, Carmen."

"I saved your ass and this is how you repay me?"

She holds a finger up. "Correction. You're *gonna* save my ass. Just as soon as you agree to Cook's terms." She grins. I look at Cook and that bastard is grinning too.

"Thursday night, you're goin' on a date. With me. And not to Pops. To dinner."

"Hardly," I scoff. Even though my heart is pitter-pattering in my chest.

Kat opens her big fat mouth. "She'll be there."

"See? You'll be there." I glare at him, trying to look pissed. On the inside, I'm happy. Jumping up and down. Somersaulting. Liver quivering. The good stuff.

"Fine."

"I'll pick you up at seven. Drive safe, gorgeous." He starts to stand. "Oh, and one more thing." I cut my eyes at him, ignoring how much that smirk of his turns me on. "Wear something sexy." He presses his lips in my hair, speaking low so only I can hear. "You have my permission."

28
AND I'M NOT YOUR PROSPECT

"You have his permission?" Emily shrieks. "What the hell does that mean?"

Putting my phone on speaker, I set it on the counter in the bathroom. "I don't know," I say, removing the hot rollers from my hair. "I guess it means I can dress sexy since I'm going out with him. You remember how possessive he got after my date with Lefty."

"Actually, the only part of that story I remember was Lefty asking if he could stick his finger in your belly button." I shiver at the reminder. Emily laughs. "That shit was funny as hell." When she catches her breath, after another fit of laughter, she says, "So since you're not going out with guys to make Jud jealous anymore, this is like a real date."

I fidget with the ends of my hair. "I wouldn't say it's a *real* date." My nerves tingle. The butterflies are back. I feel a stutter in my chest. I've missed him so much. I haven't seen or even heard from him since Saturday, and it's driving me crazy. "We're just going out to dinner instead of to the bar."

"It's a real date," Emily deadpans.

The urge to defend myself is pressuring. "We've eaten together plenty of times. He's bought me dinner on more than one occasion." I let out a breath of laughter. "He bought me groceries, Em. The only thing that makes tonight any different is that we're actually going somewhere."

"On a date."

"It's not a date. It's dinner."

"He said it was a date," she argues.

"He also blackmailed me into going."

Exasperated, she lets out a breath. "It's definitely a date. Accept it. Besides, you deserve a night out with someone decent." *That's the damn truth...* "So what *hot...sexy* little number are you going to wear?" Her animation has me grinning. Instead of telling her, I promise to send her a picture soon.

Thirty minutes later, I look down at my outfit of choice lying on the bed. Before I put it on, I turn to my reflection in the mirror and take in my freshly made face—smoky eyes. Red lips. Contoured cheeks. My hair that's now flowing in soft curls down my back. Perfectly painted nails. Smooth legs. Shimmering skin.

I could wear something sexy like Cook suggested. Maybe a tight dress or a pair of short shorts and those boots he loves so much. Hell I'm dolled up enough to pull off a more elegant look—a cocktail dress or even an evening gown. But I'm not doing either.

Cook may think he can boss me around. That he can tell me to do something and I'll comply. In the past, I have. Under normal circumstances, I probably would again. But everything I do is of my own free will.

I'm not a Prospect.

I don't need permission. Not even from Mr. Delicious himself.

29
DEVIL'S RENEGADES PROSPECT COOK

Cook stands silent in the doorway. His hands shoved in the pockets of his jeans as he appraises me. Pulling his bottom lip between his teeth, he nods a few times before meeting my eyes.

"This is because of the whole permission thing, isn't it?"

I scrunch up my nose and return his nod. "Yeah," I whisper.

"Thought so." His gaze drifts back to my outfit a moment before returning to my face. Raising his eyebrows, he nods again. "I'm impressed."

"I can tell." Taking a page from Mr. Delicious' playbook, I offer him the most mischievous, teeth baring smile I can manage.

"You're not gonna change, are you?"

"Not a chance in hell."

"Yeah, I figured that." He crosses his arms over his chest. Then brings his hand up to cup his chin. Tilting his head to the left a fraction, he keeps his face well-guarded as he studies me a little longer. It takes everything I have to hold back my laughter.

I should feel bad. I even try to. He went all out tonight. This might be the most delicious Mr. Delicious has ever looked. Hair styled to a perfect mess. Panty melting five o'clock shadow. Black sports coat over a smoky grey shirt. Dark denim jeans. And I'm pretty sure that's Gucci on his feet. Unfortunately for him, it only makes my wardrobe decision that much greater.

"You think too much, handsome." His lips twitch at hearing his own words thrown back in his face. Poking my lip out, I frown. "Are you disappointed?"

"Not at all." He offers me a small smile. I wait with a smile of my own as he struggles to find the right words to say. This is definitely a first for him. "I'm just surprised."

"Were you expecting something else? A little black dress...some heels...maybe a little more cleavage," I tease, feeling victorious as he finally starts to accept his defeat. Ronnie once said he didn't know how to lose. *Ronnie was wrong.*

A giggle escapes me and I have to press my lips together to keep from losing it completely.

He breathes out a laugh and shakes his head as he stares at his shoes. When he looks up, he's smirking. The shock has worn off. Blue eyes dance with amusement instead of disbelief. *There's my Mr. Delicious.*

"Well, gorgeous. You got me. And I don't get got very often. So congratulations to you."

I curtsy. "Thank you, sir."

Three steps later he's in front of me. His look sincere as he cups my cheek. My breath hitches at his nearness. My pulse speeds at the scent of his cologne. "Even like this, you're still the prettiest fucking thing I've ever seen." His line is repeated, but still makes my belly flip. Even if it is used as a ploy.

Smiling shyly, I look up at him from beneath my lashes as I give him the same response I did the last time he said those words to me. Right after he fucked me in the employee bathroom at Pops.

"Flattery doesn't work on a true lady." The corners of his lips tip. "And it sure as hell won't work on Wonder Woman."

"Now isn't this better than sitting in some fancy restaurant?" I ask, dipping my fry in Cook's ketchup.

"No." He narrows his eyes at me. "River Martins has the best damn seafood in the south. And reservations there are nearly impossible."

I shoot him a smile and hold out my hand. "Here, have a McDonalds fry. Best damn fries in the *world.*" He nips the tip of my finger with his teeth as he takes it. An erotic shiver ripples through me when I lick the remaining ketchup from that same finger. *So weird.*

"Besides, I don't eat seafood."

He quirks a brow. "No shit?"

"No shit." I spin to face him. Tucking my legs beneath me and leaning against the door of his truck. "I got food poison from shellfish once. Now I get queasy just at the sight of it."

"I guess Wonder Woman was looking out for you." He smirks. "Or maybe it was that ridiculous fuckin' cape."

"Hey." I point my finger at him. My expression serious. "This cape is awesome."

Shrugging, he has to agree. "Yeah. It kinda is."

"So tell me something about you. Where you from? What did you do before you became a Prospect?"

"I'm from here. I worked in the oil field." His evasive response reminds me of why I can't allow myself to feel too much for him. It's just as hurtful as it is annoying. "Tell me more," I demand, but it sounds more like a plea.

He gives me a thoughtful look. "Like what?"

"I don't know..." I drop my gaze, unable to look him in the eye. "Tell me about your family."

His silence calls to me and I peek up at him. "If you want to know something Carmen, just ask."

"But I don't want to ask," I say softly. My fingers fidget with the zipper on my onesie. "I want you to tell me because you want to."

I'm selfishly seeking a reason to allow myself to feel something deeper for him. After all, that is one of the reasons I refuse. Right? Because he's so private? It sounds ridiculous now that I repeat it in my head. I start to apologize or try to change the subject when he finally speaks.

"Her name was Elise," he starts, repositioning himself so he's facing me. Both our food forgotten. "We were together six years. She had me fooled into believing she was *the one*." Smirking, he shakes his head. "And she was. She was the one who ruined my life. My family. My checking account," he adds on a smile. I mirror his smile. But my happiness doesn't stem from his joke. It's because he's finally opening up to me.

"But she was also the one who taught me about loyalty. How important it is to stay true to the people you care about. What it feels like to be betrayed by someone you love. Without the experience, I never would've known the magnitude of giving your word. Some people live their whole life not fully understanding what it means to be loyal. But I do" He pierces me with his stare. "So do you."

I smirk. "You're a glass half full kind of guy, aren't you?"

"I learned to be." His voice drops. "Haven't you?"

Averting my gaze, I look out the windshield at the parking lot. "Jud destroyed me when he broke my heart. I may be over him, but I'm not quite ready to appreciate him for anything."

"Then you should at least appreciate the beauty of a broken heart."

"Beauty?" I face him, my look incredulous. "What the hell is beautiful about a broken heart."

Rich, cobalt blue eyes filled with tender appreciation, bore into me. "It gives you a second chance at something better." His words floor me. The intensity in his powerful gaze is enough to rattle that cage around my heart. Deliquescing the iron bars to nothing but a puddle of molten.

We stare at each other in silence. Unmoving. Barely breathing. Minds start to wander. Questions seek answers. Reality is just a hairsbreadth out of reach. The space between us is filling up with words neither of us can say.

Then his phone vibrates on the dash. Our eyes jerk to the device I've hated since I've known him. And for the first time, he looks like he hates it too.

Releasing a noisy breath, he grabs the cell, answering it with a snappy, "Yeah." I watch his eyes fall closed. His jaw tightens. "On my way," he says with no emotion even though his anger is tangible.

His look softens when he turns to me with eyes full of apology. "Bad news, gorgeous." I try to give him a reassuring smile. Letting him know it's okay. When really, it's not. "I have to go to Pops."

"Why?" I ask, shoving a cold French fry in my mouth just to give my fidgety hands something to do.

"I don't have the privilege of knowing why. It could be something as simple as gettin' Ronnie a beer because it tastes better coming from me."

His agitation and snide comment is amusing to me. So much that I actually snort. "That's the most ridiculous thing I've ever heard."

"That's the world of prospecting," he mutters, pulling the truck into traffic.

"Why do you do it?"

He doesn't hesitate. "Because it's worth it."

"Why?"

He fights a grin. "Nosey girl."

I roll my eyes. "I'm not nosey. Just curious."

"My life was shit," he says, his voice detached. "My dad was dying. Heart was broken. Only brother was fuckin' the woman I loved." His eyes slide to me. I gape back at him in shock. "You don't have to pretend, gorgeous. I know they told you."

"Kat say something?"

"No. Nobody said anything."

"Then how did you know?"

"The same way I knew you told Red we fucked." He winks at me, smothering some of that unease in his eyes. "I can read lips." I knew that. I mean, I wasn't sure, but had said it in hopes he would understand. He did. I hadn't taken into consideration that he might have read more than I wanted him to.

"And the four of you are completely clueless to how obvious you are. Here's a tip for the future. When you talk about someone, don't stare at them, make sad faces or clutch your chest. That shit gives you away."

"Well, not everyone is as observant as you, smartass." The corner of his lips barely tip. Then he's quiet.

Talking about his ex-girlfriend earlier didn't have the slightest effect on him. It was as if he was over it. Done. Accepted and moved on. But the mention of his brother and father triggers something inside of him.

"When life takes an unexpected turn, sometimes it's hard to recover," he says. My heart breaks a little at the sadness in his tone. "Watching my father slowly die and being betrayed by my brother left a huge void inside me. To fill it, I need something that can't be given. It can only be earned. The Devil's Renegades have it. And every time I answer that phone, I'm one step closer to deserving it."

"So what is this something you're searching for?"

Blue eyes seize me. Captivate me. They're filled with endless depths of conviction that reflect his answer even before he says it.

"Loyalty."

30
THE RIDE

"I did it to prove a point," I say to Kat who stares back at me in confusion. She crosses her arms and tilts her head—her jaw working overtime as she gnaws on her gum. Studying me as intently as Cook had when he'd picked me up.

"You look like a crazy person."

"Can I get a drink? Please?" She examines me another moment, then shrugs before busying herself behind the bar.

I hadn't worried about showing up to Pops looking ridiculous. Because I knew that even in Wonder Woman pajamas, I would fit in better than Cook who—to quote Red—looked like he belonged on the cover of GQ. I'd even envisioned Ronnie giving him hell. Telling him to walk the stage like a runway since he'd rather dress like a model than a biker. But the joke was on me.

The moment we pulled up, Cook lost the jacket. Retrieved his cut from beneath the seat. Traded his shoes for dusty boots. It took ten seconds for him to transform. Too bad I hadn't thought to bring something to change into. But thankfully, it was still too early for the bar to be full.

That victorious smirk he wore the entire walk across the parking lot had me wondering if Ronnie even really called him. Or if this was his way to get back at me. But after a brief, curious glance in my direction, Ronnie pulled him away from me the moment we walked in. His mood as anxious as Cook's had been.

"What is this?" I ask Kat as she hands me my drink. I take a tentative sip of the dark liquid and nearly choke.

"Something new I'm tryin'. You like it?"

"No. It's horrible."

"Hater," she mumbles, jumping up to sit on the bar. "How's the date goin'?"

I shrug. "Okay I guess." *Perfect until Ronnie called...*

"Better than the others?"

Rolling my eyes, I breathe a laugh. "Like you have to ask."

"I don't know why you even bothered with all those other guys."

"Because it was part of the plan, remember? I'm the idiot who wasted the past three months of her life dating Jud's superiors in hopes of making him feel inferior." The reminder of my stupidity has sickness swimming in my gut.

"I remember the plan. I just don't understand why you didn't just stick with Cook. He smells better, looks better and he outranks all the Eagles." I can do nothing but shake my head at her ignorance. For Kat to be a bartender, in a bar that catered to bikers, she sure didn't know a whole lot.

"He's a Prospect, Kat."

She nods slowly. Then speaks even slower as if I'm the one who's ignorant. "I know..."

"Then you should know he doesn't outrank them." She quietly regards me a moment before she breaks into a fit of laughter. "What's so funny?" I ask. She only laughs harder and louder--drawing attention to us from the few people sitting around the bar.

"You don't know, do you?"

"Know what?" My impatience grows as I have to wait for her to catch her breath before answering.

"The Eagles are a ridin' club, Carmen. Cook may be a Prospect, but he's a Prospect for the largest MC in the south. He outranks even the president of the Eagles." Surely she's kidding. "True story." She holds up her right hand. *Okay...maybe she wasn't kidding.*

Frowning, I flush with embarrassment. "I didn't know there was a difference," I mutter.

She sobers a little. "Hey, it's cool. Lots of people don't know. I thought you'd have figured it out, though."

"Well I didn't," I snap, heat flaming my cheeks. I feel like such a fool. I've suffered through weeks of shitty dates, while all along, I could've just had Cook. "Why wouldn't he tell me?"

"Probably because he didn't want you to want him just for his patch." Her lips turn up on one side as she chews her gum. "He likes you. A lot. I can tell." Before I have time to process this, or ask why in the hell she's waited so long to tell me this herself, the back door opens and the bar is instantly filled with men's voices.

Lots of men. And they're all Devil's Renegades. Many I've never seen before. But I only have eyes for Cook. He holds several beer bottles in his big hand. I watch as he dumps the bottles in a nearby trashcan. Unlike the other men who are talking and laughing, Cook remains quiet. His lips pressed in a thin lin. Brow furrowed as he turns his head to look at me.

His blue eyes are sad. A look of uncertainty on his face. It lasts for only a moment before he shields it behind a mask of indifference. The corners of his lips tip slightly, and the smile is just as desolate as his eyes.

"Seventeen of the best, Kat," Ronnie says, taking a seat next to me. "We're takin' the ride."

Kat's eyes widen. "What? Who?" Ronnie's eyes flicker to me for just a second before moving on to someone behind him.

"Kyle. He leaves first thing in the mornin'."

"Oh no," Kat pouts. "Kyle is one of my favorites!"

I turn to look at the man behind me. Wherever he's going and for whatever reason, he seems happy about it. Sliding from my seat, I offer it to him. I flash the lady behind him a warm smile—noticing the patches on her cut that brand her "Property of Devil's Renegades Kyle."

Shouldering through the crowd, I make my way toward Cook who sits at the end of the bar. He starts to stand, but then grabs me by my waists and lifts me to sit on the bar in front of him—my knees parted wide to accommodate his big body between them. He even makes sure I don't sit on my cape and choke myself before resting his arms around my thighs.

The position makes us eye level, and now that I'm so close, I notice the sadness in his eyes is deeper than I'd realized. "You going to miss him?" I ask, wanting to wrap my arms around his big shoulders and comfort him.

He stares back at me a moment before shaking his head. "No gorgeous, I can't say I will." His words confuse me, considering the pain in those beautiful blues.

Wanting to distract him from whatever burden he's suffering, I give him my best smile. "What's 'the ride'? It sure does have Kat excited."

"It's a ride we take when someone in the club takes a leave, transfers or patches in. In this case, it's a transfer."

"Patches in?"

"Transitions from a Prospect to a patch holder."

"Maybe that will be you before long."

He winks, and some of the tension in his face softens. "Hope so." Finally, I get a genuine smile and the sight of it warms me all the way to my toes. I want to kiss him. But Kat interrupts us.

"One shot for Wonder Woman," she says, placing the glass next to my thigh. "And one shot for Captain Cook." Chairs scrape against the floor as everyone stands. Cook abandons his seat then lifts me with one arm to stand next to him. An unspoken moment is shared between him and Ronnie as they stare at each other and nod. Then Ronnie speaks.

"To Kyle. A good man, best friend and a damn fine brother. You will be missed. But Mississippi will be a better chapter because of you." Everyone salutes and we throw back the shot. It burns, but doesn't compare to the heat I feel as Cook looks down at me.

I turn into him, pressing my weight into his side. "Are you okay?" I ask, so only we can hear.

He studies me a long moment before setting his glass on the bar and cupping my head in his hands. Our bodies now flush against each other. Thumbs on my jaw, he tilts my face up, leans in and covers my mouth with his in a passionate kiss.

My toes curl in my footed pajamas. The concrete cold and unforgiving beneath the thin material. But I can't help it. This is one of those kisses. The kind that shoots tingles down the back of my thighs. Makes my heart somersault. Creates a burst of fireworks behind my eyelids. Quivers my liver—just like the first time he ever kissed me.

"Prospect!"

I jump at the sound and break the kiss. Wanting to kill Ronnie for interrupting. Cook's hands still hold my head, but I manage to slide my eyes to Ronnie and give him an ugly glare. He only smiles as he looks me up and down.

"Normally, I wouldn't approve of anyone ridin' in somethin' like that." He motions to my outfit. "But for you, I'll make an exception."

Cook's hands slowly pull away from me. I chance a look up at him, relieved to find him relaxed and smirking down at me. *Maybe he just needed a kiss.* "So I can ride?" My fingers fidget with my cape. "With you?"

"Well you sure as hell ain't ridin' with me lookin' like that," Ronnie says, his breathy laugh filling the room as he walks out. I can't help but smile. Cook smiles too—that all teeth baring smile I love so much.

"Come on, gorgeous," he says, tucking my hand in his. He leads us outside and to his big, black, monster of a motorcycle.

"How did this get here?" I ask, looking across the lot at his truck.

"I trailered it here earlier. Ronnie's call was a precontrasectional." I smile at the use of my ridiculous word, but it drops to a frown when Cook says, "Capes gotta go."

"But it's the best part."

"Fine." He shrugs. "Leave it on. Just let go of me when it gets wrapped up in the tire and jerks you off the back." I make quick work of untying it from my neck.

I fold it neatly as Cook waits patiently with his hand extended and on eyebrow raised. When I offer it, I tighten my grip as he tries to take it. "Don't lose it."

"Wouldn't dream of it, babe." He smirks, tossing it carelessly into his saddle bag. I roll my eyes but he ignores it, making a motion with his finger for me to turn around. Cautiously, I turn—glancing back at him over my shoulder.

Then his fingers are in my hair. Separating the long strands into three pieces. Something like warm honey flows through my veins as he braids my hair. It's so intimate. So relaxing that I have to hold onto the seat of the bike to keep from stumbling as my eyes flutter closed.

"You like when I play with your hair?"

"Yes," I breathe on a contented sigh.

"Wish I knew that. I'd have made sure to do it more." There a note of sadness in his tone, but when he grabs my shoulders and turns me to face him, he's smiling. Placing a set of clear glasses over my eyes, he asks, "Helmet or no helmet?"

"We have to wear a helmet. It's the law."

His grin is cocky as he slides on his own glasses. "We know people. This ride is about freedom. About having earned the right to ride in places other than here. Not wearing a helmet is a way to express that freedom. And you'll find that it's pretty fuckin' liberating. But if you feel more comfortable wearing one, you can."

I cast a nervous glance around the parking lot. None of the other three women here are wearing helmets. "What if we wreck?" I ask, wringing my hands. Cook takes them in his.

"What if we don't?" He winks and my doubt and anxiety fades, replaced with the thrill of doing something dangerous.

After Cook climbs gracefully on the bike, I clamber on behind him. My knees bounce in anticipation as I slide as close to him as possible. Unlike Drake's bike, this one doesn't have a sissy bar. So I lock my arms around Cook's waist in a death grip. He chuckles as he releases the kickstand and balances the machine between his powerful thighs.

Visions of him popping a wheelie and me falling off flash in my head. Then another of me loosening my grip and flailing backwards, causing my braid to get sucked into the tire and getting dragged forehead first down the highway. Terror strikes me full force and I shiver. *So much for that thrill of excitement.*

"You cold?"

Shaking my head, I swallow hard. "No. Just a little scared." *A lot of scared.* My hold on him tightens and I try to move closer. It's impossible. I'm already on his back.

His hand rubs up my leg, over my knee and back in reassuring strokes. "You trust me, gorgeous?" he asks, smiling wide when he turns his head just a fraction and my face is there.

I nod, my chin digging into his shoulder. "Yeah, but my one and only experience on a motorcycle wasn't the best." The reminder of Drake and his wobbly riding and raggedy bike causes me to shudder again.

"Well in the MC, we ride Harleys. They handle a helluva lot better than that piece of shit Drake rides." That reminds me...

"So what's up with you not telling me you outranked the Eagles?" I ask, temporarily forgetting my fear.

"Been talkin' to Kat, huh?" He releases an exasperated breath, but he's grinning. "I'll have to remember to return the favor," he mutters, staring at Kat who waves at us from the back of Ronnie's bike. Cook gives her the finger. She points at me and gives me the finger. I'm not quite ready to release my grip on Cook to return the gesture.

Loud pipes sound across the lot as one by one, the riders crank their bikes. The noise reverberates off the walls of the building. It's powerful enough to rattle my bones. Cook is one of the last to crank his bike, then he's pushing us back with his feet.

When he has enough room for us to pull out, he angles his head so he can look at me. It doesn't take much considering I'm so close my cheek nearly touches his. "You ready?" he asks, his foot already shifting the bike into first.

"Just don't kill me," I mutter.

He breathes out a laugh. "I'll try my best, gorgeous."

With practiced perfection, Cook smoothly pulls out and takes his place in the pack. I think there's someone on the right of us, but I'm too scared to look. Instead, I focus on keeping my body glued to Cook. I'm not even on my seat anymore, I'm sitting on his.

On the first turn, I squeeze my eyes shut tight as the bike leans—just as I'd done when I rode with Drake. But this ride is nothing like that. Where Drake had bobbed and weaved and bounced us through the potholes and bumps, Cook gracefully glides us around them.

I hold my breath when we turn onto the frontage road next to the highway and pick up speed. The speedometer on Cook's bike says we're only going forty miles per hour. I remember he's good enough to handle one hundred and forty miles per hour, and it relaxes me a fraction. And when he leans against me a little and straightens his long legs to rest his boots on the highway pegs, I relax even more.

Shit he's sexy. Stretched out like a big cat. Those thick arms rippled in muscles and fully extended so those big hands can grip the handlebars. Strong, square jaw shadowed in hair tickling my cheek. He has me so worked up, I have to force my eyes to something else to keep from imprinting a wet spot on the small of his back.

We turn off the frontage road and take a side street that leads to an older part of town. As we near, our speed reduces to thirty—allowing me to take everything in as we pass. The sun is setting, making it dark enough for the district to be brightly lit with street lights and gas lanterns, giving it a look of old charm. We pass antique homes. Oversized Cypress trees. Historical buildings. All while riding in two, perfectly straight lines. The formation is something to see.

I unlock my fingers and rest my hands against Cook's stomach, easing the strain in my shoulders and tightness in my arms. But I keep my face close to his, enjoying the way my cheek feels pressed against him.

Cook effortlessly leans into the curves as we wind down road after road. I don't know how long we've been gone, but I hope it doesn't end soon. I can see why they all love it so much. It's so peaceful. And I'm already looking forward to the next time I can do it again. Although next time I ride, I'm wearing shoes. The fabric feet of my pajamas provide little protection against the vibrating foot pegs. They've been tingling for miles, and I've been too afraid to wiggle the life back into them. Fearing my movement might cause us to wreck.

Sometime later, we finally come to an intersection with a stop light. Once we're completely stopped, I twist first one ankle and then the other. Cook's hands come to my knees, then slide down my legs. When he grabs my ankles and lifts my feet, I fist his shirt in my hands. He only chuckles as he places my feet in his lap and begins to rub the life back into them.

I sigh, my shoulders drooping and my cheeks resting against his shoulder. The position is quite comfortable and I wonder if he'll let me stay like this. I decide it's worth asking.

"Hey," I say, my mouth as close to his ear as I can get it, so I can be heard over pipes. His chin lifts, his head turning toward me. "How impossible would it be to stay like this?"

A smile curves on one side of his mouth. "I got you, gorgeous." *Ohhh, he's got me again. There goes my heart, slipping and sliding all over the damn place.*

The pack starts to move. He gives my toes a final squeeze before crossing my ankles in his lap. Then we're rolling through the light. I give a smug look to the patrol car parked in the median—waiting and ready for someone to violate a traffic law so he can pounce. Not us. *We know people.* It's a powerful feeling.

Soon, the formation begins to separate. One by one, the riders branch off on their own. Each with one hand in the air, waving goodbye before they're gone. Since we're at the back, we're one of the last to break away. Cook keeps us on backroads, taking us the long way around to my apartment.

He pulls next to my car and cuts the engine. Keeping the kickstand up and balancing us with his feet as he uncrosses my ankles, but leaves my legs around his waist. When I try to pull away, he grabs my wrists and guides them over his right shoulder. Then he twists slightly, grips my arms and spins me to face him, so I'm sitting half on the gas tank and half on his lap. I'm not sure how he managed to do it without both of us landing on our asses with the bike on top of us.

"Smooth move, Mr. Delicious." I stiffen the moment the word escapes my lips. Of course he's grinning, while I stare at him with eyes the size of saucers.

"Mr. Delicious?" he asks, amused as I've ever seen him. He removes my glasses and then his own, before dropping them in the space between us. "That's a new one."

"My friend calls you that," I lie, flushing like crazy.

He quirks a brow. "Your friend? She hot?" His teasing and playful smile has me forgetting my embarrassing moment and rolling my eyes.

"Dog."

"Kiss me." The sudden demand is dark and low, quite a contradiction to who he was only seconds ago.

"Maybe I don't want to kiss you," I say, lips parted. Breath heavy. Tongue itching to explore his mouth.

"Then what do you want?"

My eyes fall to his mouth. "To kiss you." His lips quick. Mine seize them.

Slowly my hands move over his cut. Up to his shoulders. His neck. The sides of his face. Then fist in his hair. I give a slight pull, and his head moves under my touch. Angling his mouth so I have better access.

Desire sparks deep inside my core. My tongue delves deeper into his mouth. He kisses me back with the same fervor. Loosening my braid so he can run his fingers through my hair. I grind my hips into him, searching for contact and getting nothing but air.

Instantly his arm is around my waist. The other on the handle bar. His left leg lifts, the heel of his boot finding the kickstand and pushing it to the ground. As the bike leans over, he stands with me around his waist and swings his leg over the side. Not once breaking our kiss.

The journey up the stairs isn't so smooth. He pulls his lips from mine and uses the railing to help launch us up the two flights. Taking the steps two and three at a time. I bury my face in his neck—kissing, sucking and nibbling the cool flesh there.

At the door, he pulls his key from the pocket of his cut, and has us barreling through the threshold in record time. I'm untangling my legs from him even as he still walks us to the bedroom. Then I'm pushing his cut off his shoulders. When I attempt to toss it to the floor in my haste, he catches my hand. Distracting me with a kiss, he pulls it from my fingers and reverently lays it across the nightstand. But the moment it's released, those same hands aren't as gentle with me. They're possessive.

He grasps the zipper on my onesie and roughly tugs it to my navel. Then he's shoving it off my shoulders. Fingers quickly unsnapping my bra as I pull my arms free. Bra jerked from my body, he grasps my breasts, dipping his head to cover my nipple with his mouth. Causing my head to loll as he sucks hard while caressing the tip with his tongue.

I struggle to push my pajamas over my hips which are slightly wider than the opening allows. He resolves the problem by walking me backwards until the back of my knees hit the bed. With a gentle shove, I fall to my back. Landing with a bounce on the soft mattress.

The zipper is loosened by his eager fingers. Fisting the material in his hands, he jerks my clothes over my hips and pulls them down my legs. I scramble to my knees, working his belt loose. Kissing his naked chest when he yanks his shirt over his head.

Impatient, he swats my hands away and releases the button on his jeans. They're only to his hips when he crawls between my knees. Wraps one big arm around me and forces me to my back—using his feet to push his pants the rest of the way down his legs as he covers my body with his. Kissing me like a hungry man. Rocking his naked hips against mine.

He enters me on a single, hard thrust that leaves him buried deep inside me. My nails dig into his back as I struggle to find my breath. Overwhelmed at how he fills me. Stretches me. How satiny he feels. Smooth and soft against my tight walls. I hadn't realized how much more pleasurable no barrier would be than the thin membrane of a condom.

"Your pussy fits me like a glove," he growls, pulling out only to push back inside me. I mewl. My knees falling further apart, greedy for more. "That's right, gorgeous." He thrusts deeper. "Spread those fuckin' thighs. Open that sweet pussy up for me." I oblige. My legs part as much as physically possible—acting as if the damn things hate each other. "Good girl."

"Sonofabitch," I mumble, my sex inadvertently clenching around his shaft at his praise. Eliciting a guttural sound from him that's so sexy, I purposely do it again just to hear it.

In a strangled voice, he says, "Stop. It's hard enough to keep from comin' without you milking it from me."

I like the power I exude over him. It's selfish, but I've never been more turned on than I am now. Watching him struggle to keep from falling apart. Seeing that pleasure in his eyes. The desire strong enough to have him gritting his teeth and clenching his jaw to keep his control. I squeeze him tighter just to see his reaction. But he must have anticipated my actions, because he was prepared this time.

He's out of me, I'm facedown, on my knees and his hand is whistling through the air. I'm still processing how in the hell it all happened so fast when his palm crashes against my backside. I'm stunned into silence a split second before pain surfaces.

"Owwww!" I cry out, pulling myself up on my elbows so I can look at him. He's waiting for me when I do. Pulling me back against his chest. Taking my chin in his hand. Tilting my head. Claiming my mouth. Kneading the raised handprint on my ass. Then softening his touch as he parts my lips with his fingers and slowly pushes one inside me.

My, "Ow," turns to an "Oh," as he pumps one, then two in and out of me. "You like teasing me, gorgeous?" he asks, his voice velvet as he plants tender kisses to the corners of my lips. "Squeezing my cock with your pretty little cunt?" His dirty talk makes me tremble. Especially when he whispers the exotic words in my ear.

"If you want the power baby, all you had to do was ask." I don't want the power. I want to be a "lazy girl," and let him use me as he pleases. He's so much better at it than me. Obviously. He pulls his fingers out of me. I moan my protest, but he ignores it. "Stand up," he commands, delivering a light swat of encouragement to my hip.

I stand on shaky legs, my knees wobbly as I fight to keep my balance on the soft mattress. He holds my hand for support and taps the inside of my thigh. "Straddle me." He offers his other hand to me and I take it. Both excited and nervous as I position my feet on either side of his thighs.

Sliding his hands to my waist, he leans back and urges me to sit on top of him. As I do, he fists his big cock and lines it up with my opening. Slowly, I lower myself. Inch by delicious inch he fills me once again. When I'm seated, I remain still for a moment. Delighting in how good it feels. How strong his thighs feel beneath the heated handprint on my ass. The way his fingertips tighten around my waist. His beautifully chiseled chest on display for my greedy eyes.

I fold one leg under me and then the other until I'm on my knees. His eyes disappear behind his heavy lids for a moment before they flutter open to a dark blue. I'm thankful the light is on so I can see him. So he can see me.

"Fuck me, gorgeous," he demands. And fuck him is exactly what I do.

I start out slow, rocking my hips against him. Lifting my body only a couple inches before taking my time sliding back down. I wanted to tease him. To make him writhe beneath me like I'd done beneath him so many times. But at the first sign of my impending orgasm, I lose all control.

My body works him hard. Riding, rocking and moving in an offbeat rhythm in search of my release. I lean back and place my hands on his knees, lifting my body higher. Slamming down harder. Alternating my hands to tweak my nipples and palm my breasts. Watching him as he watches me. Licking his lips when I touch my chest. Flaring his nostrils when I stroke my clit. Fisting the sheets. Kneading my thighs. Gripping my waist. Anything to keep his hands busy.

"Come here." He drags me up his body. Leaving a wet trail of my desire across his chest. Then I'm sitting on his face. Riding his mouth. He's fucking me with his tongue. And I'm coming hard. My nails scratching the wooden headboard. Moans echo off the walls of the room.

When I find my breath, I'm on my knees at the edge of the bed. He's standing behind me. Impaling me. Hands spreading my cheeks. Exposing me to him. He touches me there and I tense. I look over my shoulder to see him wet his fingers with his mouth. A deep flush spreads over me. Unable to look, I turn away and concentrate on how good it feels when he fucks me hard like this.

His wet fingers spread moisture over the one place on my body that's forbidden. But this time I don't stiffen from his caress. It feels too damn good. When he presses one finger against the tight ring, I gasp.

"No."

"Hush, baby." His demand is as gentle as his touch. His drive slows to long, measured thrusts. He strokes my back. Hips. The back of my thighs. Pressing his finger against me again once I've loosened up.

Surprisingly, it doesn't hurt when he pushes the tip inside me. Actually, it's the opposite. It feels forbidden and wrong, which makes it that much more pleasurable. "Push back against me," he encourages. I do and he groans, deepening his touch. "My sweet, sweet girl."

I whimper. Whether it's the "my" that has me feeling so precious or just the praise, I'm not sure. But something about his words has me feeling like I'm special. Someone worthy. Someone loved…

"You're gonna come like this. While I'm fucking you. Fingering you. Telling you how good you feel. How sweet you taste. How sexy you look. How perfect you are…"

"Cook!" I scream, my orgasm rocketing through me. His gentleness subsides as he gives me just what I want. Knowing how much I love the way he pounds me while I come around him. His finger inside me only heightens the pleasure, if that's even possible. It's rough. Raw. Almost cruel. And so damn perfect.

I collapse on the bed just as something warm covers my back. The feel of his release and the sound of his passion is enough to keep me trembling with aftershocks. Soon, our loud breaths are the only sound in the room.

The bed dips as Cook stands. He returns a few minutes later, and presses something damp and warm against my back. The intimacy of him cleaning me has me swooning. Hard. When he's finished, he kisses his way to my shoulder then nuzzles my neck.

"Hey you."

I wiggle my fingers at him, unable to move more of my body than that. "Hello."

"You sleepy?"

I'd laugh if I had the energy. "I'm always sleepy after you fuck me. You wear me out."

"You like it." He smiles against my cheek.

"I love it," I admit.

He rolls me to my back, and it's my favorite post-sex moment. There's nothing quite like seeing that sated and happy look on his face. But this time, it's not there. It's replaced by the sadness from earlier. The pain maybe even a little greater.

"Hey," I say, wide awake now as I reach up to cup his cheek. "What's wrong?"

His eyes close as he turns his lips into my palm. He presses a lingering kiss there, before flashing me a reassuring smile. But it's not real. His eyes don't lie. Something is definitely wrong.

"I need to make a few calls. I'll be back shortly."

"Are you leaving?" I ask, a hint of panic in my voice. He's quiet a moment.

"I just need to step outside, gorgeous. I promise I'll be back." He gives me no time to respond before he leaves, grabbing his jeans and shirt on the way out. I start to follow him, but decide against it. Crawling under the covers, I give him the space he obviously needs and wrack my brain.

This all started at the bar. He was fine when we arrived, but something happened while we were there. Was it the news of Kyle leaving? Are they closer than he let on? Or was it the ride? Did he regret taking me?

Maybe it's the anniversary of his father's death. Or his girlfriend's betrayal. Could that be what this is about? Her? Is he still nursing a broken heart? Bandaging an open wound? *No.* That couldn't be it. He's clearly over her.

What if it's about that moment we shared in the truck? That speech on second chances. Did he realize I might be his second chance? *Because, I'm pretty sure he's mine.* Is he scared of what he's feeling? *What I'm feeling.* Is it the fear of falling? *Just like I'm falling.* Or is he afraid because he already knows?

Like I'm afraid.

Because I know...

I'm completely and most definitely in love with him.

Having an epiphany is exhausting. One minute my mind was going crazy. I was sweating. Anxious. Ready to scream my love for Cook to the mountains. If I could just find my voice. Then the next minute, I was asleep. Snoring. Dreaming. Picturing little Cooks running across my yard wearing Ninja Turtle underwear.

But something thick and hard, seated deep inside my core, woke me. My eyes opened to a set of cobalt blues filled with the same emotion I felt in my chest. In that moment, I knew he loved me.

Now, with my hands in his hands. My arms stretched above my head. His body moving in and out of mine. I truly feel like I belong to him. Like this is the moment. The perfect time to say out loud, what I've been refusing to admit.

"I love you."

His eyes flutter closed as he buries his face in my neck. "Say it again," he pleads. His voice barely a whisper.

"I love you."

I never imagined sex between us could be any better. Any more intimate or special. But there's something so much greater about making love to the one person you're in love with. The kisses are deeper. The connection stronger. The cradle of your face in their hands. The look in their eyes. The freedom of a heart beating without the confines of a steel cage.

Cook makes love to me in a way that can't be described. Each caress is felt with my heart. Every kiss touches my soul. We come together in a beautiful oblivion where the only thing that exists is one another.

He holds me in his arms. Embracing. Petting. Kissing. Lavishing me with the most tender touches I've ever felt from his strong hands. The moment is beautifully perfect. Or it could've been. If only he'd have said, he loved me too.

31
THE PROSPECT: THE MEMORY

Sleep didn't come as easy the second time around. Judging by his constant rubbing and kissing and touching, I'm guessing Cook didn't sleep much either. I'd hoped it was because he was planning the perfect way to tell me he loved me. I held tight to that hope. It was the only thing keeping my heart from shattering. Just because I knew, beyond a shadow of a doubt, that he did love me, I still needed him to say it.

When he stirs from bed just as the sun starts to come up, I turn on my side and watch him. Taking pride in the claw marks etched on that muscular, toned ass of his. He moves silently around the room. Checking his phone. Dressing. Holding his cut in his hands, and starting at it a long time before pulling it over his shoulders.

He takes a deep breath, bringing his hand to his face before turning to me. He looks surprised to find me awake.

"Hey," he says, his expression dubious as if he's not sure I'm actually awake.

"Hello."

"You're awake."

"No shit." A smile tugs at his lips. "You're leaving." It's not a question.

He nods. "I am."

"You going to see Kyle off?"

He pierces me with a steady gaze as he slowly shakes his head. Then, in an even tone, he says, "I'm going with him."

I sit up, pulling the sheet around me. "When are you coming back?"

Again, he studies me a long moment as if he's trying to find the right words to say. "I don't know."

My mind scrambles to put the pieces of the puzzle together. Pain begins to form in my chest as each piece clicks into place—revealing a reality that I'm forced to accept. "You're transferring too, aren't you?"

"Just until I get my patch."

Hope soars inside me. "You should be getting that any day though, right?" I may not know a lot about the MC, but I'd learned from Kat that Cook had more days of prospecting than anyone she'd ever known. And that he could be getting a patch at any moment.

He takes a seat on the bed next to me. "I should've had it months ago, but I fucked up," he says, releasing a breath as he shakes his head. "I'd been prospecting nearly a year, and I did something really stupid." His eyes find mine. "For Delilah."

I don't like that he did something for her. I don't like that he's even mentioning her name. When I think of her, all I can see is her and Cook. *When he's in town, I suck his dick.* Now he's transferring there. To her town. And she may suck his dick.

"I don't want you to go," I blurt, my response earning me a knowing smile from Cook. He tucks a strand of hair behind my ear. And even though I want to be mad, I curl into his touch.

"Because you'll miss me or because you're scared I'm gonna fuck with Delilah."

There's her damn name again. Ugh. "Both."

His smile widens. "Well, like I said, I fucked up and did something stupid that involved her once. I won't do it again."

"What did you do?"

"A patch holder told me to not let her out of my sights. I did. And she got hurt. The result was pretty bad. For both of us. She spent a week in a hospital, and I've spent the past eight months trying to prove myself again."

"So how long do you have left?"

His smile is gone. The sadness is back. Seeing him hurt makes the pain in my chest that much worse. "I don't know." He picks up my hand, kissing my fingers as he speaks. "Could be days. Could be weeks. Months."

"Months?" I ask in disbelief. He nods slowly. "Where does that leave us?"

"If you were mine, you could come with me."

"But I'm not yours," I whisper.

"You could be." His low, dark voice holds a hint of hope. But I have a feeling he knows what I'm going to say even before I say it.

"I don't want to be second."

222

Surprising me, he nods in understanding. "You shouldn't be."

His hands cup my face, as his eyes slowly study every feature as if he's memorizing what I look like. "You told me you loved me last night. Did you mean it?" I try to drop my head, but his hold refuses to let me.

Meeting his eyes, I blink back my tears. "You know I do."

"Then wait for me." I'm shocked by his request. "Wait for me until this is over. Then I swear I'll treat you like you deserve to be treated."

I shake my head, pulling away from his hold. "I don't think this is the kind of lifestyle I want, Cook." He frowns in confusion, prompting me to continue. "The late nights alone. The interrupted moments. You being at someone else's beck and call."

"It won't always be like this," he defends, reaching out for me. To avoid his touch, because I can't think clearly when I feel it, I stand.

"Really? So even after you're back and you have your patch, you won't go if they call? You won't leave me to be with them if they need you?" He doesn't deny it. "I don't want to be with someone who loves something else more than they love me. Especially when I love them so much." My voice cracks on a sob as the tears start to fall. "I love you so...fucking much. It scares me."

He's on his feet. I can't move away from him fast enough. Lips are on my lips. But the kiss is chaste. Then his forehead is pressed against mine and we're both breathing hard. "I'm so sorry, gorgeous. So fuckin' sorry. I swear on my life I'll make this up to you." His thumb swipes across my cheek, catching my tear.

"Say it," he demands. "Say it again."

"I love you," I breathe, closing my eyes as he wraps his arms around me.

I'm expecting him to hold me. Tell me he's not leaving. That he chooses me over the club. Proving that for once in my life, I'm the most important thing to someone. Instead, with one last lingering kiss to my forehead, he turns his back to me and walks out--like he's done so many times before.

That sole patch on his back is now a faded orange. Branding him property of Devil's Renegades. Reminding everyone that he's their Prospect. And nothing more than a memory to me.

32
HOME

The first week after Cook left was a lot easier to handle than I thought it would be. I focused on work. Enrolled in classes for the upcoming fall semester that started the following week. I avoided the bar and Kat's texts and calls. I didn't want to hear her apologies or promises that he'd be back soon. I found a way to deal with it myself.

I just pretended he was still in town. That he was with Ronnie, doing whatever it was they always did. That at any moment, I would come home to find him in my house. Or wake up to him making love to me. He never showed, but he did call.

Every day.

At the exact same time.

Eleven P.M.

Not a minute after or before. As if he was reminding me before I went to sleep that not a day went by that he didn't think of me. But I couldn't bring myself to answer the phone. No matter how much I missed his voice. I wouldn't settle for a ten-minute phone call in place of his presence. I wanted more. I was worth more.

The strength it took to watch his name flash across my phone and not accept it, came from knowing the call would abruptly end the moment the club needed him. At the word "Prospect," he would be theirs. And I would be forgotten and left to suffer his absence alone.

The second week was worse. I started to really feel the effects of his leaving. The days were getting long. The nights even longer. I'd been clinging to the hope that he'd get his patch and return, then fulfill his promise of making it up to me. But he never showed.

Kat had stopped texting and calling, too. The last text had simply said she was here if I needed her. I didn't. The only one I needed was Cook. I needed his arms. Him to tell me he loved me. See it in his eyes. Then have him prove it to me by not only coming back, but staying. All I got was his daily calls. That still went unanswered.

When an entire month passed, I knew it was over. Even if he did show up, I couldn't forgive him for walking out and leaving me for so long. And I couldn't blame him for it either. He'd worked so hard to earn his place with the Devil's Renegades. In his words, he had fucked up. Now he was paying the price. So was I.

I never gave him an ultimatum. Deep down, I knew not only that it wasn't fair, but that I was incapable of being so selfish. He was passionate about the club. He needed it. And because I loved him so much, I had been willing to give him the space he needed to do what he had to do. But I never imagined it would take this long. Or hurt this much.

One month and one week later, I decided it was time to move on. I was tired of being the one to make all the sacrifices. He had his club. I had no one. He had a patch waiting for him at the finish line. I had nothing. All this hard work was going to be worth it to him. Not only would he find what he went searching for with the Devil's Renegades, but he'd have me to. In those first few weeks I would have taken him back. But not anymore.

Swallowing my pride, I called my parents. Of course they already knew about mine and Jud's split. My job. Apartment. How hard I'd been struggling to make it. Their pride in me would have brought tears to my eyes, had I not have cried them all for Cook.

When I told them I was coming home, their joy had me feeling a spark of happiness for the first time in weeks. My dad insisted on buying me out of my lease, and I didn't protest. I was too ready to move on. To get back home. To surround myself with people whose love and attention I didn't have to fight for.

I quit my job. Unenrolled from my classes. Packed my clothes and personal belongings that would fit in my car—leaving what little furniture I had behind. I delivered the apartment keys to my manager. When she'd asked if there were ever any copies made, I swallowed back my emotions and paid to have the locks changed. Scared Cook might come back and surprise the new tenants by breaking in on them as he had me so many times.

As I pulled away, I said goodbye to the only place I'd ever considered mine. The feeling was nostalgic. I had some good memories there. A few bad ones too. Long nights spent alone, and some spent with him. He was my Mr. Delicious. My biker bad boy. My Cook. My love. He could've been my second chance. That beautiful part to my broken heart. Now, he's just gone.

"Who's calling you?" Emily asks, scrolling through my Facebook newsfeed. She's sitting at my desk, while I lay on my bed—staring at the name that flashes across my screen.

"Nobody." I drop the phone to my chest and let it vibrate against my heart that, for some reason, still beats a little harder every time he calls.

"I'm so glad you're home. I've missed this."

"What?" I tilt my head to look at her. She has her face buried in my computer screen. "Facebook stalking from my account or having me around?"

"Both."

The day Cook left, I'd called Emily. She'd listened to me cry. Said all the right things. Promised to support if I decided to wait for him or move on. Just like a best friend should.

When I came home, she was here to greet me. Stayed for dinner that night with me and my parents. We'd sat up late talking and she ended up staying the night. She hasn't left yet.

For the three days I've been home, it's been like old times. The two of us hanging out in my childhood bedroom that still looks like it did the day I graduated high school. Lilac painted walls. Shelves filled with pageant trophies and academic awards. Princess canopy bed. Posters of rock bands. Fuzzy rugs and stuffed animals. A plate with leftover crust from the PB&J my mom brought up to us earlier.

"Who is Denny Deen?" Emily asks, looking closer at the computer screen of my old desktop.

"Denny Deen?"

"Yeah. Redhead. Hot. Posing in a pic with a guy named Cook."

My heart skips at the mention of his name. "I had her hidden from my timeline, Em."

"I know. I unhid her. Who is she?"

"That's Red. The girl from the river who told me about Cook's ex." *Damn.* Saying his name hurts even worse.

"Can't escape this guy, eighteen exclamation points," Emily reads. "Operation 'Lose The Prospect' is an epic fail when it comes to Cook."

Before I can stop myself, I scramble out of bed to look. Red is beaming while Cook smirks in the background. He doesn't look like he really wanted to take the picture. It's as if Red ran over and snapped the picture in front of him before he could protest.

"What the hell is operation 'Lose the Prospect?'"

"I think it's when a Prospect watches the ol' ladies and they try to escape him. Kat said Red was infamous for that." After what Cook had told me about fucking up with Delilah, I'm sure he wasn't going to let Red escape. "He looks sad," I whisper, wondering if it's because he misses me.

"He looks fucking hot." I can't help but smile at Emily's shock.

She had never seen Cook. Months ago, I had promised to take a picture of him to send to her. I never did. Now I wish I had. Not just so she could have given her approval, but so at least I'd have that to look at when I wanted to cry and feel sorry for myself. I'd managed to do that enough without a picture, though.

"Why didn't you tell me he was so fine?" she asks, both our faces now buried in the screen.

"I said he was delicious."

"We have to find a better word. One that's hotter than delicious." With a sigh, I force my eyes away and fall back on my bed. "Or asshole," she quickly adds, minimizing the screen and turning to face me. "Jerk. Fuckwit. Douchebag." I turn my head to look at her and she rolls her eyes. "He's really not that hot, anyway."

"Yes he is," I admit on a frown.

Unfolding her legs from the chair, Emily lays next to me on the bed. Resting her head on my shoulder and wrapping her arm around my waist. She exhales loudly and peeks up at me from beneath her lashes. "You okay?"

"I'm fine."

"Then why are you crying?"

I brush the tears from my cheeks with the back of my hand. "I didn't realize I was," I say on a laugh. "I'm okay." I nod and shoot her a smile. "Promise."

"You're lying, but it's totally cool. Because do you know what happens when you're sad and you lie about it?" I shake my head. She sits up and beams down at me. "First, you get ice cream for the sadness, and wine for the lie."

"Wine for the lie?"

"Yep." She winks. "Cause nothing will make you tell the truth like throwing a good drunk."

The next several hours are spent doing just that. I got full off of ice cream, drunk off of wine and Emily passed me Kleenex as I cried and admitted the truth. I love Cook. I miss him. Every day the pain gets worse. He'd once told me time had a way of healing. But it will take a lifetime to get over him.

33
SECOND CHANCES

It's been two months and six days since I've seen him. I'm still living at my parent's house with Emily who pretty much lives there too. We'd always talked about getting a place and living together. In some sense, I guess we finally do.

I'm now a full time student at UGA. Today was my first final, and once the perfect score was posted, Emily had insisted we go out to this tiny bar not too far from home, and have a drink. Or five. Which is the number I'm on right now.

"That guy is checking you out." Emily juts her chin in the direction of someone at the end of the bar. There are only two people in the place besides us. I can only guess at the one who is "checking me out."

"I'm a lesbian," I say, tossing back the buttery nipple shot and chasing it with a beer.

"Well, you're in luck because he might be a girl."

I laugh, turning to the man who's anything but a girl. "Look at that Adam's Apple." I point unashamed, even as the man looks right back at me. "No way he's a girl."

"You sure are drinking heavy." I look to Emily and notice a hint of concern in her eyes. "Is it because it's after midnight and he didn't call, or because he did call?"

"Oh, he called." I summon the bartender for another round. "At eleven. Like clockwork. As always."

"Are you ever going to answer?"

I shrug. "Maybe."

"When you do, give me the phone," Emily says, holding up her fingers to ask the bartender for a double. "I've got a few choice words for that delicious little prick."

A little buzzed, and feeling silly, I grin at her. "What would you say?"

Emily hands me a shot and takes one for herself. We hold it up in a toast. "Hello Mr. Delicious," she says, her proper voice making me grin wider. "May the fleas of a thousand camels take residence in your undergarments, and may your arms be too short to scratch."

I nod in acceptance of her Googled speech, and lift my glass to hers. But before we even clink them, the thick liquid begins to shake from the vibrations of what could be an earthquake. The bar quiets as a loud roar draws nearer. The thin walls shake with the force. Glasses rattle. It sounds like a train is passing through the building.

"What the fuck is that?" Emily asks, squinting her eyes at the endless row of white lights lining the building. I toss back my shot and grab another—knowing exactly what it is.

"Motorcycles."

"Oh yeah...I heard there is some kind of rally or something happening in Florida. I guess they're passing through." Emily crosses her legs, bouncing her knee in excitement. "Maybe I can get one to take me for a ride." She wiggles her eyebrows at me, then thins her lips at my expression. "I mean, fuck them. Stupid jerks," she mutters, burying her face in her glass.

The door swings open and the men pile in. I've seen a few bikers since I've been home, so it's not the sight of them that has me nearly falling off my stool. It's the patch they're wearing—Devil's Renegades.

At least fifty of them enter. Every one of them focused on me. I'm not breathing. I don't think Emily is breathing either. We just sit silent as they gather around us. I recognize a few, but only know one by name. Ronnie—standing tall and proud and stoic at the front.

Then I feel him before I see him. My heart spikes. Stomach flips. Toes curl. These are the tell-tale signs that he's near. The crowd parts. My eyes gravitate to his. Emily's jaw drops at the sight of him, but somehow I manage to keep my shit together.

It's like the first time all over again. His hair is a perfect mess. Long, sculpted arms hang at his sides. Thick, muscular legs covered in faded jeans. Dusty boots on his feet. Leather vest. Black T-shirt. Head tilted. Chin slightly raised. Full lips curved on one side. Sharp, riveting eyes that are the deepest color of blue. They watch me with interest and sparkle with amusement as they drink me in. Then he speaks in that voice that still has the power to quiver my liver.

"Hello gorgeous."

Ohmylordhavemercy.

"I called you," he says, his eyebrow slightly raised in question. "A lot."

Emily slaps at me with the back of her hand. Repeatedly hitting me as she stares at Cook with an open mouth. I finally have to grab her hand in mine to still it. Cook's gaze never shifts from mine despite the commotion.

I glance at his cut that is now covered in patches. Although I can't see the back, I know what's on it. The reaper with the hooded eyes. The name Devil's Renegades. And the bottom rocker that reads, "Louisiana."

Clearing my throat, I straighten my spine and meet his eyes. "I see you have your patch."

"I'd rather have you." His response derails me a moment. But I quickly recover.

"But you don't have me."

He shoots me a cocky smile. "Baby, I've had you since the moment you walked in that bar."

"Maybe." I shrug, sounding braver than I am. "That changed when you left me."

"Now I'm back. And I'm here to make it up to you. Just like I promised I would."

Something akin to anger festers inside me. How dare him think he can just show up with his army and tell me what he's here to do. This isn't Pops. Or Louisiana. Which reminds me.

"How did you know where I was?"

"I know people." He's grinning again. Cocky and smug and pissing me off.

"We're through, Cook." Emily's hand moves in mine and I tighten my grip. "It's been over two months. The damage is done. I've moved on." For some reason, my eyes flit to the guy at the end of the bar.

An evil smile slowly spreads across Cook's lips. *He knows my game.* Dragging his eyes from mine, he looks at the guy and lifts his chin. "Sup?"

"Not much man. How you doin'? I'm Gary. Love the bikes. I used to ride—"

"Get out," Cook says, in a voice just above a whisper. Gary's boots scrape across the floor as he scurries out of the side door. Cook looks back at me. Victory flashing in those blue eyes. "You were sayin'?"

"What are you doing here?" I grit, trying to sound angry, despite how impressed I am at his show of authority. And how wet it makes my panties.

"I'm here to make it up to you."

"There's no..." My free hand flails in the air. "Making it up to me."

"You sure about that?" *No...but he damn sure it.*

"Yes, I'm sure."

"What if I told you I'll give it all up." I stiffen.

"You'd miss it."

"Not as much as I've missed you."

"But you love the club," I whisper.

"I love you more." There's no smile. No grin. Just honest conviction in his words. I'd swoon off my stool if I wasn't too busy keeping Emily's hand from trying to push me to him.

"I don't want you to give up your club for me." I frown. "I would never ask you to do that."

"Then I won't. I'll have you both."

I shake my head, my hand nervously wringing Emily's. "I can't be second."

His face softens. "When I told you this was something I had to do, I meant it. I needed something. It took me six hundred and thirty-seven days to get it. Now that I have it, it means nothing without you."

Dropping his voice, he promises, "You will never be second, gorgeous. Not to me. That's why they're all here. So there's no mistaking where my loyalties lie or what order my priorities are in. You first. Club second. Or if you want it to just be you, then I'll hand them my patch right now. Either way, it will always be you, Carmen."

My lips trembles. "You'd do that? For me?"

"I'd do anything for you."

I'm sure Emily thinks I'm crazy for not flying from my seat and kissing this handsome devil. She probably wonders how anyone could hesitate and not take this man at his word. But Emily wasn't the one who spent the past two months crying herself to sleep. She's not the one who's been burned. Or has trust issues. So I'm sure she'll never understand my next words.

"Then prove it."

The moment the words slip past my lips, his hands are fisted in leather. There is no sadness or loss in his eyes as he pulls the cut from his shoulders. Only triumph. Happiness. Love. He looks at me like I'm his greatest achievement. And he's anxious to throw away something he's worked so hard for, just to get me in return. Because he loves me. Because he finds me worthy.

My feet find the floor just as he hands his patch to Ronnie. I snatch it from his fingers and press it into Cook's chest. "Put it on," I demand. My voice shaky. He gives me a curious look, but keeps his arms at his sides. "Just put it on." I push him a little harder for encouragement, impressed when he stiffens to keep his balance.

Eyes on me, he slides it back over his shoulders. "I would never ask you to do that," I say. He quirks a brow. "I mean, I wouldn't say it and actually mean it." *Yeah. That makes no sense either.* His lips tip in lopsided grin. I fidget with my shirt, trying to figure this out. Searching for a way to be happy and keep my heart safe at the same time. I'm pretty sure it's not possible. That's why I have to trust him.

"I'm really scared," I say, my eyes brimming with tears. My chest tight. My resolve crumbling. He takes a step toward me and slides his hands up my arms. Across my shoulders. Up my neck. Holds my head and tilts it to meet his eyes.

I've missed his touch so much. I've longed for weeks to feel his hands on me. His mouth on mine. His thumbs on my cheeks to catch my falling tears.

"Don't cry, gorgeous," he whispers. "And you don't have to be scared. I've got you."

He's got me.

His lips touch mine in a soft, but brief kiss. He pulls away to gaze back down at me. "Say it."

"I love you," I say without hesitation.

"I love you too, gorgeous. More than you could ever know. But I'll spend forever proving it to you."

I press my hands against his vest, tightening my fingers into the soft leather. "Why?" I ask on a sniff. "Why were you so willing to give this up for me?"

He kisses me again. My lips. My eyes. Cheeks. The corners of my mouth. Then he looks at me with those warm, blue eyes and gives me his signature heart melting smile. "Because you're my second chance."

About the Author

Kim Jones is just a girl who enjoys writing books, dogs, Merle Haggard, taking long vacations and never doing laundry.

You can stalk Kim here:
http://www.kimjonesbooks.com/
http://www.facebook.com/kimjonesbooks
http://www.twitter.com/authorkimjones
Instagram: @kimjones204

Other books by Kim Jones:

Saving Dallas
Saving Dallas Making the Cut
Saving Dallas Forever

Red
Devil's Love

Clubwhore
Patchwhore

Sinner's Creed
Sinner's Revenge

I knew the man in front of me was doomed.

This was a test. I had to prove my loyalty. The club had my pride, now they wanted my innocence.

The knife I held in my hand would be kept as proof that I was guilty of murder. It wouldn't help my case that the man was begging for his life, on his knees in front of me. We were the only two on the video. It was everything they needed. My fingerprints, my weapon, and my face. The club would use it against me if I ever turned on them.

I wasn't scared to take this man's life. I knew he deserved everything he got and so much more. What scared me was knowing that if I did this, there would be no saving me from the depths of hell, from the fiery roads of eternity or the haunting sounds of this man's screams, which I was sure would give me nightmares for the rest of my days.

But, this club is all I know. I'm out of options. Either I prove myself now, or I walk away and never look back. I look up at my grandfather, who gives me a nod of encouragement. His black eyes are full of hate. They have the same effect on me now as they did when I was seven. He is the only man I fear, and the only man I don't want to disappoint.

The club means something to me because it means something to him. He is all I have. He has molded me into the monster I've become. If I knew for sure that not becoming a killer would ensure me a spot in the afterlife away from him, I would take my life right now. But, I know there is no place for me but hell. With him. For eternity.

I can only hear the man's screams, but I see my grandfather mouth "pussy." He is growing impatient. I have to make a decision. So, I ask myself, *Is killing this man worth pacifying the demon-possessed grandfather who raised me? Is taking a life really worth seeing the small, temporary sparkle of pride in his eyes that I've never seen in my twenty-one years? Is it worth the small mustard seed of hope that this will make him love me?* You're fuckin' right it is.

I kill the man with the brutality that the club expects, stabbing him multiple times until his face is unrecognizable. I let the faith I have in my grandfather's love fuel me. I let images of him smiling and telling me he loves me fill my head, and block the sight of the face I am butchering.

When I am finished, I search for him in the crowd, but he isn't there. When I finally notice the men around me, the body is buried and the evidence has been collected. They all wear a look of pity on their faces. Their eyes apologize for what my grandfather is, and what I have become. They can keep their guilt. They can save their sorrow. My cold, dead heart is at the point of no return.

The hell I once feared is now a desire. Satan isn't there anyway. He is here. His eyes are black as night, his heart is cold as ice, and the words *Sinner's Creed* are tattooed on his back. The same poisonous blood that runs through his veins runs through mine.

Hell is my home and Satan is this man, the only father I know. And if evil is he, then evil am I. I don't need his pride. I don't need his love. He wanted a monster; he got one.

I am the spawn of Satan.

I am the son of Lucifer.

I am Sinner's Creed.

Made in the USA
Columbia, SC
09 October 2024

43379329R00130